AMBER

WITHIN
You

To the muses, and all the shapes
they've ever taken.

CONTENTS

For trigger warnings, please skip to the end.

A PAUSE TO START

"Your task is not to seek for love, but merely to seek and find all the barriers within yourself that you have built against it."

RUMI

CHAPTER ONE

"Well?"

Maya glanced around the space. Six by fifteen feet max. More shed than flat, really: you could see the gaps where the wooden structure clung to the solid brick of the house behind it. Tiny kitchenette, the faint hum of a generator, small desk, and where was…

"The bed?" she asked.

The man pulled aside a curtain which covered the brick wall, revealing a small alcove hewn into the stone. He flashed a smile. "Cosy, huh? Keeps it nice and toasty in winter."

Right. Not bloody likely.

"Loo's outside. Back end of the garden. No need to worry about it getting backed up."

"And water?"

"Shower's round the back of the flat. Recycled rainwater, of course. There's an outside tap on the house as well, you're free to use it so long as you don't go mad. Then we'll charge. Or cut you off. You know what it's like."

She did, now. Strange that mere months ago she'd never given a second thought to fresh water.

"My, you're a hard sell. I haven't got all day, you know. You taking it, or not?"

The paper notes rustled against her hand as she pulled them from her pocket. So antiquated. And yet… her palm seemed to throb faintly, as if in memory of the chip which lay dormant inside it, nestled against sinew and bone. Perhaps non-contactless forms of payment did have a lot going for them.

"I'll take it," she said.

A drizzle enveloped Maya as she found her way through the grey streets later that afternoon. She longed for her Thinsulex jacket. It had always been perfect for this kind of weather, but it would have stood out like a sore thumb in these parts of London and probably made her a target for pickpockets. No, passing it on to Jolene had no doubt been the right call, even though she'd only be able to wear it in the garden for the same reason. Without its protection, the rain crept under the upturned collar of the double-breasted, black coat Maya wore, covering her long maroon skirt in a fine mist. Did she look the part? This wasn't like any other job interview she'd had.

Jolene would have told her not to worry. Maya already missed her and her quick smile, the way she always radiated warmth even with one of her kids endlessly pulling at her skirt-tails. Five of them. How did she do it? It still blew Maya's mind a little – how Jolene and Mike had welcomed her into their home despite the lack of space, how they'd made her a part of their family on nothing but a word. If only she could have stayed. But as lovely as they'd been, it wouldn't have worked. Too vivacious, too chaotic – the day-to-day turbulence of a big family would have sucked Maya straight in and stolen all her attention. It would have become a distraction.

Still, her pulse quickened from more than the walk. Here she was. All alone again.

The pub stood at the end of a narrow alleyway. It must have been beautiful in its heyday, black facade rising proudly from cobblestones. But now the glossy paint peeled in shreds, the golden lettering on its side reading only *'pe a Ancho'*. *Hope and Anchor*, Mike had called it, but it didn't really look that full of hope. A thick patina of grime and neglect frosted the windows, obscuring any view inside. It was a sight she was fast becoming used to. None of the few businesses which remained in the Ring seemed keen to advertise their services. Perhaps they didn't need to.

She found the side door Mike had described easily enough. Brushed down her jacket and skirt, put on her brightest, friendliest smile. And knocked.

The seconds stretched. She knocked again. She could feel her heart thudding against her ribcage. What if this had all been a big mistake? What if Mike was wrong, if nobody was here anymore? What if they turned her away? What if—

The door crept open, just wide enough for her to take in the shape of a man blurring into the gloom. Tall, black, shaved head and a decidedly unfriendly expression as his eyes flicked over her. "We're not buying."

She barely caught the door with her foot. The impact collapsed her smile momentarily.

The man frowned. "I said we're not interested."

"Well, it's a good thing I'm not selling anything, then." Maya pasted the bravado back on her lips. "I'm here to see Don."

"Are you." His gaze settled on her, intense, unwavering. "He's busy."

"Listen, could you not just… please, I'm not messing you about, I swear." She dug in her coat pocket for the letter and thrust it at him. "Mike sent me, I've got a reference and everything, could you maybe give this to him? I'm sure he'll want to see me when he reads it." Hopefully. "And I'm happy to wait." She glanced down. "Although this door is kind of heavy."

The pressure on her foot relented slightly. He grabbed the letter. "Fine. But you wait out here. Door closed."

She breathed a sigh. "Great. Thanks—what's your name?"

"Juan."

"Oh," she said. "Don and—"

"Yes, yes, very funny." He raised an eyebrow, nodding sharply at her foot. "Well?"

"Oh," she said again, "right."

The door slammed shut in her face, reverberating as much with the force of his glare as with its own weight.

Well. This was going swimmingly. At this rate, she wouldn't have to miss Jolene for very long. She'd have to turn tail and head back if she couldn't get a job and make enough money to pay her rent. Maybe she'd have to abandon the entire plan. What had she been thinking? It had seemed like such an exciting prospect in the warmth of a safe room in the Zone, surrounded by nothing but books and ideas. A challenge, sure, but a real one, for once. To get to know a world which wasn't so carefully constructed and edited, where people's thoughts weren't managed by what the screens told them each day. But the reality already felt sharper than she could have anticipated, sharper than the edges she'd glimpsed in Mike and Jolene's house. Who was she, to think she could just step out of one world and into another? That she could keep herself safe? She knew none of the rules here. How long was she meant to wait in front of a closed door before calling it a day? What if it never—

The door opened abruptly. This time, the extra light in the background allowed her to make out more than Juan's vague shape: the clean cut of his cheekbones, the corded rope of muscle beneath his long-sleeved shirt. He wasn't just tall but built, full of the kind of strength you wouldn't want to come across in a dark alley but would gladly have by your side. Either way, without the pissed off expression on his face, he could have been an attractive man.

He was sort of attractive even when he looked pissed off, to be honest.

"Come on up then," he said, gesturing to the stairway behind him.

He took her to a small office at the top of the staircase, waved her inside and vanished down the corridor without a goodbye.

"You'll have to forgive Juan," said the middle-aged man who got up from his desk. "He forgets his manners sometimes when there's unexpected guests. Very cautious." He smiled, stepping towards her with an outstretched hand. "Don. Short for Donald, but I prefer Don."

"I'm Maya." She shook his hand. His grip was warm and firm, his posture relaxed as he leant back against the desk. He seemed in every way like Juan's opposite – short with silver-streaked dark hair and deep-set lines cut into white skin, exuding a quiet sense of peace which instantly put her at ease. "And I wasn't expecting to be a guest."

"No, I can see that." He lifted the letter. "It's more that he expected you'd offer a certain kind of service that we don't allow here, if you get my drift. You're lucky I happen to be in, I rarely am these days. How is Mike? It's been a long time."

"He's fine. Working non-stop to keep his family afloat, I don't know how he— Wait, what? He thought I was a prostitute?"

"As I said, you'll have to forgive him."

"Right." Maya bristled. She was buttoned to the neck, for heaven's sake. She brushed down her skirt again. "And who exactly is he, to jump to conclusions like that? I mean, I know you own this place, but…"

Don laughed. "Your boss, if you'd still like that job you're asking for?" He tilted his head, a smile playing over his lips. "My right hand. Runs the place and very well at that. I do very little around here, really. I'm rarely in." He spread his hands. "Think of me as a decorative feature."

Shit. Maya bit her lip. "Sorry. I didn't…"

Don laughed again. "I can see why Mike sent you. You've got some grit there. But maybe not quite enough caution? I think the two of you will get on perfectly." He folded his arms over his chest. "If you do still want the job?"

"I do. Yes. Thank you."

"Fantastic. Juan! See, the timing's just right, one of our girls had to leave us the other day. Not the nicest part of town." He shot Maya a quizzical look. "I won't begin to ask what a girl like you is doing here."

"A girl like me."

"Hmm. Mike says you came all the way in here from the Counties? Just to find work?"

"Yes," Maya said, her fingers curling against her palms. "Things are pretty desperate out there."

It had seemed a reasonable enough story. After all, the Ring was still a part of London. But surely beyond the physical boundaries of the city, out in the countryside and beyond, life would be different yet again. Pretending to be from there should cover any blatant lack in knowledge she let slip about the running of things here. Anything which would make her stand out like a sore thumb.

"Of course. But see, I could've sworn your accent…" He smiled a little. Shook his head. "It's very… polished. Ah, *vale.*" He turned to the door where Juan had appeared. Don stepped close to him and continued speaking in Spanish in low tones for a moment. Even if Maya had remembered any of her long-forgotten lessons, she would have been hard-pressed to catch a word of their quickfire exchange.

She did catch Juan's gaze over Don's shoulder, though. He was scrutinising her with the same intensity as on the doorstep. It made her skin prickle uncomfortably.

In fact, he looked so cross she half expected an argument to break out in front of her, but it never did. Instead, Don clapped Juan on the shoulder with a murmured, "Gracias, hermano," and turned to her. "It's a shame I can't get to know you better, but I was nearly out the door. As I said, lucky you caught me at all. And just as lucky that Juan's happy to show you around, isn't it?"

"Of course," said Juan, sounding like he'd just as soon bite into a lemon.

"Thank you." Maya shook Don's hand again. "I know it's a lot to take on trust, but you won't regret this. I owe you."

"Best not," Don said at the same time that Juan barked, "Come on, then."

He was already three steps down the corridor and past a closed door to their right by the time Maya caught up with him.

"Don's right," he said. "Better strike those words from your vocabulary if you want to stick around here for a while."

She frowned. "It's not like I'm throwing them around willy-nilly. Mike said he's—"

"I don't know Mike," Juan interrupted, "and I don't care."

He opened a door which led to steep wooden stairs. "Upstairs is the office and where I live. Not much reason for you to be there." They descended into another dimly lit corridor. He pointed at the doors leading off it as they walked past them. "Kitchen. Storage. Utility." And finally, pushing past the swinging double doors: "Front of house."

Like the corridors, the main area of the pub was clad in dark wood, from the bar to the flooring to the booths which flanked the front door and ran along the sides of the building, nestled beneath the obscured windows. The low-energy wall sconces hummed with subdued light, candles set out on the table ready to offer a cosier atmosphere once lit for the evening. It was a far cry from the bright, minimalist decor of bars inside the Zone, where glass-panelled fronts displayed their customers for any passersby to see. This felt, at once, like a step back in time and a step into obscurity, a reminder of classic films and books Maya had once dug from the library's archives. The thrill of cracking the codes on the ones which weren't meant for public consumption... Her eyes trailed over the bottles lining the back of the bar, a handful of familiar brands drowned out by countless unmarked ones. How many people brewed moonshine in their backyards to make a living around here?

"You look like you've never seen a pub before," said Juan. He pointed to the door at the far end of the room. "Toilets and back garden through there. We keep the generator outside."

"Maybe I haven't," Maya said, injecting a playful lilt into her voice. "Or maybe I'm just impressed with what you've done with the place."

"So help me…" He planted his hands on his hips. "Don likes to think of it as a haven."

"And you?"

"It's a business. Doing something with the place isn't exactly my priority."

"Right." Maya brushed a finger along the bar. It came away spotless, not a speck of dust clinging to her skin. She met his eyes. "A haven from what? The outside?"

"The outside. The rules which don't exist outside."

"You mean you create a haven by having rules here."

"Yes."

"Such as no working girls?" She crossed her arms. "Tell me, just what about me made you think 'prostitute'?"

He stepped behind the bar and leant on it with both arms, fingers clasped loosely together. The movement made his sleeves ride up, exposing the sharp lines of his wrist bones. "Who said I thought you were?" He raised an eyebrow. "Maybe I was simply saying that we have everything we need here." His gaze cut straight through her. "Bothers you a lot, though, doesn't it?"

Maya could have sworn his lip curled upwards slightly. Or maybe it was a trick of the light.

"Well," she said, "either way I'm not, but I am here to work. So what's the job?"

Juan straightened. "I would have had you doing dishes, but Don wants you front of house." He gestured towards her coat. "Take that off." Then, in response to her affronted look, "I need to see if you're dressed properly."

Could have said please. Under his eyes, her fingers seemed to swell, clumsily tripping over the small buttons of her coat. She didn't know why – the white shirt she'd worn underneath wasn't quite as old-fashioned, but it was also modest. No, it was the sense of being watched, of being assessed…

"That's fine. Wear something like that." He stooped to rummage in a drawer and pulled out an apron which he tossed across to her. "Come back tomorrow, five pm. We open at six. I'll get someone to show you the ropes. Don't be late."

He motioned to the front door.

"Thanks," said Maya. "I'll see you then." Halfway there, she paused and turned around. "Wait. You haven't explained the rules."

This time, there was no mistaking the half-smile which spread over his lips, though it gleamed with a grim determination.

"Start with one. Be decent."

CHAPTER TWO

What did that even mean – be decent?

Maya turned the question over in her mind as she lay in her little alcove later that night, scribbling notes in the small journal she'd taken to carrying around with her. She would have known what it meant in the Zone. Once upon a time, it had been one of her mother's favourite phrases. Be decent. Be polite.

But she'd also written notes on her phone in the Zone, never once worrying about how much energy it used or what might connect to it. Now it lay switched off beneath her pillow, ready to be an emergency beacon only, a last means of contact with the civilised world. People here had long since reverted to outdated forms of communication, with energy so severely rationed. If you had the option of either powering a phone or a stove…. Well. The choice was obvious.

More importantly, it was traceable. And she had no wish to be found.

Was there a black market for generators which weren't powered by solar or wind energy? Old style ones which burned fossil fuels? There had to be. Was that decent or not? Jolene had shown her just how hard it was to keep a household running without all the electronic mod cons which made life easy: washing everything by hand, sweeping the floors with a broom. Everyone had owned them, once. All those empty houses stretching along the roads had been connected to a flourishing mains supply of energy which powered the whole of London.

But that had been before her lifetime.

'The Ring and the Counties returned to a traditional way of life,' the history books had told her, when she'd learnt about the Regression in school. 'But some of us were called to a higher purpose, and so the Zone was formed, right in the centre of our capital.'

Maya still remembered the teacher excluding her from class for digging into the details, for asking why too many times. Why did some people get to stay? What made them special? Why couldn't anyone in the Counties or the Ring prevent the next plague or find better ways of maintaining their energy supply? It didn't make sense. Why lock them all out and create physical barriers around the Zone? Didn't it lock people in as well? And if people outside the Zone kept getting ill with new diseases, why didn't anyone here want to help them?

Asking all those questions wasn't decent. The teacher made that very clear. As did the headmaster. As did, later that day, her mother – the flashing anger in her eyes and her raised voice left Maya in no doubt. Did she want to get thrown out of classes and never see her friends again? Did she want to get banned from the Academy forever, to pass up her chance to become a top-class engineer or a scientist who would make a breakthrough discovery one day? Most importantly, did Maya want her mother to get into trouble and vanish like her father? Wasn't it enough that one of them was gone?

She didn't explain how those last two points were connected to asking too many questions, but that wasn't necessary. The threat hung thick in the air, a palpable presence which soaked into the plush furniture like a fog and lingered, lingered. Even to this day, the sight of a Chesterfield sent shivers up Maya's spine.

It had been a long while until Maya dared to ask why again with someone else present. What it was about Stuart that had opened her up – who knew. A feeling. A knowledge engraved in the wrinkles which softened his face.

"Why didn't we work together, if it was all falling apart?"

Stuart had looked at her, a smile playing about his lips which didn't quite crinkle the corners of his eyes. And told her that was an excellent question.

The library had become her favourite place from that day on.

The pub was a different place at night, still dark and cosy but also filled with the din of people's conversations, the clattering of glasses and cutlery. For somewhere nestled amidst the backstreets, it got far busier than Maya had expected. By seven pm it rivalled a teeming town square.

Juan barely said hello before passing her on to Irene—"Call me Rina"—a white woman in her early thirties with short-cropped, black hair and brown eyes. Maya liked her immediately. Although she ran Maya through a dizzying list of to-dos and how-tos, she had a knack for explaining them and threw in the odd joke for good measure. The regulars obviously shared Maya's impression, greeting Rina warmly as they filed into the pub, settled into the booths and lined the bar.

An hour had seemed like plenty of time for her induction, but it flew by and soon Maya was juggling orders for drinks and trying to remember the – thankfully simple – menu, all the while keeping track of dirty glasses and tables which needed clearing. The challenge grew as the place got busier and busier and the background noise swallowed people's requests so Maya had to lean in close to catch a word. She couldn't mess this up, not with Juan looming behind the bar, undoubtedly watching her every move. She confirmed each order twice until they all merged into a cacophony, tangling and twisting. And who would have known how physical it would be to run back and forth within the same small space? She'd been in decent shape, hadn't she? Still, a couple of hours in and her arms were aching, a trickle of sweat running down the nape of her neck and curling her hair where it spilled over her upper back.

Perhaps it was inevitable, then, that the tray full of dirties would slip as she swerved to avoid a group of men squeezing past the bar. She tried to save it, but the balance was already lost, glass after glass falling as if in slow motion and shattering on the hard floor right before her eyes.

The steady hum of the pub broke just long enough for a loud series of cheers and claps to mark her fuck up, then resumed. Maya sighed and brushed a wet tendril of hair off her forehead with the back of her arm.

"It's all right," Rina said. "At least they were empty. Here, let me show you where the dustpan and brush live."

Juan watched them clear the mess from behind the bar, a frown etched on his face.

"What?" Rina crossed her arms and frowned back at him. "You said to throw her in at the deep end."

Oh, thanks.

Juan set the dishcloth down and looked pointedly over to the far corner where a man was gesturing for another order. Rina rolled her eyes and took off.

Juan picked the dishcloth back up. Gestured towards the line of dirty glasses. "Wash these."

"Guess you've got me where you wanted me in the first place. Doing dishes," Maya murmured as she turned the tap on. "Not sure what it is you've got against me."

Juan took the first glass from her, drying it with a swift, practised motion. The light arced off it when he set it back on the counter. "Who says I've got anything against you?"

"Throw her in at the deep end," Maya mimicked.

Shut up. She really needed to shut up.

"Has it occurred to you that this might not be the kind of place where we have the luxury to ease people in gently? Or maybe that I'm stress-testing you?"

"Different things, surely." She thrust the next glass at him. "And? How's the test going? Proving insightful so far?"

"Yes." His slim fingers folded around the glass slowly, as if the pub around them was a calm oasis, not a storm. "Very."

Maya bit her lip. "I'm doing my best."

"Yes," Juan said, without missing a beat. "I can see that."

Why did everything about him have to be so measured? She'd been prepared for him to be critical after yesterday but not for this settled watchfulness, this quiet confidence he carried about him like a cloak. As if it was ok to appraise people and then come right out and own up to it. As if it was abnormal to be riled when you were treated like some kind of experiment. Abnormal not to be so calculating. And yet, she couldn't argue with some of what he'd said. This wasn't home. Maybe she was expecting too much. Maybe she'd overestimated herself.

She took a deep breath. She needed to get better at letting things roll off her back. How long had she been working at it by now? Years. Endless years. Long before she first stepped foot outside the Zone, she'd made a commitment to herself. But something about Juan set her back, made it a hundred times harder to shut up and smile. And besides, hadn't he started it? She had put her best foot forward yesterday despite his irritability, had been unfailingly polite – she didn't deserve this.

Still, there was nothing for it. She slowed down her movements as she washed the rest of the glasses, avoiding his gaze. Thankfully, she was saved from further awkward conversation by Rina returning to call Juan to some emergency in the kitchen. She wasn't saved, of course, from overhearing his sharp instruction to, "Keep an eye on her." Like she was some sort of errant puppy that might ruin the carpet, not a full-grown woman.

"What's with him?" she asked once he had disappeared around the corner.

Rina laughed. "He's all right. Grumpy, but there's far worse." She looked Maya over, head tilted to the side. "You think he's got it in for you."

Maya began stacking clean glasses into the shelf behind the counter. "I'm that obvious, huh?" She smiled wryly. "I don't know, it's just been non-stop since I've met him. Like he's trying to dissect me."

"Don't take it personally, he's like that. Likes to vet people who have any sort of access here. Takes it all very seriously. If you're good, you're going to be good in the long run." She grabbed a couple of glasses and began pulling pints. "Thing is, he's pretty solid once you're in. Pays you. Full wage and on time.

Far more than can be said for a lot of bosses round here. Hell, he even lets me swap my shifts around when I've got exams coming up, even if it means we're short. That's practically unheard of."

"You're studying?"

"Yeah. Substation technician exam. It's a lot. But it'll be a game-changer if I can swing it."

"They're the power hubs that route energy from the wind farms, aren't they?" Maya said, feigning ignorance. Everyone inside the Zone knew about the star-shaped network of metal arteries which pulsed energy and life from the far reaches of the country into their glowing bubble. Well. Everyone who had ever studied engineering, that was. The rest just took it for granted.

"Wind farms. Solar farms. Offshore. Onshore. This close to the centre, it doesn't really matter where it came from, it's more about bringing it all together. I mean, it does matter when you get into the technical detail, but you get my drift."

"I've heard it's tough to even get a foot in the door."

It was Rina's turn to smile. "Hell yeah. Are you surprised? Of course they're worried about sabotage. Can you imagine what all that juice would fetch on the black market? Trust me, Juan's got nothing on their background checks."

"But you passed them anyway."

"I did. Always helps when you know people."

"Do you ever…" Maya hesitated, then pressed on. "Does it not ever feel really unfair to you?"

Rina shot her a look. "To know people?"

"No, I…" Maya shook her head. "I meant the energy. All of it going inside."

Rina shrugged. "Fair. Unfair. It is what it is. It'll be unfair to ditch this place for all it's given me if I manage to move on, won't it? Thanks for all the flexibility, Juan, off I fuck." She placed four full pints on a tray. "But I've got a three-year-old at home. Gotta be solid for her, no? Does me no good wondering if it's fair."

Would she still think the same if she knew? All those socialite dinners Maya's mother had dragged her to as a child. The long, stacked tables. The dazzling light of the chandeliers arcing off the glasses. The elaborately arranged food.

"Does you no good either," Rina said and handed her a pint full of water. "Here." She pulled out a stool. "Take a breather while he's gone. Get through tonight, fix the world tomorrow."

Maya sighed and sat down.

She did get through the night. By the time Rina flashed her a smile and a "Well done!" on her way out of the door, Maya's clothes stuck to her in a sweaty mess. She itched to get out of them, but there was one more table to wipe and another, and then, finally, the night was officially over.

She headed back to the bar, rinsed the cloth and hung it up. Her fingertips were wrinkled from all the washing, and her arms ached when she pulled the apron over her head. She shrugged back into the warmth of her coat, grabbing her bag from the storage space beneath the counter. Juan stood beside her, bent over a small book and scribbling steadily. Probably their takings for the evening.

"Goodnight," she said, as she walked past him.

Only the sound of her boots accompanied her. Never mind. She was far too tired to care, anyway.

"Sometimes people who come through connections, they also come with expectations. To be treated differently to the rest of us. Better."

Maya paused, already halfway to the door. She should keep walking. She was definitely, definitely too tired for this.

"That's not me," she said instead.

"No." His pensive tone urged her to turn towards him, though any extra movement seemed like a waste of energy right now. "It isn't, is it."

She looked at him across the distance of the pub. The wall sconces glowed dimly, wrapping them both in shadows.

"Why are you here?" Juan asked.

Her thumb found the edge of a thread in her pocket, rhythmically pulling it back and forth. "None of your business."

Juan smiled and dropped his gaze. Looked up again, eyes piercing straight into hers. There was something mesmerising about the gesture, something hypnotic. "You're too soft," he said, voice low. "You won't make it here if you stay that way. In here, maybe. But not past that door."

What on earth was she meant to say to that? "It's not your job to toughen me up."

Juan smiled again. Pushed himself off the counter. "No, I suppose it isn't." He walked over and leant across her, pulling the heavy front door open with one hand as though it weighed nothing. Its bell resonated with a crystal note singing into the dark of the night.

"Goodnight, Maya. I'll see you tomorrow."

CHAPTER THREE

She'd never thought of herself as soft. All her life she'd been too many edges, never quite slotting into the smooth social flows which ran everything inside the Zone.

"I don't know what I did to deserve this!" her mother had shouted one evening. Maya had stolen into the host's office while they attended a dinner party inside his Kensington mansion. She couldn't have been older than fourteen. Fifteen, maybe? "Haven't I taught you anything about how to behave in polite society?"

She had, of course. Maya knew the rules. But dinner parties were also incredibly boring, and she knew Uncle Derek was one of the most acclaimed virologists around. The office door stood slightly ajar. The temptation, once she'd been excused from the table to nip to the loo, was too overwhelming. And the papers which she pulled from the file drawer's depths, well, they were too fascinating, too new, too foreign; a glimpse into a different world. They told stories: stories of pandemic after pandemic, of diseases sweeping the world. Naturally, they told only a sliver of those stories, a slice of reality wrapped in abstract medical language which kept her guessing at answers. But they told stories nevertheless: of attempts to find vaccines, to identify different strains of disease, to sequence genomes and discover new drugs. She skimmed them hungrily – and just as she noticed that they grew sparser as the publication years rolled by, her mother found her.

Maya kept stealing into secret spaces from that day, always on the hunt for further clues. Although she found many more shards over the years to add to the mosaic, vast gaps fractured the bigger picture. At some point, buried in digital files on geopolitics and global warming and early 21st-century history, the realisation sank in: she would never complete the puzzle in a library. There were too many unspoken stories, too many silenced stories. Stories which lived outside the Zone, out in the Ring, in the Counties. In the daily wheels which kept on turning to bring them fresh food and all that bright, sparkling electricity for the virtual reality systems.

In the people who kept them turning.

She had never thought of herself as soft. Was it soft to long for the truth?

To be fair, life in the Zone had definitely spoiled her for life out here in the Ring. Her draughty shed-flat was a far cry from the cosy bed in her mother's apartment. Instead of golden sunlight which flooded through regal windows in the morning to rouse her, she woke to her back screaming bloody murder from another night in the stony alcove. She quickly learnt not to fling her arms out wide in a stretch first thing only to be met by unforgiving brick. At least the curtain held the draught at bay enough so she could keep the portable heater switched off for now. She was doing her best to stretch out those long September days, knowing full well that every ray of sunshine she didn't use would be worth its weight in gold if allowed to slumber in the battery until colder days came along. Well. Worth far more. Gold possessed little value since the market crash which had heralded the start of the Regression.

Most days Maya was too busy trying to figure out how things worked around here to feel lonely. She soon learnt to memorise walking routes by heart. If only she could have used her phone to map a path around the intersecting streets which time had stripped clean of signage, but it wasn't worth the risk of being tracked. Besides, a close call with a pickpocket at the food market near Victoria Park's allotments showed her that it would have disappeared in a flash: amidst the bustle of people scrambling for the largest loaf of bread, she almost didn't feel the hand sneak into her pocket. Maya elbowed the man swiftly and yelped which deterred him – thank fuck – but the moment left her shaking, her heart a fierce gallop. Nobody asked if she was ok. Beyond some glances, nobody even reacted.

Absurd that less than five miles away this would never have happened. Nobody needed to steal in the Zone. And even if they had tried to, well… They wouldn't have had the chance to try a second time. Of course, the shadow of the Enforcers loomed here in the Ring, too, a much more visible presence in many ways. But the men in clean-cut, armoured uniforms with weapons pressed to their chest showed little interest in interfering in the day-to-day skirmishes which affected people. They hung around like grey clouds in the sky. A reminder.

Maya dashed away whenever she saw one, just in case. She soon learnt to avoid the old railway stations where they congregated.

How lucky she'd been to stumble across her tiny shed. Of course, some nights she longed for a room in one the abandoned houses she regularly passed on her way back from the pub. But they didn't have the same cast-iron gates with heavy chains; they didn't sit in a garden embraced by wildly overgrown hedges which even the fittest, most limber man would have trouble climbing. Getting used to outdoor showers was a small price to pay, surely. She could afford to shiver her way through her late-morning wake-ups. Without a reliable way to dry her hair, she stopped wearing the dark brown curls down – far simpler to wrestle them into a braid which fell between her shoulder blades.

Her body changed in other ways, too. She'd always been tall but never toned, preferring time in the library to throwing herself into a VR gym. Now her strength built with each passing day. Soon, she was lifting full trays of glasses without her arms protesting the move.

She fell into a rhythm at the pub, getting to know her coworkers as time passed. Gus in the kitchen cooked a mean stew and always made sure everyone took back their share of the leftovers at the end of the night – a relief on those chaotic days when the local markets didn't have enough to go around. Evelyn was always five minutes late but scrubbed the cutlery until it gleamed like silver. Everything inside the pub was a little like that, worn around the edges but impeccably clean, unlike the alleyways outside. The leather on the booths cracked with its age, but it smelled only of old smoke from decades long gone: nobody lit up inside the room. Probably another one of Juan's unspoken rules. Maya had walked past some other pubs by now, and it certainly wasn't the norm.

She struggled to get to know the regulars. Why on earth had she ever dreamt that it would be easy? A natural turn in their conversation, an instant connection, and she'd suddenly find out all about people's lives outside the Zone – hah. How naive could she be? A request for a pint, an order for some stew, and Maya, the eternal social butterfly, wittily responding with a 'sure' – that was more like it. Any clever comment she might have made fell prey to the fast pace of the evenings, popping into her head on her way home. If only she could be more like Rina, who excelled at the kind of rapid banter which might have opened doors to some heart-to-hearts. Maya was fast becoming friends with Rina herself, but that was clearly all Rina's doing. Whenever Maya drifted off into her thoughts, Rina would be there with a quip and a smile, easing her into some common ground, finding topics of conversation during their breaks. It was so much harder with the others. Sure, Maya slowly picked up some names here and there, but people came to the pub to talk to each other, not to the bar staff.

Well. Except for how everyone took their time to speak to Juan.

Perhaps it didn't help to have him working so nearby, either. For some reason, his presence made it hard to stay focused. Instead of thinking about what she could say to build rapport with the next customer, Maya often caught herself watching Juan. He seemed a different person when chatting to people at the bar, warm smile ready on his lips as he poured drinks with slick movements. In a way it made sense – a place like this would never have thrived without some social skills at the helm. But Maya couldn't quite reconcile the watchful man who handed out neatly lined-up pay packets at the end of each week with this jovial hub of the community. Which one was the front? Neither? Both?

It was the mystery which intrigued Maya. It had nothing to do with the fact that, when in a good mood, Juan was remarkably easy to look at, relaxed, liquid strength flowing through his gestures, smiles crinkling his eyes even as they smoothed away all his other lines. She wasn't that shallow. It had nothing to do with the fact that the rich timbre of his laugh trickled molasses down her spine the first time she heard it. With the way the deep shades of his skin blended into the dark wood stretching behind him, only to gleam subtly when the light hit them just right. And it definitely had nothing to do with those moments when – to a jolt of adrenaline – he caught her looking, how the easygoing expression slid away momentarily to reveal something deeper: not the stern formality but something alert and incisive which cut straight through to the core of her.

Did he watch her, too, when she wasn't looking? She threw out the idea as fanciful. He was too busy. Sure, he was keeping an eye on her to be certain she was doing her job, but beyond that, why would he be stealing glances at her? For one, he didn't seem the type to ever steal anything. No. He'd be taking it like he had earned it – and he probably had. Skittishly looking away like she'd been caught with her hand in the cookie jar, that was Maya's territory.

Now if only she could drop this fantasy that she'd absorb people's life stories through some strange osmosis. It would never happen unless she started somewhere, and she needed to stop finding excuses. She began by capturing observations, just some hasty squiggles in her notebook about the regulars whenever she wasn't run off her feet. Or when she wasn't lost in inappropriate thoughts, as it were.

"You're catching flies, my girl."

Maya shook herself from her reverie of watching Juan pull pints. He was wearing a button-down shirt tonight, sleeves rolled up to the elbow. The crisp contrast of the white fabric against his skin threw the muscles of his forearms into stark relief.

The elderly lady in the booth smiled, revealing the gaps between her teeth. Somehow, they didn't detract from the gesture. "He's a bit of all right, isn't he? Ah, if I had my time again…" She winked. "Shame those days are over."

Maya felt heat rise to her cheeks. "I wasn't…"

The woman clucked her tongue. "Don't worry about it." She patted the seat beside her. "Sit down. I've been watching you race about, you deserve a break. No, really, don't worry about it, nobody but me even noticed. All too busy thinking about themselves to be observant. Always that way in life."

Maya sat with some hesitation. "I'm Maya," she said.

"I know. You're the word of the town."

"Really?"

"Nah. Not really. All too busy thinking about themselves, remember? But I'm old and bored, and I like to watch people sometimes. Precious else to do round here but knit." She lifted her work in progress, yarn spooling over needles in tight loops. "Bethany, but you can call me Beth."

"Hi Beth." Maya cast a sideways glance to the bar. "Not sure I should be joining you, to be honest. Don't think I'm meant to chat to the customers while there's orders open. He'll have my head in a minute."

"Nah," Beth said again. "Bark's worse than the bite with that one, trust me."

"People keep saying that, but I'd rather not put it to the test. He does write my paycheck."

"Worst comes to worst we'll pretend I was asking you for another shandy." Beth winked. "Besides, maybe a little rebellion is just what you need to grab his attention."

"Can we… not talk about him, maybe?" Maya frowned. "Or myself. I'd much rather hear more about you, to be honest."

"Now that's music to my ears! Usually you young folk just want us to listen with all our wisdom, don't you?" She propped her chin on one hand. "Tell us all about your struggles like we know nothing about them, then tell us we know nothing and don't understand you?"

Maya smiled. "I don't know. I think the more you listen, the more you learn."

"Or the more you watch? All right, all right, I'm only teasing you, don't look at me like that." Beth ran a hand through her short, silver hair. "You're not wrong, of course. Don't think I knew that when I was your age."

"What did you know?"

"How to tap into our neighbour's power supply and siphon off enough energy to keep the house warm for the baby, but not so much that he'd notice. How to get the baby to sleep on the nights when it's still just too cold. My dad taught me. The siphoning, not the baby. My nana taught me about the baby. You carry them, wrap them in your coat. She knew nothing about siphoning. Always found it mighty strange, said in her time nobody worried about how things worked, they just used them. When it went wrong, you called someone to come round and fix it. They all had to learn very fast when things changed, but she just didn't have the head for it. Nah, she was always very glad my grandad did."

What was it she'd been worried about a minute ago? Something to do with Juan. It didn't seem important anymore.

"Tell me more," Maya said with rapt attention.

"Good evening, Bethany. How is my favourite girl tonight?"

Maya jumped at the sound of Juan's voice so close to her ear. How long had she been listening to Beth?

"Taking up all my staff's precious time, I see?"

"Sorry," Maya said. "She was just—I mean, I was just taking an order. For shandy."

Juan turned to look at her, raising an eyebrow. He was near enough that she could have traced its clean arch. "For half an hour?"

"I was teaching her how to brew it," Beth cut in sweetly.

Juan smiled and straightened, gaze settling on Beth. "Yes, that seems likely," he responded, just as sweetly. "You probably make a better one than our suppliers as well."

"Of course." Beth grinned. "Now where are your manners, my boy?"

Juan laughed. "Tragically lost whenever I'm away from your dearest tutelage." He bent across the table, lifting her weathered hand and bringing it to his lips in an exaggerated, courtly kiss. "Is that better, milady?"

"Much. At this rate you'll have earned your present"—she raised her knitting needles—"in spite of all those long, lonely hours you leave me sitting here by myself. You know, it's almost as though you forget me at times. As if you don't appreciate all the effort, every ounce of love that goes into creating this."

"Never. I lie awake every night dreaming of the day I shall wear it." Juan flattened his palm against his breastbone. "It warms my heart to think of how I'll always be able to carry you with me once I've been gifted with the fruits of your labour. Even when circumstances force us apart. You must know this."

Beth laughed, the sound surprisingly clear for all her roughened edges. A bit as if she'd distilled her youth into it.

Juan turned back to Maya. "Was I too subtle earlier? Don't you have somewhere to be?"

"Ah, lay off the girl," said Beth. "Only giving an old woman excellent customer service like back in the day."

"You're not old enough to remember pre-Regression times. Nobody is."

"Yes, but she's far too sweet to be hard on, isn't she?"

"I'm going to go wash the glasses," Maya said quickly and rushed away before Beth could make things very awkward for her.

Maya's mind buzzed with everything Beth had told her throughout the rest of her shift. As soon as she'd cleared the last table, she slid into a booth and pulled out her notebook. She'd never remember everything if she waited to get home. And this was everything she'd been waiting for: the kind of story which didn't just help her understand the past better but which could help others inside the Zone understand the present, if only she captured it well enough. The kind of story which made it harder to ignore that people out here were just that – people like them, with families and lives. Not the faceless crowds that everybody clapped for on a Friday night, in organised gratitude.

The second she hit her flow, Juan's voice broke her concentration for the second time that night. "What are you doing?"

Maya didn't look up. "None of your business," she said and kept writing.

"I thought we'd moved on from that a little."

"Had we?" Maya asked distractedly. "I hadn't noticed."

The silence which followed grew thick until it smothered her thoughts. She sighed and put down her pen to look at him. Rude. That's what she was being: rude.

He was still watching her. Gaze resting on her. Contemplative. He looked even taller when she was sitting down than he normally did. Somehow less intimidating in his height than he'd appeared on the day she'd met him, though.

"Sorry," she said. "I'm probably making you stay down here longer than necessary. Should really be doing this at home. I'll let myself out."

Juan shook his head. "I don't mind. I was only trying to work out what would possess anyone to stick around at this hour."

"Would you believe me if I said the heating is way better here?"

"Hmm." Was that a frown? "Well, it usually takes me half an hour to finish everything up. You can stay that long. I don't sleep much, anyway."

"All right. Thanks."

She watched him walk back to the bar in silence. A hush had descended over the room now they were alone, amplifying the creak of the floorboards, the rustle of his clothes. In the far corner, an antique clock ticked away the seconds on a shelf. Everything about the moment felt slow and small, like a trickle of sand running through outstretched hands.

"Juan?"

"Yes?"

Maya hesitated.

"Nothing. Never mind."

There was no imagining the bemused smile which curved his lips then. Not even at a distance.

"Was that a scarf?" she asked abruptly. "What Beth was knitting."

He laughed. "Jumper. I get one every year. They're hideous. No idea where she gets the yarn from." He shrugged. "They're warm, though. Comfortable. Counts for something."

"Yes," Maya said. "It does."

CHAPTER FOUR

She stayed late most nights after that. Some days, she also arrived a little early – it wasn't as if she had anywhere else to be. Back at home, there had always been social commitments to duck: a study group, a virtual games night, her mother's dinner parties. She'd thrown most of them over for time at the library or in her room, but now she found herself without invitations for the first time in her life. The pub increasingly felt like home, though, that echo of familiarity, like being wrapped inside a cloak, like being tucked away somewhere out of sight. And perhaps Maya and Juan had moved past their initial tension, too. He'd stopped picking her up on minor mistakes during the evenings, and they spent the additional time they shared quietly absorbed in their respective tasks.

Much though her curiosity about him still urged her eyes to track his movements, she couldn't bring herself to break the silence of the evenings by starting a conversation. There was something almost magical about their stillness, something delicate and tranquil. Like neither of them were making any effort to be anything other than who they were in those moments. Like neither of them were asking each other to be anything else, either.

Maya let the atmosphere sink into her bones. She felt at peace in it, in a way she'd only ever glimpsed in the library before.

Spending time in his presence certainly was a far cry from listening to another one of her mother's rants right before bedtime. She slept so much better these days, even on her concrete bed of stone.

No, she couldn't break the spell of their evenings by prying, by invading his privacy with brash questions. This was yet another version of him, one she hadn't seen before. Quiet, but not watchful. Relaxed. Settled in whatever he was doing, in himself. A steadiness to him which she'd been missing since she first came here. There was a kind of intimacy, too, in stealing glances at him when it was only them. It deepened the captivation of each little moment. The absent-minded path of his fingers across his bare scalp while he was concentrating on the logbook. The reverberation of low sound whenever he cleared his throat and the way his Adam's apple moved.

The knowledge that if he caught her at it, she couldn't pretend they'd accidentally crossed gazes in a busy room.

One thing was certain: she definitely still spent far too much time thinking about Juan. He probably didn't give her half the headspace. In fact, he sometimes seemed almost surprised when she got up to leave and said goodbye. As if he'd entirely forgotten she was there.

Oh well. So long as he was comfortable around her.

The leaves gleamed in the bright October sun, a vibrant shock of golds and reds on the trees when she arrived one late afternoon.

"Oh, it's you," Juan said and stepped inside without waiting for her. She barely caught the door. "Lock that behind you."

"Good afternoon to you, too?" she called after him. But in the time it took her eyes to adjust to the gloom of the pub, he had already vanished. Maya shook her head and locked the door. What had got into him? She hadn't seen him this sour-faced since their first meeting.

She tracked him down to the courtyard where he was kneeling beside the exposed innards of the solar generator.

"What's wrong?" She dropped to her knees.

"Blasted thing has gone and developed a short. Think I've narrowed it down to the inverter." He narrowed his eyes at the generator as if he could stare it into submission. "And that's about as far as I got."

Instinct took over. She scanned the instruments scattered all over the ground and grabbed the multimeter. "May I?"

"Be my guest."

She removed a panel. "God, who put this thing together?" How long had it been since she'd sat in lectures? Somehow it felt like a lifetime ago, all the memories of poring over diagrams resurfacing with a grey tinge to their edges. Still, the tests were simple enough to run – even in a system which must have been patched together with detritus from the refuse pile. It only took her a few minutes.

"There." She pointed at a junction. "The transistor has blown. Just needs replacing and it should run. Although strictly speaking you need to replace that entire circuit board, really. It's a shambles."

"Very likely," Juan said, voice dripping with sarcasm.

"Ok, well, just the transistor, then. Shall I swap it out?"

"Sure." His tone didn't lift. If anything, he sounded more biting, more bitter. "Thanks for your help. I'll go right over and grab a new one from the transistor fairies, yes?"

Maya looked at him, stunned. It was just a—

"Maya," Juan said impatiently, as if he could read her thoughts, "where exactly did you come from?"

"I don't understand." She shifted, rubbing her palms against her knees. He hadn't mentioned her cover story or asked why she was here for ages. Almost as though he was respecting her privacy, too. "You know where I came from. I'm Mike's niece from the Counties. I couldn't find work so I came—"

"Cut the crap. Nobody from the Counties is stupid enough to believe transistors grow on trees. And you are many things, princess, but stupid isn't one of them."

Maya frowned. "Was that an insult? Or a compliment?"

Juan stared at her, forehead still furrowed into deep-set lines. "Probably both."

"Wow," Maya said with some heat. "Thanks. Well, listen, I didn't break your transistor. I'm just trying to help."

Juan closed his eyes and pinched the bridge of his nose. She saw the sigh more than she heard it: the ripple of it as he breathed in, then out, tension flowing from his muscles like a current into the earth. "I know."

They fell silent for a long moment.

"Are we not on the grid?" Maya asked.

"Yes, but do you have any idea how erratic it is? No, don't answer that. Suffice to say, we can't afford for the backup to go down. I might as well shut the doors now." He grabbed the multimeter, sticking it back into the canvas bag beside him. "We'll have to wait for Rina to come in. She might be able to patch it."

"She's not in today, remember? She left early yesterday because her daughter's sick. You said she could stay off today if she wasn't any better."

"Yes, of course. Of course."

Maya stared at the circuit board. For all that it hadn't been fair of him to be so snarky, the weight in his words banished any resentment which still clung to her. This wasn't about her. She could almost hear the thoughts ticking away inside his skull – everyone connected to the pub, everyone who depended on it to stay open. If only she wasn't such an amateur. If only she were creative enough to patch faulty circuit paths without replacement parts, if only she knew how to fix things outside the rigid structure she'd always taken for granted… If only she wasn't falling so desperately short.

"I could try and get her," she suggested.

"No." Juan shook his head. "It's how close to opening time? Half an hour? She'd be here already if she could be, you know that. Besides, you're right, the transistor needs replacing or the whole thing will blow in a week." His fingers drummed a gallop on his thigh. "I need you to open up. Can you do that?"

"Me?" Maya said. "I mean – doesn't it make more sense to stay closed for today?"

Juan's lip quirked. "Sure. In the same magical universe where transistors grow on trees." He brushed the dirt off his hands and got to his feet. "Must be lovely there."

"Maybe not as lovely as you imagine." She followed suit. He knew, didn't he? Or at least suspected. And still he wasn't really digging. "I'm happy to help, just not sure I'm the person for the job."

"Gus will help if you need it, I've no doubt. But you're much more in tune with the flow at the bar than him. Better with the customers, too. Worst comes to worst it'll be slow service, but they'll cope."

"Sure, but what if the grid does go down?"

"Then you close. No other option, the battery won't last the night. Kick them all out and we start again when I'm back. Don't kick out Gus, obviously. Have a candlelit dinner with him while you wait for me or whatever helps you pass the time. What else?"

They slipped back inside the pub. Maya struggled to follow his movements in the dim light, the imprint of the sun still clinging to her eyes.

"It's just… two months ago you were watching me like a hawk and only trusting me to wash glasses."

"I've revised my opinion." Juan rummaged in the lockbox he kept in the bottom cabinet, his back turned towards her. "You should be happy."

"I am." Probably best not to think about how happy. Or what exactly he meant by that. "But…"

"But what?" He rose, turning to face her. In his outstretched hand lay two keys: one for the front door, the other for the heavy, antiquated cash register.

Maya coiled a strand of hair around her finger. Tugged at it, caught herself and tucked it behind her ear. "What if they kick off?"

"Who? The staff?"

"The customers!" She'd never seen a fight break out, to be fair, but it had always puzzled her, given the reputation of the area. Altercations in broad daylight were a common occurrence – she'd run into them more than once. The pub, on the other hand, seemed to inhabit a parallel universe, one in which tolerance and peace were the norms.

"They won't. Not as long as they know I'm coming back."

"Right," Maya said, pressing her lips together. "The mere threat of your presence intimidates them into compliance."

Juan flashed her a wide smile. "Obviously."

"Is that why we don't have a doorman?"

"Obviously."

"Well, I'm glad you've got such immense confidence in your invisible presence."

"You don't seem to share it." The fine lines around his eyes crinkled. "I'm hurt."

"Why do I get the sense you're not taking me seriously?"

Juan's smile softened as he dropped his gaze, his eyelashes smudging like coal against his skin. He really needed to stop doing that so much; it did terrible things to Maya's stomach. Maybe that was the real reason he didn't need to worry about the customers: he'd charmed them all into submission.

"It's less about my invisible presence," he said, "and more about Don's sphere of influence, if you really must know."

Maya's brows drew together. "What do you mean, influence? In what way?"

"I don't have time for this." He pressed the keys into her hand, then rested his palm on her shoulder. She could feel the warmth of it heavy against her clavicle, her skin tingling beneath his fingertips even through the thick cotton of her dress. "You can do this. It'll be fine. I'll see you in a few hours. Just don't let the place burn down."

And before she knew it, he had shrugged into his coat and was halfway to the door.

"Great!" Maya called after him. "I wasn't even worried about that!"

Gus was happy to help, but Gus was also Gus – far more interested in staying away from people than in mingling with them. On his suggestion, Maya rigged up the specials board, writing 'No table service, order at bar!' in big, looping letters. Evelyn agreed to split herself between running food from the kitchen and her usual dishwashing, collecting glasses along the way. All in all, it wasn't a bad setup, but the pace soon stretched them and Maya felt like it was her first day all over again.

"Hey sweetie," a male voice interrupted her just as she was trying to speed-rinse ten glasses. "Where's the bossman gone?"

Maya glanced at the man who'd sidled up to the bar. Ash brown hair, wide-set eyes and a rough five o'clock shadow. Had she seen him before? "Not your sweetie," she said and returned to her task. "Juan's out on business, he's left me in charge. Can I help?"

He leered at her. "Pretty rapid promotion, that. What did you do to get there?"

So much for good behaviour sustaining in the absence of a certain someone's presence. "I worked," Maya said sharply. "I behaved. Did you want to order something?"

"Pint of lager."

"Sure." She flipped a glass the right way up and pulled the tap handle. He was still staring – even with her gaze fixed on the golden bubbles streaming steadily downwards, she could see the grin on his face.

"Oh, I bet you behaved."

Maya forced herself to look him straight in the eye. "Did you want that beer, or not?"

"Don't be that way. I'll give you a good tip and all."

Maya bit her lip. She was out of her depth here. Apart from a couple of overenthusiastic schoolboy crushes in her teenage years who she'd easily evaded, most men had treated her with respect. This was new. What was the best strategy with someone who wouldn't take a hint? Confrontation seemed to be escalating things…

"I think I'd rather you took your pint and left." She plonked the glass down in front of him with one hand and held the other out for payment.

Wrong call. The cold press of coins was swiftly followed with a clammy grip of her palm. "Can't take a joke, can you? New position's gone to your head already? Or have you always been such a—"

"Leave the girl alone already, would you?"

The man let go of her and turned to the speaker, a middle-aged, black man with salt-and-pepper hair and a pair of spectacles balancing on the knuckles of his left hand. "Just making conversation."

"Well, and she's only doing her job, so why don't you give her some space to get on with it?"

Her assailant studied him for long, tense seconds before slinking away in a huff. Not without shooting Maya a look of pure vitriol, though.

"Thanks," she said, her shoulders dropping.

"Leroy," said the older man. He unfolded his glasses and set them back on the tip of his nose. "Looks like these will live through another day. Good, good. They weren't cheap."

"Thanks, Leroy." Maya chucked the coins in the register. It clanged shut. "What would you like? On the house."

"Ah, in that case, you should have a nice Glenfidditch right there. Near the top."

Maya scanned the shelf until she found the bottle of aged whisky. A layer of dust blew clean off it. "I'll remember to set tighter parameters next time," she said ruefully, pouring two fingers' worth. "Let's hope Juan doesn't check it too often, huh?"

Leroy chuckled, a gravelly rasp. "I doubt he'd mind. You've earned way more than that tonight, I've seen how you've been holding it all together. You could always pretend you gave yourself a little treat."

"He'd definitely mind me drinking on the job."

"True." Leroy took a sip. "Though dealing with that charmer just now, you'd be forgiven for turning to drink." He tilted the glass. "Thanks. This is beautiful."

"I'm glad." Maya released a breath. "Wish I could say I actually dealt with it myself. Thanks again for stepping in, anyway."

Leroy shrugged. "We're a community, aren't we? Where will things get to if we can't be that? It's hard enough." He settled more comfortably on the bar stool. "Where *is* Juan?"

"We had some supply issues he had to sort."

"Those must be some issues. Can't remember last time I didn't see him at the helm. Must have been years? Come to think of it, maybe I never have…"

"I'm sure he'll find a solution," Maya said, willing it to be true. She paused, studying Leroy for a moment. She'd definitely seen him before tonight, although they'd never spoken. He cleaved to the bar, always in the same spot, often the catalyst for Juan's laughter. "This pub is his life, isn't it? He never leaves."

Leroy hummed an affirmative, letting another trickle of whisky seep past his lips.

"How long has this place been open? It seems a bit like—"

"Maya, we've got the dinner glut, can you give me a hand running it out? It's too much."

"Of course," Maya called across to Evelyn, who was balancing three plates on each hand. "Excuse me."

By the time they had finished serving, Leroy was huddled in conversation with a small group of men. She never got her answer.

CHAPTER FIVE

"Why don't you head home?" Maya asked Evelyn, blowing out the last candle before placing it back on the table. "I'll finish off, I have to wait until he's back, anyway."

Gus had left half an hour ago, not long after the doorbell jingled the last customer away into the night. Now a velvet silence stretched through the building, wrapping the empty spaces in its threads.

Juan should be back already.

"Well, you don't have to tell me twice." Evelyn grabbed her coat off the rail. "We did awesome tonight if I say so myself, but hell if I'm going for a repeat of that tomorrow." She shook her head. "Madness. Hope you don't have to wait too long. It's late."

"That's ok," Maya said. "Goodnight."

"Night."

The moment the door shut, Maya collapsed in a chair. Her body ached from pure exertion, but underneath it lay a different heaviness, a coiling, twisting tension in her belly. It was late. Why wasn't Juan back?

She breathed in deeply, the smell of soot from extinguished wicks mingling with the acrid tang of cleaning fluid and the errant spill of cider between floorboards. He would come back. He had to. Years, Leroy had said, and someone who'd spent years keeping an institution afloat didn't just vanish all of a sudden.

45

She was only feeling this way because she wasn't used to being in charge. Of the pub, of herself, of anything. Because the empty pub felt eerie, claustrophobic and expansive at the same time, creaking in all its shadows. But people like Juan didn't just vanish all of a sudden.

Except that any disappearance was sudden, wasn't it? People were there until they were not.

What a stupid thought. This wasn't productive. She forced herself to her feet and back behind the bar, digging through the drawers until she found the logbook for the cash register. She'd watched him often enough to know the process. How soothing, meditative, almost, to run the notes and coins through her fingers, counting even as the tiredness of the day caught up with her, slowing her movements. Two, four, six, eight…

The crystal note of the doorbell cut clean through the trance she had dropped into.

"Oh, you're still here," Juan said, and something unravelled inside her, coils of tension unspooling into relief.

"Well, yes." She dropped the coins and strode towards him. "What did you expect?"

He shook his head. "Go home."

"Did you get the transistor?"

"Yes." He took his coat off. "Go home."

"Is everything all right? You seem—"

"Go home, Maya," he said sharply, looking at her for the first time. His eyes were shuttered, his lips a compressed line. She might as well have imagined the playful man who had left earlier. "I can take it from here."

"Fine," Maya said. But it wasn't fine. The twisted coils woke back up in her belly, churning like iron snakes. She shrugged into her coat, buttoning it closed at a snail's pace. Dragged her feet on her way across the room, pausing by the bar for a long minute. Anything to give him a chance to change his mind and talk.

"Goodnight," she said at the door.

Outside, the night opened, dark and wide. The full moon cast slivers of pale silver onto the pavement, the leaves on the trees shivering in shadowy dances. Maya huddled deeper into the hood of her coat. She shouldn't feel so hurt. It wasn't as if she'd done anything special tonight – she'd only done the decent thing. Rina would have done it in her place, too. Gus would have, as would Evelyn. Well, maybe not Evelyn, but push come to shove someone else would have filled the gap. She knew that. She needed to get over herself – he didn't owe her an explanation or a rundown or a thank you, even. It wasn't personal. His coldness might not even be anything to worry about at all. Maybe he was just tired. Tired and fed up after a long day full of unexpected, genuine crises, and here she was, blowing his silence out of proportion. She always did that. Blew things out of proportion.

If it had been a windier night, she wouldn't have noticed it. As it was, the noise cut into her concentration with the sharpness of glass: a crunch of gravel on stone which didn't come from her own boot. She ground to a halt. The road before her wound uphill in a tight turn, a stretch of black trees rising against an old iron fence to her left. Their shadows loomed like cavernous mouths.

Maya backed away two paces, hesitating. Was there someone there? Just a squirrel? She'd been down this path so many times…

He was on her before she knew it. She couldn't see anything, just thick wool right in her face as they scuffled, as he tried to wrestle her down. She stumbled, kicked and fell. Felt the cobblestone hard against her cheekbone, the stab of adrenaline in her veins. Her stomach turned over, a sickening lurch. She punched and kicked, aimless, uncoordinated, more flailing than fighting, but somehow, somehow she was suddenly free, stones gripping beneath her boots as she stumbled to her feet.

She ran. Didn't look back, didn't turn around. Just ran. She didn't know if she was being followed or where she was even going, but it didn't matter, she couldn't take the chance. She nearly fell again, skirt twisting around her legs until she hiked it up, and then she finally saw the familiar door of the pub and threw herself against it, hammering away at the wood when it didn't give way immediately. She tried to call out, but her lungs were too full of air, pulling in deep, heavy gulps of oxygen. The night swam around her. What if she was being followed? What if Juan was still out back and didn't hear her? What if he was upstairs and—

The door gave way and she tumbled inside, would have fallen if not for Juan's arm steadying her. "Maya? What happened?"

She closed her eyes, sinking against the wall in relief, shaking as she heard the door fall shut. Something like a sob tried to force its way through her throat, but she gritted her teeth and swallowed it down.

"Maya?" He didn't sound cold now. He sounded worried.

Her tongue tasted metallic, like burnt pennies. When she brought her hand to her mouth, it came away red. Must have split her lip.

"You're safe," Juan said, and she clung to the steadiness of his voice. He was crouching down in front of her. "Are you hurt? You look like you're bleeding."

Why was she sitting on the floor? She couldn't remember sliding down the wall. "I'm fine," she mumbled, pushing herself to her feet. The sense of disorientation was slipping away, reality sharpening around the edges. "Just my lip. Shit. He got my bag."

"Forget about the bag." Juan reached behind himself, picking something up off the floor as he rose. "Who did?"

"I don't know. I couldn't see anything. It all happened so fast. One moment I was walking down the road and the next—you have a gun."

"Yes," Juan said calmly, flicking a switch on the weapon before tucking it into the back of his waistband. "Of course I do."

"I don't like this place!" Maya burst out. God, she sounded childish. Childish and overdramatic and ridiculous, and all the things she'd always tried so hard not to be. "And don't you dare tell me I chose to be here."

And, unbidden, the tears began to flow. She tried to brush them away but more took their place, and then more, every single one of them unwanted.

"Ok, ok, I won't," said Juan and pulled her into a hug.

Embarrassingly, it only made her cry harder.

She had never missed her mum more. There was a memory, somewhere, a memory from before she was doing everything wrong all the time, a memory of night time stories and warm, cocooned safety, and she longed for it now. Longed for home. But no, she was here. In a strange pub, in a strange place, in a strange man's arms. Who had a gun.

She buried her face against his chest, smelling woodsmoke and musk, feeling the scratch of wool against her cheek. It was a comforting scent, strange but steadying somehow, and Maya drank it in until the sobs had subsided to small hitches of breath.

"Sorry," she said and pulled away. "God, you must think I'm stupid."

Hand still on her elbow, Juan guided her to a table. He grabbed a bottle and two glasses from the bar, pouring out two fingers of golden liquid. Then he wrapped some ice inside a cloth and brought the whole lot over. "Drink."

The whisky stung her lip and burned going down, making her cough a little. But its fumes rose warm in her throat, chasing tendrils of heat into her lungs.

"I hope that wasn't the good stuff," she mumbled. "Wasted on me right now."

"Total swill," Juan said. "Don't worry." He poured himself a measure and knocked it back. "Clearly the day for it."

Maya spluttered a wet laugh, surreptitiously wiping her face on her coat sleeve. The fabric was covered in dirt now, anyway. "Sorry," she said again.

"Don't mention it."

She pressed the ice to her lip, dulling its ache. Now that she was sitting across from him, she could see the concern etched into his forehead. It seemed to trickle beneath her skin, stripping away layers which wrapped her more intimately than clothes. She shifted in her chair, playing with her glass to avoid his gaze.

"So where did this happen?" he asked after a long moment's silence.

"Up the hill. By the park."

"A little way away. Is that close to where you live?"

"No. I'm on Oriel road. Near the old hospital."

"That's a good forty minutes' walk from here. You walk home alone for forty minutes every night?"

Maya looked up. He was staring back at her, aghast. "Yes," she said and dropped the ice. "What else am I meant to do?"

He covered his eyes with both hands. Rubbed his forehead, shook his head, and pushed himself to his feet. "Right, well, you aren't anymore from now on."

"What do you mean?"

"I mean, I'm going to walk you home from now on. Come on."

Maya bristled. "I'm not a child."

"I never said you were. But, frankly, it's a miracle that something like this hasn't happened before if you've been traipsing around the streets for hours every night."

"So it's my fault now? What happened?"

"No, of course it isn't— That's not what I meant at all."

"Traipsing," Maya said emphatically. Something was roiling inside her, bubbling up in a heat which wasn't nearly as smooth as the whisky.

"Yes." Juan pinched the bridge of his nose. "That was a poor choice of words. As you might have noticed, today doesn't seem to be my day."

"Well, join the club!" She slammed her glass on the table. On second thought, she picked it back up and ran it over to the bar, rinsing it vigorously under the tap before splashing water on her face. She scrubbed at the tear tracks until she felt clean again.

"It's just not safe," Juan said when she was finished. He was right beside her, dropping the ice in the sink. "That's all I meant. It's not safe for a woman to walk around out there on her own at this time."

"I don't see you playing bodyguard for anyone else."

"That's because they either live around the corner or they have someone picking them up at the corner. Evelyn? Two streets over from here. Rina? Her father-in-law meets her on his way home from late shift." He looked down at her, a frown creasing his brow. "Besides, they know the area. They're used to it, the way things are here. I should really have checked before how far you were going."

"Right," Maya said bitterly. "Because I'm too soft."

"Maya…" Juan sighed. "That wasn't an insult."

"Wasn't it?" she bit back, trying hard not to feel guilty at the plaintive note in his voice. She grabbed his coat off the hook and thrust it at him. "Well, let's go, then. Seems like I don't have a choice."

They walked in silence for the better part of the way. Around them, the night hung like a dense curtain, ominous even with the moon peering over the clouds at regular intervals. Of course, it would have been a lie to claim that Juan's presence wasn't a relief. Every shadow seemed deeper after the attack, darker, every sound louder, sharper. The fissures in the old pavements swallowed their footsteps as they moved over them, the ivy crawling up the buildings testament to their neglect. In the sanctuary of her own mind, Maya could admit to it: the utterly stupid part of her which had always delighted a little in these walks home, had found them romantic in their quiet isolation. For as long as she could remember, she had loved the night: the warm sparkle of the energy bubble which enveloped the Zone, a constant shimmer in the sky far above her mother's roof garden. She had always wondered at the stars beyond. It never got truly dark in the Zone the way it did out here, where the pitch black garden tripped her up on the way to the toilet when she woke at night.

The sheer idiocy of it. Like any of that made her impervious to danger. Like she'd blocked the very possibility of it out, the moment she stopped actively thinking about it. Like she was just that used to being safe.

Talk about blind spots.

Her anger trickled away with each step they took, as if she was leaving a trail of breadcrumbs for him to follow back home. Not that he needed it.

"Did the transistor fit?" she asked eventually.

"Yes."

"Where did you get it?"

"I'd prefer not to talk about it."

The gravel crunched beneath her feet. Where had the gun come from? She'd never noticed it before. Had he taken it from the lockbox before he left that afternoon? How had she missed that? Surely she would have seen it if he carried it on him all the time. She'd paid such close attention to the fit of his clothes.

"I'm sorry if I made you feel like I was blaming you," he said, as they turned the corner into Oriel road. "That wasn't my intention."

Something inside her eased with the words. "I know. I just hate that you were right. I don't belong here. I don't know what the fuck I'm even doing here half the time."

"Why did you come, Maya?"

She sighed. He had asked twice already, in different ways. Maybe the third time should be the charm. "Would you believe that I thought some things are worse than danger?"

"Are they?"

"I don't know." She ground to a halt outside the iron gate which blocked off the passageway leading to her shed. Nestled between two houses on either side, it was easy to miss. "It's probably too early to tell. 'Sleep on it, especially if it's made you overwrought.' That's what Stuart would have said."

"Who's Stuart?"

"Probably the closest thing I've had to a father," Maya admitted.

"He sounds wise."

"He is. He also said I was bonkers for wanting to head out here. Helped me arrange it all the same. Said I needed to do what I needed to do." She fished for the keys in her pocket. "Thanks anyway. For opening the door. And for walking me. I'm sorry if I made a shit day worse for you."

Juan shook his head. "Not your fault. I was feeling far too sorry for myself, anyway. I should take it as a reminder that things could be much worse."

That didn't seem like him, to feel sorry for himself. Even less so to admit it. "Tomorrow will be better."

"Yes." The darkness obscured his expression, blurring away any clean lines. He lifted his hand as though he might touch her face – but then, just as quickly, he dropped it again. "It wasn't an insult. I find you very charming. Refreshing. Goodnight, Maya."

"Night," Maya whispered, watching him turn around and walk away. Her heart was still thumping a staccato beat against her ribcage when she closed the shed door behind her, long after he'd dissolved into the night.

CHAPTER SIX

Leroy was talking to Juan. Maya could see them from the corner of her eye, leaning towards one another over the bar as she collected plates across the room. Nothing spectacular so far, except when she next raised her eyes, they were both looking straight at her, staring. She slipped a smile on her lips and Leroy matched it, raising a hand in greeting.

She was still shaking off the lingering unease from the moment when she returned with a bare tray from the kitchen a while later.

"—lot of nerve, showing your face here again," Juan was saying in a low tone.

"Sorry, mate, what are you on about?"

Maya recognised the voice a split second before she caught sight of his face: the guy who had bothered her the night before. Juan was standing next to him, one hand resting on his elbow. Leroy sat at the bar, gazing into his whisky as if it held the secrets of the universe. Ah. It all made sense now.

The man caught sight of her and raised his eyebrows. "Listen, I don't know what stories your little girl's been telling you, but I'm sure we can clear up any misunderstanding."

"No, you listen," Juan said softly. "We can do this the quiet way, or the very loud, public, everyone in here will know you've crossed me–way. I can assure you, I much prefer the quiet way. It's definitely in your interests, too."

And, seemingly applying no pressure, he led the man away.

Maya turned to Leroy. "What on earth did you tell him?"

"Only the truth."

Maya watched the door rock on its hinges as it fell shut. She should stay out of it. That would be the wise thing to do.

She set the tray on the bar and took off after them.

The space right outside the door was empty, but as she headed towards the canalside, she could hear them arguing. She turned the corner just as Juan slammed the guy into the brick wall, one arm twisted behind his back.

"—and if you ever set foot over my threshold again, you'll regret it. Understood?"

Maya didn't catch the mumble which followed.

Juan twisted the man's arm more sharply. "Understood?"

"Yes! Yes, just let me go, damn it!"

Juan loosened his grip. The man stumbled away from him, grinding to a halt a safe distance away when he spotted Maya. He glared at her, then at Juan. "Enjoy your little whore," he said. "Just remember, they always drop you in the end."

He spat at her feet and fled.

Maya watched the tight clench of Juan's fists gradually relax into openness. "I didn't ask you to do that," she said.

"I didn't do it for you. I despise men like him. He had no right to treat any of my staff like that." He shook his head. "And besides, if I don't enforce some simple rules on behaviour, we might as well have a free for all. We'd be overrun by his type. They have no place in my pub."

"Yours?" Maya said gently.

"In all but name."

"Hmm. Don likes to think of it as a haven, was it? You're just running a business?"

"You've got a good memory," Juan said. "Was that him? Last night?"

"I didn't even think—" Maya stared at him, lips parted. Why hadn't it occurred to her before? "I honestly don't know. It was so dark."

"I suppose it doesn't matter at the end of the day. He won't be back." He crossed his arms. "You should have told me."

"When? You weren't exactly chatty when you came back. And then what happened rather took over."

Juan sighed. "Yes, fine. I take your point."

For a while they stood in silence, the water lapping at the sides of the canal in quiet ripples the only sound cutting through the night. "How often do you have to enforce the rules like this, anyway?"

"More often than I care to," said Juan. "What are you doing out here, Maya? Have the tables developed the skill to wait themselves?"

"I was worried."

"Don't be." Juan stepped closer, giving her a gentle nudge in the pub's direction. His presence folded around her as they wandered over to the door, the dark wrapping them inside an invisible cocoon.

"Ok, I won't be." Maya lifted her eyebrows. "So long as you're not."

He studied her for a long moment, door suspended mid-push, the warm spill of light from the inside illuminating his face. It wouldn't have taken much to reach out and touch his cheek.

Then his hand was at the small of her back, ushering her inside.

"I'm going to the growing co-op tomorrow," she said casually. "The one in the Lee Valley. Rina says they're having a late harvest celebration. If you'd like to come."

"I'm doing accounts. But thanks. Be careful."

"Ok," Maya said. Shame. "I will be. Hey, Beth. Another shandy?"

The harvest festival turned out quite different from what Maya expected. For one, instead of starting with a celebration, it started with – well, harvesting. A man waved Maya, Rina, her husband Ben and her daughter Solace through the front gate, another guided them to a stretch of land and handed them a big basket each. The ground was bursting with green shoots which thrust through the soil, alternating lines of carrots and beetroot, as Maya soon discovered.

Solace promptly climbed into Rina's basket. Maya laughed. It was impossible not to love the fierce bundle of energy, her open joy at the endless discoveries which surrounded her. It took a bit of to and fro, but eventually Rina sold the task at hand, convincing Solace to leave the basket in favour of digging into the soil with bare hands. She rubbed the earth between her fingers and squealed in delight when she successfully submerged her entire hand, flinging handfuls around her as soon as she broke the surface.

Maya couldn't blame her. The experience thrilled her, too, albeit in a more restrained way. She'd never dug around in the earth like this. In the Zone, the carefully curated roof gardens and stretches of flowers by the pavements had always been off-limits, like wilderness wrapped in glass. Even the parks were delicate, static arrangements of beauty, to be witnessed and seen, not to be grasped. Sure, she had sneaked the odd touch here and there as a child, but always in the knowledge that she'd soon be dragged away. And of course, countless virtual reality programmes allowed people to explore natural environments, from forests to beaches to vast grasslands. But this was different, the gritty grain of the earth between her fingers a much subtler texture than any sensory glove could replicate, the cool density of the carrots as they slithered from the ground, the coarse skin of the beetroots against her own.

Solace had it right.

"You ok?" Rina asked, her lips curving. Her basket was already a quarter full where Maya's barely had a handful of vegetables in it. "Did they not grow these where you're from? You're studying each one like it's a miracle."

"No, no, of course they did," Maya said and chucked a bunch of carrots into her basket. "Just amazed how well they're doing in London soil, that's all."

"It's not that bad. Just needs a little love and tenderness."

"It used to be marshland though, didn't it?"

"Yeah. It's a bit strange. How none of this was cultivated for so long back in the day? I mean, these fields have been here forever now, I can't imagine this not being an allotment. But I know it wasn't, I've heard the stories. Hard to imagine that you'd pass up a perfectly good floodplain and not grow anything on it, you know? What on earth did they use it for?"

"To take walks?"

"Walks." Rina scoffed. "Can you imagine?"

Maya could, actually. Walks by the river had been one of the few welcome breaks from the confines of the high rises which loomed above the Thames in the Zone. For her first date, unremarkable as it had been otherwise, they had gone for a walk by the river. The rushing accompaniment of its tides might even have made it romantic, with the right person by her side.

"Different times, I guess," Rina said. "The whole area must have been teeming with people. My nan used to show me pics. Don't think I'll ever wrap my head around it, how you can feed that many people in such a small space."

"Decent supply lines, probably."

"Yeah. Now most of those go to the Zone. But look at this, though." She spread her arms wide. "We're all right."

"Great crop of carrots this year," Ben agreed, wandering over to them from the far end of the row.

"Carrots for bunnies," Solace said with a serious nod. "Sol find bunnies." She grabbed two carrots off the ground and took off at speed.

"Solace, no!" Rina shot to her feet.

"It's all right," Ben said. "I'll keep an eye on her. You keep chatting." He jogged after Solace.

"You just want to avoid your share of the digging, don't think I'm not onto you!" Rina shouted after him. She brushed her dirty hands together and grinned at Maya. "Honestly, men."

"Well, at least he's not sitting in a pub downing pints," Maya said.

"True," Rina agreed. "I got me a good one. He loves her to pieces." She crouched back down. "Not sure what I'd do without him, to be honest. Definitely not studying anything, that's for sure."

"You do so much. Your job at the pub, the studying, and now on your free day you're here, doing this."

"Free day? Where are we, in some mythical fairytale?" Rina smiled. "Don't get any of those as a mum, anyway. I don't know. It's knackering some days, don't get me wrong. But you've gotta get ahead while the world provides. You can't take it for granted. Or you end up like one of those sad sods that try to break into the fields before harvest and make off with a bunch of produce at night time. I mean, much easier to get involved and do your bit, no?"

"Do they patrol this? At night?"

"Yeah, they've got a rota, except when it's too cold to get far with nicking anything. Not much left to nick at that point, anyway. Ben sometimes does a shift. They keep the foxes out as well. Those bastards are the worst. Burrow here, burrow there – not to mention the hens."

"It must be nice." Maya rubbed some grit off a carrot. "Being part of a community."

"That's why I brought you here, silly. So you can be a part of it, too. You seem a bit lonely, sometimes."

"I… It's all still very new." Maya hesitated. "Thought it would be easier to find my feet."

"You must miss them a lot. Your family."

"Sure. I mean…" She swallowed. Did she? Her fellow students, whose names had always blurred into the background? Her ex, Ren, who might have been her path to getting to know the people behind those names, if she'd not backed away from the relationship so soon? Her mother? "It's just me and my mum, anyway. And a good family friend. But yes, they're far away now."

She did miss Stuart. He'd always made her feel understood in not feeling understood.

"No phone lines out there?"

"No, all collapsed. Not a priority area to maintain them. I haven't seen as much active infrastructure work as I have since I came here." Strange, how the lies just tripped past her tongue. They tasted all the more acrid the easier they flowed.

"Well, you're here now. Let's build you a new family."

Maya bit her lip. Best move on. "Have you always lived around here?"

"Pretty much. Was just me and my mum and my nan for a long while before I met Ben and we moved in with his family. My dad used to work at the substation in Edmonton, but there was an accident when I was nine."

"I'm sorry. You must miss him."

"It's a long time gone, now. I've got the memories." Rina looked over to where Ben was jumping over rows of carrot greens next to Solace. "We used to all cuddle up in bed together, on the mornings when it was too cold, me, my mum and him. We do that now with Sol. It's nice to pass it down."

Maya felt a pang deep in her chest, a tightness behind her sternum. Had her parents ever done that, when she was little? She tried to picture it, her mother's perfect coils dishevelled by sleep, but the image blew away like gossamer threads in a strong gust of wind.

"And how long have you been working at the pub?"

"Oh, a while. I started a couple of years before I had Sol. Friend of a friend knew of the position. Glad I got in there, the previous place I was at was a hellhole. No way would they have let me work until my due date. No way would I have wanted to, to be honest."

"It's an odd place, isn't it? So…"

"Peaceful?"

Maya laughed. "That wasn't quite the word I was looking for, but in a way."

"Busy but calm. I know what you mean, don't worry. He's turned it into something in a class of its own."

"Do you think that's him or Don?"

"Hmm. Hard to say. One doesn't go without the other."

"What does he do, anyway? Don, I mean? I haven't seen him since I started, but he's clearly an influence somehow. Does he only drop by outside opening times? Also, there's no way that pub alone is keeping him flush with what the margins are." She knew that now, having dipped into the books. "Does he own more than one? What's in it for him if it's not money?"

"I've heard rumours, but I try not to stick my nose in," Rina said, a note of hesitation creeping into her voice. "Way I see it, they pay my bills and they treat me well. Sometimes I don't need to know everything. Don't dig too deep."

Maya frowned. He'd been such a warm, inviting presence the first time she'd met him. How instantly she'd felt at ease around him… She felt a little less at ease, now.

"Honestly, you think too much!" Rina said. "You'll tie yourself in knots one day. World is complicated enough without you trying to find hornets' nests. Ooof!"

Solace had careened into her, throwing herself bodily into Rina's arms.

"Mummy cuddle," she said with satisfaction.

"Yes, Mummy cuddle," Rina agreed, wrapping her arms around her. Her eyes met Maya's over Solace's shoulder. "Don't question what's good. Embrace it. There's always time for the other stuff."

And Maya did, at least for the rest of the afternoon. They dug through the soil until it was barren, emptying baskets into big storage crates near the outbuildings. Everyone got allocated a share to take home, and then they huddled around a spread of freshly baked beetroot bread with carrot soup and pumpkin wine and an unexpected campfire. Rina assured Maya it was perfectly legal despite its polluting impact, a rare exception of tradition combining with practicality. The ash would become a vital ingredient to keep the soil fertile in future years.

The crackle of flames was another thing the virtual realities hadn't got right. Nothing could have imitated the way Maya's skin grew hot unevenly, the way the fire danced bright sunspots into her eyes which lingered as shadows when she glanced away. When the group broke into song, she didn't know any of the tunes, but they surged like the blaze, rising and shifting, carrying something to the skies like the motes of ash which floated into the distance. Solace danced around in circles at a safe distance until Rina strapped her to her back, where she fell asleep in the blink of an eye. Maya lost track of time. The sun was beginning to sink past the horizon when Rina reminded her that she was meant to be at work. A few hasty hugs later and she dashed off, grateful that she wasn't far away from the pub as she ran along the canal.

She got there just after six, all out of breath. Thankfully tonight seemed to be a slow starter: apart from a few customers in the booths, the pub was still empty, only Juan and Leroy at the bar. Juan raised his gaze as she approached in a half-run.

"Sorry I'm late," she said. "Won't happen again. Here, that's for you." She set a bottle in front of him. "It's pumpkin wine."

"I run a pub. Do I look like I need more alcohol?"

"Fine," Maya said. "Would you like some carrots instead?" She dropped a couple of bunches on the counter. "Or beetroot?" A couple of those followed swiftly.

Juan's lip twitched. He slowly pushed the vegetables back at her. "I'll stick with the wine, thanks."

"No problem."

"Your skirt is covered in mud."

"I'm glad you noticed. Would you like me to take it off and serve people naked instead?"

Heat rushed to her cheeks the moment the words spilled past her lips. Where on earth had they come from?

"No," Juan said, eyebrows lifting. "That might be taking it a step far. But maybe remember a change of clothes next time?"

"Right." Maya swept the vegetables back into her bag. "I'm really sorry I'm late."

"No problem."

"I'll just go grab an apron."

"Take your time." He raised the bottle. "Thanks for thinking of me."

"Of course," she said, face still flushed. Damn it, what was wrong with her? "I'll get going, then."

"Right."

"Right."

There was a soft sound from the far end of the bar, like a smothered cough. As Maya sped off to the kitchen, she thought she heard Juan tell Leroy to be quiet, but she couldn't be sure. But maybe Rina was right, and this was just one of those things… better left uninvestigated.

"He's looking at you, kid."

"What?" Maya ground to a halt on her way past Beth's usual booth. "Who?"

"You know who."

Maya turned around. Juan was facing the back of the bar, tidying shelves. He was definitely not looking at her.

"Stop messing with me," she said.

Beth set down her knitting with a crinkle in the corner of her eye. "A little bird tells me you always stay late now. People are talking."

"Well, there's nothing to talk about. Sorry to burst your bubble."

"Would you like there to be?"

Maya sighed. "Beth, with all due respect for your desire to relive your wild youth—"

"I never had a wild youth, you know that by now, my girl."

"—the wild youth you wish you'd had—"

"Better."

"He's just walking me home because it's not safe," Maya said. "That's all."

And it was, wasn't it? They still barely spoke on their walks back to her flat. Never mind that the comfortable ease which had defined their evenings often felt cut through with something else, nowadays. Something which urged her towards questions and held her tongue for fear of it tripping up in equal parts.

"That's still a lot of time to invest in someone each night," said Beth.

"And he's obsessively invested in keeping this place a danger-free zone, isn't he?" Maya pointed out. "No prostitutes. No smoking. No fist fights. No weapons. Hell, even the steak knives aren't particularly sharp." Not that she'd call the meat they got here steak, exactly. She scraped a splash of dried wax off the table's edge with her thumbnail. "Are people really talking?"

"No. I just said that to get you to pay attention."

"Honestly, you're terrible."

"I know," Beth said with an exaggerated nod. "I'm sorry. You didn't answer my question."

"Which one?"

"Don't play coy. Would you like there to be?"

"It doesn't really matter," Maya said. There was another trickle of wax, but she forced herself to meet Beth's gaze instead. She had nothing to feel embarrassed about. "I don't think he's interested. I bet he wasn't even looking right now, was he? Before you called me over?"

"No. I just said that to get you to pay attention."

"Bethany…"

"But he does, sometimes. Always when he thinks you're not watching. He forgets about little old me sitting quietly in the corner, seeing all."

"Or maybe you're just saying that to get me to pay attention?"

"Oh," Beth said, her lips curving warmly, "I would never do such a thing."

"Honestly, Beth! How you made it to this ripe old age I don't know." Maya bit her lip. "Sorry. I shouldn't have said that."

"Don't be. You were just being truthful. I'm taking terrible liberties with you and you are quite right to push back."

Maya released a deep breath.

"You have to forgive an old woman. There isn't much that entertains me anymore."

"I know. It's the only reason you get away with it."

"You still haven't answered my question."

"I don't know," Maya said. It wasn't quite a lie. Was it? "And if I did, I wouldn't tell you."

"That's probably very wise." Beth's smile stretched wide. "You're a clever girl all round. It's why I like you. I bet it's why he likes you, too. And in all seriousness"—her voice dropped, as did her smile, something insubstantial slipping away with them like a veil—"he does watch you sometimes when you're not looking. Of course, what he's thinking is anyone's guess with that poker face of his. But he's a man, so in my experience the possibilities are limited." She picked up her knitting. "Just in case you might like to know. What do you think – does the colour scheme work?"

The main body of the jumper was almost complete, olive green and cinnamon brown alternating in an argyle pattern with lilac accents.

"It's lovely," Maya said.

CHAPTER SEVEN

She wasn't feeling so great.

She hadn't felt brilliant when she woke, far later than usual and long after lunch, her morning trip to the outside toilet an icy shock to the system. At first, she had put the freezing cold down to a turn in the weather – after all, they were rapidly approaching December. But as she slunk along her usual route to work, huddling deeper into her coat in a futile attempt to chase a hint of heat, she knew she'd miscalculated. Not only did the shivers reverberate through her very bones, but her muscles felt like they'd been dipped in liquid lead, each strand coated with heaviness so that she could barely lift her limbs. The evening air bit at her lungs as though she were inhaling snow crystals, yet there was no snow in sight.

By the time she reached the pub, her teeth were chattering a staccato beat far beyond her control. The warm blast of air which greeted her from inside only sped up its pace.

Juan took one look at her and frowned. "You look terrible."

"Charmer." Maya coughed. She leant against the wall near the bar. Maybe she had inhaled snowflakes. Invisible, metallic snowflakes which were spinning like cogs in a wheel and shredding her bronchi from the inside. "Sorry. I didn't—" She coughed again. "I think I'm a bit under the weather."

The back of Juan's hand pressed blissfully cool against her forehead. "You don't say. You're burning up."

"Sorry," Maya repeated. "Shouldn't have come in. Didn't realise." She closed her eyes, trying hard not to shiver. "Just give me a minute and I'll head home."

"Not on my watch, you won't," Juan said.

"It's still light."

"Not the point. There's no way I'll let you go home like this."

"What's going on?" a familiar voice cut in.

"Nothing," Maya said to Rina in what she hoped was a reassuring tone. "Just having a party. Just me and this wall."

"She's ill," said Juan. "I'm taking her upstairs to rest." He grasped Maya's elbow. "Come on. Can you get started down here, Rina?"

"Sure."

"You are?" Maya would have protested, but it seemed like an awful lot of effort right now. "Oh, Beth is going to love this."

"What on earth does Bethany have to do with it?" Juan asked, sounding as irritable as he did perplexed. "Come on. Can you walk, or do you need a hand?"

"This is total overkill, you know." Maya broke into a fit of coughs. "Course I can walk." She promptly took three steps, only for her knees to buckle treacherously on the fourth. Juan caught her before the stumble could turn into a fall.

"Of course," he said. "Total overkill."

"Ok, maybe a hand with the stairs wouldn't be so bad."

"I'm glad you see it that way." He looped an arm around her waist, taking most of her weight as she held on to his shoulder. "Thanks." This last to Rina, who was holding the double doors to the corridor open for them.

"No problem. Feel better, Maya."

The stairs might as well have led up the tallest skyscraper for how long it took her to climb them, even with Juan half-carrying her. By the time they reached the top, Maya was past arguing. All she wanted to do was close her eyes. Hadn't she been curious about his rooms at some point? It didn't seem to matter now. All that mattered was one thing, and that was—

"That's a lovely sofa," she said, but he led her straight past it. "Hey, why—oh, it's a bed."

She sat down heavily. Sank back into the covers. Had she meant to lie down? "An actual bed. With sheets and everything."

It was, too. No bare brick in sight, no alcove or curtain, just soft, cool cotton. She turned her cheek into it.

"Yes, they generally come with those," Juan said, lifting her legs and shifting her across. Maya's boots still hung heavy on her feet, but she couldn't bring herself to care.

She closed her eyes and buried her nose in the pillow. It smelled of the same musk as his shirt, unfamiliar but comforting. Soothing. She felt so hot. Too hot. Too cold. "Beth will have a field day."

"What is this thing you have about Beth?" His footsteps retreated, stilled, returned. She must have been lying here for an aeon. Why wasn't she asleep yet? "Are you delirious already?"

"…always a bit delirious around you," Maya mumbled. Or maybe she didn't. That didn't make much sense, did it? Maybe it did.

"Ok, ok. Here, take these." Something hard pressed against her lips. Pills. Then a glass. She swallowed, his palm a chill guide at the back of her neck. "Get some rest."

And the world slipped away.

Maya blinked awake into the darkness. She was so hot. Her clothes stuck to her uncomfortably, wet against the small of her back. She turned her head. A soft spill of light flowed towards her from the other side of the room. A lamp on a chest of drawers. It swam away into vagueness. She blinked until it refocused. This wasn't her shed. This wasn't home.

"—very ill," Juan's voice filtered across. He was standing by the door. Right. The door. His door. His bed. Why was she in his bed?

She managed to sit somehow, pushing herself up with shaky arms to slide off the mattress. Where were her boots? The ground felt cool, even through her socks. It also seemed surprisingly pliable, shifting like quicksand under her feet as she walked towards the door. How stupid. Who would want quicksand flooring? Juan must have lost his mind. She opened her mouth to tell him so – and collided with something hard at shin-height. There was a loud crash as something toppled to the floor. She wobbled, knees giving way, and barely caught herself on the coffee table as she fell.

Juan wheeled around. "What are you doing up?" A second later he was by her side, lifting her. "You should be in bed."

"How long have I been asleep?" Maya asked. The words came out slurred and distorted. "Why are you so cold?"

"You have a fever," Juan said. "You need to sleep."

"Didn't say how long."

"Only as long as your shift. Rina's just leaving. Come on."

"I can't take your bed," she protested as he laid her back on the soft surface.

"Of course you can."

She liked his voice. A gentle sway. Like leaves rippling within the trees.

"Where will you sleep?"

"I have a lovely sofa, don't you remember?"

"You do?"

"I do. Very comfortable."

"Oh," Maya said. Her eyes felt very heavy. She glanced across the room. Rina stood in the open doorway, arms crossed. She smiled reassuringly at Maya, but something was off about her eyes.

"It's ok," Juan said. "Sleep."

She slept.

She woke in a furnace. Everything was too bright. When she opened her eyes, shards of light stabbed agony into her sockets. Through the white fog, Juan's face swam into view, deep lines etched into his forehead. He looked so worried… She should ask him what was wrong. How she could help.

Something cool brushed her forehead.

"Hi," she whispered. It hurt. Everything hurt.

"Shhh," said Juan.

Her eyes fell closed again.

Her mother was calling her. Maya tried to hear what she was saying, but her voice was so faint, soaked up by the trees thrashing their leaves about in the blazing sunlight. On the other side of St James' Park, Stuart was walking a golden cocker spaniel. She waved at him and smiled, before kneeling back down in the grass. No point getting distracted when she had a job to do.

She focused on the lines in the sand before her, on digging neat trenches, but her shovel kept breaking. She let it go and dug with her fingers, revealing row after row of bright, sparkling mirrors. Their silver shine reflected the green of the trees, shivering shades of emerald and jade into a verdant kaleidoscope. She raised one of them to the skies and it moulded to her palm, sinking into the skin like a glove.

"It's an ancient burial site," Ren said over her shoulder. "Didn't you know?"

"Of course I do," Maya said, suddenly annoyed. "But it's still my job to plant these!"

Ren laughed. "You're not planting anything. You're excavating."

Maya turned to protest. Ren—Juan looked her straight in the eye. "Well, aren't you going to give it to me?" he asked.

"Give you what?"

He gestured to the ground, lip curving. Confused, eyes still locked with his, she stuck her hand in the earth, digging, digging. The soil wrapped around her arm like a silk ribbon until she was elbow-deep, still nothing but grains of sand slipping between her fingers.

"Why aren't you helping me?"

Juan smiled, shook his head. He brushed a wet tendril off her forehead. "Deeper," he murmured.

She redoubled her efforts, breathing heavily, sweating with it. Finally, her fingers brushed against something cold and metallic. She grasped at it in desperation, again and again and again, until she finally pulled the object from the ground.

"Thank you," he said, taking the gun from her and rising to his feet.

"Hey!" Maya shouted, her stomach churning. "Where are you going? What are you going to do with that?"

Juan smiled and walked away. Maya ran after him, trying to catch up, but the ground swallowed her movements as though she were wading through treacle, never reaching, never coming a step closer. There was a wrenching twist to her guts now, a panic which wrapped its fingers around her throat as she watched Juan stride towards Don and hand him the gun. Don turned it over with a tut, removing the magazine.

"It's empty," he said, and they both turned to Maya, fixing her with unmoving stares.

Her mother was calling her from a distance. Her voice was so faint.

"You need to wake up, Maya," said Don.

The light cascaded through the treetops above her, blinding like a knife. She blinked, confused. The glare hurt, but all the leaves had vanished and there were no trees. "Need to wake up," she repeated.

"No, you don't," Juan murmured. "It's ok. Go back to sleep."

Reality came and went in hazy flashes. Soft sheets against her cheek. Chill moisture against her forehead, on her lips. The room: arcs of sunshine on dark floorboards. A chair. A bedside table. The sound of paper rustling. A sharp scratch to the back of her hand, a dullness, a pain, something strange sticking, lodged firmly. Someone breathing. Breathing in the dark.

It hurt to breathe. Then a little less.

She was kissing Ren by the river. Her mother hugged her, lips brushing her brow.

Maya opened her eyes. The light from the window above her didn't hurt this time, casting the large room in a gentle glow instead. Next to the bed, Juan sat with a book spread on crossed legs. She tried to lift her hand, but it hurt; on closer examination, she discovered a cannula embedded deep in a vein, its plastic piping running to a near-empty drip beside the bed.

She must have made a noise because Juan looked up from his book and promptly set it aside. "You're awake." He reached over, fingers trailing her brow. "Fever's not come back. Good. How are you feeling?"

Maya opened her mouth, but it was stuffed full of cotton, her tongue impossibly huge. "Water," she managed eventually.

"Of course." He rose, then paused. "I don't suppose you're hungry yet, are you?"

She was, actually. It was a strange sort of hunger, smothered in exhaustion but no less deep an ache, as though her very cells yearned for energy. She nodded weakly.

"Be right back."

She watched him walk out of sight, if not out of earshot – the expanse of the room must contain a kitchenette. The smell of warmed bread wafted across to her alongside clanging noises. They lent the world more solidity.

"It's good you're well again," Juan said when he returned with a plate of toast and a glass of water.

Maya raised her eyebrows.

"Fine, better, not well," he amended, propping her up so she could sip the water. "Trust me, if you'd seen yourself two days ago, you'd agree."

The water tasted like liquid heaven, drenching her dry tongue and soothing her parched throat. "Two days?" she whispered. "How long—" A fit of coughs racked her body. She drew shallow breaths until the pain receded.

"Try not to talk, you need a lot of rest still. Here, have some more water. You've been down for a little over a week. Fever kept spiking, despite the meds. I'm glad the antivirals worked in the end, it was a bit of a gamble. Always is, with these things."

Maya's eyes followed Juan's to the drip. Where on earth had that come from? She wet her cracked lips. Maybe that thought could wait.

"Here, have some toast."

He had smeared some kind of jam on it, sweet berry flavours which exploded in her mouth like fireworks. Maya closed her eyes, savouring its sugary kiss on her tongue. Despite its deliciousness, she only managed a few small bites.

When she was finished, Juan checked the drip, deft fingers moving to the cannula. "I'll need to take this out now. Ready?"

Maya nodded, wincing as he slipped the needle from her skin, then sighing with relief. Her hand felt at once lighter, freed. Exhaustion still blanketed her, beginning to pull her under with its iron weight. There seemed little point in fighting it, so she closed her eyes and sank back into sleep.

CHAPTER EIGHT

When she next woke up, she was alone in the room. The shadows had lengthened, the light filtering through the window dim and tinged with a reddish hue. She desperately needed to pee.

She pushed herself up on her elbows and into a seated position, scanning the room. On the far wall, the kitchenette stretched, cupboards, a sink and a small icebox nestling against the wall. Next to them, a closed door beckoned. The bathroom?

There was no way in hell she was going to call Juan for help to go to the toilet. None. Besides, she was feeling stronger anyway – the weary lassitude which had drowned out everything the last time she woke had faded to a background noise. When she moved, the blanket brushed against her bare leg. Somehow she'd lost half her clothes, leaving her dressed in only her underwear and the thin vest top she layered under her shirts for warmth. Maya bit her lip. It was totally reasonable, of course. Nothing funny about it. And what else could he have done – let her roast in peace for a semblance of modesty? Best not to think about it. Maybe Rina had helped with anything too intimate if there was something fair left in this world…

No way in hell was she going to call him for help. She slipped from beneath the sheets, her wobbly legs taking her about halfway across the room before she had to admit defeat and sink to her knees for a break. That was all right, though, she could crawl. Nothing wrong with crawling. She could just crawl there and crawl back. All in good time.

She made it to the door which thankfully did lead to the bathroom, a simple set-up of a toilet with a basin beside it and a glass-walled shower in the corner. With the sink so nearby, she even managed to rinse her hands afterwards. She hung on to the door while she hitched her underwear back up her hips with trembling fingers, and then…

And then she could only sit on the floor, head resting against the doorjamb as the world spun around her in dizzying colours. Damn it.

"Maya? Maya, where are—"

Fuck. She buried her face against her bare knees, willing the floor to swallow her up.

"What on earth are you doing out of bed?" Juan's hand settled on her arm. "Are you all right?"

"Great," Maya said. In the background, she could hear the tap running. She must not have turned it off properly.

"You should have called," he said, but there was more warmth than reproach in his voice.

Maya let her head sink back against the doorframe. She couldn't quite bring herself to open her eyes. "This is humiliating."

"You're ill."

"No, I'm disgusting." And she was, her vest top glued to her in all the wrong places, her hair stringy and greasy where it fell into her face. Her mother would never have stood for it. Every inch of her felt sticky and uncomfortable, and she needed to strip off her skin and slip into a whole new one right bloody now.

"It's nothing to me, honestly."

"It is to me, though," she said, rubbing her face with both hands. That felt disgusting, too, as though it were covered in a thin layer of grime. "Maybe that's stupid, but you say I've been in bed for a week, and I've never—" She bit her lip. It was all wrong.

"It's a lot, I know," he said. "A lot to take in. If it helps, it worried me, too, seeing how sick you got. It must be disconcerting, to wake up like this and not know where the time's gone."

She opened her eyes. On closer inspection he didn't look his usual polished self either, dark circles smudging hollows under his eyes. "I didn't even get to worry," she said.

He laughed. "I know. That must feel especially disconcerting for you."

She pursed her lips. "It's not nice to make fun of an invalid."

He rose and stepped past her to turn the tap off. "Do you feel strong enough for a shower?"

"I…" Maya glanced at the glass doors in the corner. It was probably a hot shower, too.

"We'll keep you decent, don't worry. Or I can ask Rina to help later, if you'd prefer. Another couple of hours at most till she's here. Your call."

Maya wrapped her arms more tightly around her legs, shivering in the draughty air. It seemed silly to hold out for Rina. What was it that had her so worried? How much time had she already cost him? A whole bloody week of sleeping on the couch. How much money? Who had been covering her shifts? And here she was, turning the whole thing into a scene.

"Maya?"

"Well, I've come all this way already, haven't I? Shame to waste a long-distance crawl and all that. Yes." She sighed. "A shower would be lovely."

"You crawled."

"Don't." Maya let her forehead sink back against her knees. "It made sense at the time."

"I'm sure it did."

She tilted her head to the side to look up at him. He looked impossibly tall from this angle. "So how are we going to do this?"

"Come here," he said, dropping down and lifting her to her feet in one smooth move as though she weighed nothing. He'd done that before, hadn't he? When he'd taken her up the stairs, and then when she'd been drunk with fever. It was sort of nice, now the details weren't drowned out by a haze: the way his arm snaked around her waist and his palm spread wide over her belly to anchor her. The solid curve of his shoulder as she clung to it, and the ripples of muscle beneath her fingers as he half-carried her to the shower, her feet barely kissing the floor.

Sort of nice, and sort of something else. Something which licked hot trickles of uncertainty up her spine.

Juan folded her into the shower like a paper doll, her limbs slipping into the safety of a seated position anew. He disappeared for a split second and returned with a huge towel, holding it over her so she could strip beneath its makeshift canopy. Maya's fingers tripped clumsily over the fastenings of her bra and struggled to slide her underwear over her hips, but of course that had everything to do with how weak and unreliable her muscles still were. And nothing with… anything else.

"Ready?"

She nodded, and he pulled the towel away, bending over her to turn the water on.

"I'm not looking," he said, quite unnecessarily.

"I know," she murmured, a shiver prickling over her skin. What would happen if he did? Nothing. Nothing. She didn't have the energy, anyway.

The glass door closed, rapidly fogging up as hot water cascaded over her shoulders and her head, running in rivulets down the expanse of her back. Maya inhaled the steam, breathing deeply. When was the last time she had sat under a hot shower? She could barely remember. Maybe if she closed her eyes and leant back against the glass, listening to the pitter-patter of each drop, she could pretend that things were different. That she was in a warm, safe place, not the crumbling ruin of a pub in the crumbling ruins of a city. That she was well and happy, not sore and tired, the skin on her hand still throbbing faintly beneath a plaster. That any minute now, Juan would open the cubicle and brush her hair back softly, his lips…

"Maya?"

Ok, maybe that wasn't such a productive train of thought. "Yes, I'm fine. Sorry. I'll be quick."

"Take your time. Just tell me if you feel faint."

"I'm good," she said, but truth be told, the steam was getting a bit heady. She grabbed the soap and finished the rest of her shower more efficiently, scrubbing her hair until each strand squeaked between her fingers. When she was done and Juan had wrapped the towel tightly around her, they began the slow journey across the room. This time, she only made it as far as the bathroom door before her legs buckled completely. She couldn't possibly protest him carrying her the rest of the way. Nor could she still her pulse, the way it bloomed wild in her throat when he lifted her fully, cradling her close.

She rested her head against his chest and prayed that he couldn't hear its thunder.

"I need some clothes," she said, once she was sitting on the bed and hiding behind a glass of juice.

"Right." Juan stared at her for a long second, utterly motionless. "I didn't think—let me have a look." He started rifling through the wardrobe, then the chest of drawers. "I should have asked Rina to bring something in before you woke up, but I didn't—"

"It's ok," Maya said. "I'm not fussy."

"Good." He flung a rather oversized sweatshirt beside her on the bed. "Because this is all I have." A much smaller scrap of black fabric followed, like a hasty afterthought. "Don't ask."

The jumper was blatantly his, and Maya could have fit in it twice over. The underwear... clearly wasn't.

"I'll go make some tea," said Juan.

It wasn't any of her business. It wasn't. Whatever speculations Beth dreamt up in her free time aside, Maya had no reason to feel so... She was just being childish. It was only a pair of underwear at the end of the day, a perfectly fine, clean pair of underwear, and that was all that mattered right now. Who cared whether the woman who had left it was blonde or brunette or black-haired? Who cared whether she had legs which rose to the sky or a laugh which filled any room? How often she must have slept in this bed to bother with leaving lingerie behind? What they had done together, right in this very spot?

Maya had no right to even be wondering about any of this. It was just a pair of underwear. She pulled the clothes on – at least the jumper swallowed her whole. When she tried to run her fingers through her hair, though, they stuck amidst tangles.

"Do you have a comb? I mean, not that you need one, but—"

"I do." He strode towards the cabinet with unerring focus. "There you go."

Maya took the plain, wide-toothed comb, eyebrows chasing her surprise. He had no hair, no need to use it, ever. Why would he remember where he kept it? "You knew exactly where that was. Why? Unless that's another don't ask—ah, damn it."

She had promptly dropped the thing, all fumbling fingers and no fine motor control.

"Let me." Juan scooted his chair closer to the bed. Maya let her arms flop in her lap, tilting her head for easier access. He ran the comb through her hair, his movements slow. Methodical. Gentle. "It was my mother's."

Ah. Now that made sense. A keepsake. "She's not around anymore."

"No." He untangled a particularly thick knot with his fingers. "I would do this for her sometimes when she wasn't well. She broke her wrist when I was about ten. Twelve? It's so long ago now. It took months to heal. Her hair would have been a mess if she'd left it, so I brushed it out for her most days, learnt how to braid it. Took much longer to do than yours. But it wasn't so bad. She would always sing while we did it."

"Why didn't your father do it?"

He withdrew, setting the comb on the bedside table. "It's good that you seem to have turned a corner. Let's keep you heading in the right direction. You should rest."

Maya looked at him. The evening sunlight which streamed through the windows brought out the rich red undertones of his skin, lending a burnished cast to his cheekbones.

"Juan?"

"Yes?"

"I— Is this normal? For people to get so ill around here?"

"Is it where you are from?"

"No." She cast her mind back, grasping at memories. "It's… we have hospitals. People go early. It's all very well managed. We get shots. Vaccines," she clarified, at his drawn brow. "To prevent anyone from getting sick with communicable diseases. I mean, of course people get the odd cold and old people develop conditions and die, but it's all… very tidy. Contained. I'd never even dreamt… I went by the old hospital near my place the other week, to peek inside—"

"Why on earth would you do that?"

"I was curious. Anyway—"

"Curious. Of course."

"Anyway, my point is, it was a shell. Just a shell. And I can't quite wrap my head around that, it's just so… That's normal?"

"Pretty much. Most people build up some strength when they're young, but not everybody makes it. A lot of kids go early."

Her head spun with his words. That time Rina had been off work, looking after a sick Solace. How insistent Juan had been not to call her for help with the generator. And yet, he sounded so calm about it. Like it was just a fact. "But that's not fair. So what, if you don't have anyone to look after you, you're screwed? If you're not lucky enough to be able to fight things off by yourself, that's it? I mean, where did you even get all that stuff you used on me?"

"Maya. Will you do me a favour?"

"Yes, of course."

"Stop thinking. Rest." He grabbed the book she'd seen him reading from the bedside table and passed it to her. "Read if you can't sleep, but give yourself a break."

She turned the book over in her hands. It had been a while since she'd held the weight of a solid spine in her palm. It was deliciously worn, cracked leather bending beneath her fingers. "What is it about?"

"I'm not sure," he admitted with a wry smile. "I don't think I was giving it my full attention." He spread the duvet over her, then rose and turned towards the door.

"Thank you," Maya said. "Even if it's unfair, I'm still… I'm grateful for all this. I'm not taking it for granted."

"No problem." He watched her settle back into the pillows. A long moment stretched into thin air. "Have you found your answer yet?"

"What answer?"

"Are there worse things than danger?"

She hugged the book against her chest. "Never answer life-changing questions straight after a crisis."

His lips curved. "Is that another nugget from Stuart?"

"Yes."

"Wise man. You were lucky to have him."

"I thought you told me to stop thinking. You're not really helping."

"Yes. You're quite right." He opened the door. "I'll be in my office. Call me if you need me."

She was going to read the book, but its warm weight against her chest soothed her like a second blanket. Before she knew it, she had drifted back to sleep.

"Maya, are you awa—well, the light is on, so she must be. Didn't I tell you to call me?"

Maya looked up from her book, blinking away the brightness from the small bedside table lamp. Juan and Rina stood in the doorway.

"I figured you were downstairs," she said. "Was I wrong?"

Juan's lips pressed together.

"He's been sticking his head up the corridor every fifteen minutes, though, just to see you weren't calling," Rina said. "Been driving me mad. Hey stranger." She strode across the room and dropped down on the side of Maya's bed, enveloping her in a hug. "You're a sight for sore eyes."

"I'll get you some dinner," said Juan and disappeared.

"Bless him, he's worse than a mother hen," said Rina. "Mind you, I can't blame him after this week. He said you woke up earlier, but you were fast asleep when I got here, so I just wanted to stick my head round the door, now we're all done for the day. How are you feeling?"

"It's closing time? Sorry, my sense of time is totally warped." Maya shook her head. "You should go home. I mean, it's nice you're popping by, but I don't expect—"

"Don't be silly, I've been worried! What's an hour here or there? I've had far worse nights of sleep, trust me. You look a lot better."

"I feel a lot better." Maya coughed weakly. "Just the tail end now. Be right as rain soon enough."

"Good," Rina said. "You gave us all a fright. People have been asking after you."

"They have?"

"Well, yes. Beth and Leroy and the other usuals. And Gus and Evelyn, obviously. You've been missed. I've definitely missed you. Running the show just hasn't been the same. Don't get me wrong, your replacement was lovely, but nowhere near as quick."

"You've had someone in to help?"

"Just for the moment. I sort of insisted. It wasn't like Juan was able to pull any extra weight, even if he'd wanted to. I think he was too tired to argue. He spent half his time up here, glued to your side, worrying himself sick. So it's been a bit of a weird vibe downstairs. Everyone's noticed him being gone."

"Worrying himself sick."

"Well, you know. In that way of his where you need to know him to realise that's what's going on because he's putting on such a solid front." She paused for a moment, forehead furrowing. "Actually, I lie. He was proper snippy with us at points. You know, service too slow, food not right, and so on."

"He feels awfully responsible for everything that goes on here."

"Hmm. Yes, but that's not it." Rina flicked a strand of hair behind her ear, resting her chin on her hand as she studied Maya. "I don't think I've ever seen him this way before."

Maya brushed her hands over the duvet cover. It was a surprisingly lovely quality for this place. Really thick thread count. It wouldn't have looked out of place in her mother's apartment. Only the guest room, of course…

"Anyway. So we got some help in, a friend of Evelyn's, and it's been ticking over ok, but I'm looking forward to having you back when you're ready. I need someone to help me get some Christmas decorations sorted for once! I keep meaning to do it every year, but Juan is totally indifferent, Evelyn is too lazy to make a start, and Gus hates the idea of bringing even more people together than normal. Although I think he secretly likes the chance to jazz up the menu a bit. I'm thinking let's go the whole hog this year. We can hunt down some ivy and holly, and maybe even some mistletoe, bring a bit of tradition and magic back to town. What do you think?"

"Sounds great," Maya said. "Looking forward to it."

"When you're ready. I'll drop by with some clothes tomorrow. Make you a bit more comfortable in the meantime."

"Oh, that's fine. I'm sure I'll be home soon enough to get my own back."

"No, you won't," Juan cut in, suddenly appearing over Rina's shoulder to hand Maya a bowl of soup. "You've said yourself your flat is a freezer. I'm not sending you back there to get secondary pneumonia. Another few days at least."

"Do I get any say in the matter?"

"No."

"I can't keep sleeping in your bed!"

"I don't see why not. It's a bed, it's meant to be slept in."

"Exactly. By its owner."

"The sofa is fine."

"It's a sofa," Maya mimicked. "It's meant to be sat on."

"You could always share the bed," Rina suggested calmly. "Since you both seem to care so much about its originally intended purpose and all."

Juan shot her a withering glare.

"And that's me out of here," Rina said. "Have a good night, you two, wherever you end up sleeping. No need to tell me or anything. I'll be back tomorrow with those clothes."

And she left them, awkward silence hanging like a dense fog in the air.

"Maya…" Juan said.

"No, it's ok," Maya said. "Take the damn sofa. I'm just—I just feel guilty, is all."

His gaze softened. "You don't need to."

"And it's not nice to be told you have no choice over your own whereabouts."

"No, I— No, it's not. I'm sorry. Of course you have a choice. But I'd really rather you didn't go back there by yourself just yet. Symptoms with these viruses come and go in waves. You could easily get worse again."

She couldn't really argue with that. "Fine."

He parted his lips, hesitated, then closed them again. Continued to look at her silently for a long moment.

Maya trailed her spoon through the pale yellow soup. It was thick, fragrant with the scent of parsnip and winter spices. "You wouldn't enjoy being in my place either if it were you."

"No. I wouldn't."

"Is the sofa really that comfy?"

His lip curled up a touch. "It's a sofa. It's meant to be sat on. I'll live."

Maya laughed. The noise came out a bit wet, sticking against the sudden lump in her throat. She thrust her spoon into the bowl, concentrating on the bouquet of flavours against her tongue. For someone who hated the idea of bringing people together, Gus certainly had the skill to make it happen. "Rina wants us to decorate the pub for Christmas. Create an atmosphere. Make it special."

"Be my guest. I won't stand in her way." He covered a yawn with the back of his hand. "As long as I get some sleep first."

"Right," Maya shoved a couple of spoonfuls of soup into her mouth, swallowing quickly. "I'll eat up."

She finished the soup while he was in the bathroom before rinsing her mouth with some water and turning off the light. Her eyes tracked his movements when he re-emerged, shifting shadows coalescing into a solid shape which glided through her vision and sank away behind the back of the sofa.

"Night, Maya."

"Night," she whispered.

In the dark, Rina's words crept back to her, as if they slithered through gaps in the floorboards. What if they had shared the bed instead? All she'd seen before the sofa had swallowed him had been an outline. Had he undressed? If he were lying next to her, if she reached out and touched his chest, would her palm meet the silk of skin?

He couldn't be further than six feet away. The night wrapped around them. So close and intimate.

Maya shifted, the sheets brushing against her legs. A rustle drifted across from the sofa. Like he was settling. Or struggling to, maybe.

Her pulse echoed within her neck. This was ridiculous. She was still sick and needed rest. Besides, he hadn't even tried to look at her in the shower. She'd been the one in there, dreaming. She needed to get a bloody grip.

He wouldn't have, though, not even if he had been sorely tempted. That wasn't him. That wouldn't be the decent thing to do, now, would it?

She listened to his breaths slow and smooth out into infinity. It took her a long, long time to get to sleep.

CHAPTER NINE

"I'm bored," Maya said, plonking her book on the bedside table.

It was only the following day. She had woken with such a burst of added strength that even navigating the shower by herself – albeit with Juan insisting on hovering outside the bathroom door just in case – had proved unproblematic. Rina had been and gone, dropping a duffel full of clothes right before lunchtime. Now the afternoon stretched before Maya, filled with endless swathes of books in bed. If she could have spoken to a younger self, she would have laughed at the notion that she could ever be bored when surrounded by books. But something about the enforced isolation made it impossible to focus, her mind repeatedly slipping off the words and out of the window in flights of fancy. She had probably been lying still for too long.

"I honestly don't think I need to be in bed any longer," she said.

"I know you don't." Across in the kitchen, Juan's spoon clinked against the cup as he stirred milk into his tea. "But we had a deal."

"That was before I woke up feeling this much better."

"I know you disagree with me on this." He ambled over. "But a deal is a deal."

"Well, this deal needs renegotiating then, because it's outlived its sell-by date."

"Its what?"

"Never mind. I mean, it's not applicable anymore. External conditions have changed. Make me a new one, or I shall get up."

Juan ducked his head on a smile. Took a leisurely sip of his tea. "You *are* feeling better."

"Yes!"

"It's still important that you rest."

Maya opened her mouth, only for her body to betray her with a cough.

Juan raised an eyebrow. Maya crossed her arms and did her best not to look sullen.

"Fine." Juan set the tea on the table. He grabbed a chair and swung it around, sitting astride it so that his arms lay across the backrest, chin resting on his arms. "What stipulations do you propose this new deal should entail?"

"I don't know," Maya said. "Entertain me?"

"Vague asks rarely lend themselves to strong negotiations. Entertain you, how? Would you like a dance? A song? A story? An interactive theatre production? Instructions on how to become a better bookkeeper?"

"This is already better than before."

"Nor does setting the bar low."

"See? I'm learning heaps already. And you're finally talking for a change."

He arced an eyebrow. "I talk plenty, Maya."

"You so do not. Ask Rina if you don't believe me. You're shut as an ancient chest of drawers."

"That's almost poetic. Is it also possible that you're just bored?"

"Maybe. Where on earth did the bookkeeping come from?"

"That's what I should be doing instead of having this conversation." Juan grabbed his cup and took another sip. "But go on, it can wait. Let's renegotiate your deal."

"You've walked me home how many times? If you're so chatty, then why do I know precisely nothing about you?"

"You've never asked."

"Because I knew you wouldn't answer!" She glared at him. "Fine, maybe that's it, then. Let's play twenty questions."

"And you do know things… Twenty what?"

"Except different."

"Clarity is another helpful asset when negotiating, you know. At least if you're the one making the demands."

"Very funny," she said. "We each get twenty questions to ask each other."

"You mean we have a conversation? Only shorter?"

"Which we must answer honestly."

"Ah." He stretched the vowel as though he was deliberating. "I see."

"See? You're backing out already. Fine. Ten each."

"I was doing nothing of the sort. I was negotiating." He shifted the mug of tea, cradling it in both hands. "Never give away things for free if you don't have to. Ten questions it is."

"Are you getting a kick out of messing me about right now?"

"I'll give you that one as a bonus question because I don't think you meant to start yet. Yes, a little."

"Never give away things for free, huh?" She caught herself quickly. "I mean, you said never give away things for free. Now you're doing it. How contradictory. Full stop."

"Nice save. And it's still important to incentivise people."

"Let's just strike rhetorical questions from the count."

"Shall we?" A silent laughter danced within his eyes.

"You're having way too much fun with this."

"Maybe. I thought that was the whole point." He schooled his face into a serious expression. "Do correct me if I'm wrong."

"You're infuriating."

"Am I?"

The pillow beside her lay so very close. He would never see it coming. But no, she was an adult.

"You haven't asked me a question yet," he said.

"That's because you won't let me think through the noise of you being a smart-arse!"

"You did want me to talk. Am I not pleasing to you?"

"That's definitely a question," Maya said before she thought better of it. "Yes. You are."

His grin vanished, chased away by something softer, something quiet. Maya could feel her pulse, a deep thud in her neck, suddenly thunderous in the silence. She wet her lips. "Except when you're being a bit of an arsehole, which is most of the time."

"Well, that's all right, then," he said, his eyes tracking the movement. "We wouldn't want you to get too comfortable."

She certainly wasn't that. She was all tied up, all of a sudden, tangled in the invisible ribbons which tethered their gazes to one another, soft yet unyielding. Why was he just sitting there, looking at her? Shouldn't he be… doing something? Something more?

She cleared her throat. "How did you come to be here? I mean, running the pub. People talk about you as if you've done it forever, but you must have started somewhere."

"I met Don. He gave me the chance to make my way to something more solid than what I'd had before, as long as I was willing to put the work in. It was too good an opportunity to pass up."

"What were you doing before?"

"Grafting. Anything going. Physical labour, mostly. Picking up what I could on the side."

"What do you mean, on the side?"

"Skills. Knowledge. Connections."

"Right," she said. "That's funny, because you do seem to know everyone, but most people around here also seem to have close family ties. You don't, unless I've missed something. Do you have siblings?"

"No."

"But you grew up here. In London?"

"Yes."

"Is your family originally from here?"

"No."

"Where are they from?"

"South America. Venezuela. Colombia."

"You're all single-word answers."

Juan raised an eyebrow. "That's because you're asking closed questions. That was number seven, I believe."

Damn it. "Fine," Maya said. "Why did your parents come over here, then?"

"My grandparents. Both sides fled a wave of social unrest that took over around the time of the Regression. Many people did. Trying to make a better life for their children, the age-old story." His lips curved, but the lines around his eyes didn't join them. "Funny in retrospect. Who would have thought the land of milk and honey would turn out to be just a colder, wetter version of what they left? They might as well have kept the sunshine."

"The great leveller."

"Sorry?"

"I read an old article once, on global geopolitics. It described that entire period as a universal leveller between first world countries and second and third world countries. Ironically, by sharpening the social divides across the developed world. Further to fall from the standard of living people had got used to here, you know. So many rich countries cut off from all the usual trade and influence. All that migration and social unrest and chaos. And suddenly you can maintain your affluence by leaning on the people who are right around you, or by equalising it all at a lower standard. I guess we didn't equalise. I wonder how many places did."

"You've read some interesting things in your time."

"It was contraband," Maya said. "Stupid phrase, anyway, developed world."

"Yes."

"That wasn't a question."

"I know."

Maya studied him. "So if it was your grandparents who came over, and there was a whole community that came with them, you must have at least some extended family over here. But you're not in touch with them. Why?"

"I left home early."

"Why?"

"You ask some pretty personal questions."

"That's not an answer. And besides, I wasted most of my questions on my own stupidity. You got off lightly. You can give me this one, surely."

Juan sighed, gaze skittering off to the side before locking on hers anew. "Because my father wasn't nearly as wise as your Stuart. That's ten. Where was yours?"

"My what?"

"Your father."

In hindsight, she should have known this game would be a terrible idea. "I don't know," Maya said. "My mother would never tell me. I don't remember much of him at all. Just flashes. I must have been very young."

"What were you doing before you came here?"

"Training to be an engineer. I was in my final year of study. Rigorous course, five years of it. A lot of abstract development work, mind, so half of it is probably useless around here." She shrugged. "Full of transistor fairies."

"Your father wasn't around. Your mother was. I'm guessing no siblings, you would have mentioned them before. Was there anyone else you left behind who meant something to you?"

"No, no siblings. Just Stuart. And Ren, I suppose."

"Who is Ren?"

"My boyfriend." Damn it. "I mean, ex. We split up some time ago."

"Why?"

"It just wasn't working. I mean, he was perfectly fine on paper. We studied together, he was clever, well-liked, attractive"—oh, what the hell was she doing, tying herself in knots here—"but he just didn't get it. I tried to talk to him about what we wanted to do when we graduated, and he was just so… He didn't question any of it. Where we were meant to go, into these pre-arranged placements to work on finding even more ways to funnel even more energy the way of people who were already drowning in it, when out here—"

Damn it, he hadn't asked about any of this. Why couldn't she just keep her mouth shut? Stick to the bare minimum when answering, the way he'd done? She should have known he'd hook into every area of her life she didn't want to think about, let alone share.

This had been a terrible idea.

"I really messed up my chance to ask questions earlier, didn't I?" She willed her lips into a smile. "We should have taken turns or something. Please, be gentle."

Juan studied her, that same incisive gaze which had cut her apart in the early days. "Am I making you nervous?"

"Yes. Of course you are." A terrible, terrible idea. "That counts."

"Fair enough." He swirled the dregs of his drink around in his cup, making a face and putting it aside for good. "What is your happiest memory?"

"Happiest is a tall order. Any superlative is. I— Can I get back to you after I've thought that through for a week?"

"One of your happiest memories," Juan relented. "One that springs to mind."

"Ok. Right. So…" She rifled through the images which rose. "So we used to go to all these functions when I was little. You'd probably struggle to imagine them, I doubt there's anything like it here. Very formal affairs, everyone dresses up to the nines, strict timetables for meals, just full of rules and gloss and pomp. I remember this one time that we went, it was at some gallery, I think, by the river, with this wide-open space outside it. And they had a band playing, this beautiful soulful music, piano and strings, and everyone inside was just… sitting there. Like they were frozen in their chairs, locked in this tiny, enormous adult world, like they couldn't even hear the music and—"

"You felt trapped."

"I…" She held his gaze for a long moment. "Yes, actually." Damn it, she couldn't think straight when he looked at her like this, like he was staring right inside her. She closed her eyes, focusing on the memory. "Anyway, I sneaked out somehow – I did that a lot, my mum always hated it – I sneaked out, and it was a warm summer night. And they had fairy lights – they're small, bright lights, purely aesthetic, not functional at all, utterly useless but utterly beautiful. All strung up above the square outside the doors in row after row. And beyond it, the glowing bubble of the Zone, so the sky was like ink covered in gold shimmer and tiny pinpricks of white sparkles, all above me. And the music was streaming out these doors in the background, and I… let it move me. I mean, I was too young to dance with any grace anyway, but it didn't matter, you know, it was just me and the sky and the music and the lights. It seemed to go on forever. I seemed to go on forever."

She opened her eyes. Juan sat motionless on the chair, chin firmly tucked against the backs of his hands. She couldn't quite put her finger on his expression, something sombre but delicate about it, like a door to an immutable place had opened before her.

"Sorry," she said, brushing a strand of hair behind her ear.

"Don't be." A warmth sank into the melody of his voice, lifting into his eyes. "Whatever for?"

"Is that one of your questions or rhetorical?"

"Rhetorical."

"Good, because I think you're running out."

"Then I'd better make use of them," he said, straightening. "How did you get into reading contraband articles?"

"I don't even remember. I've always wanted to know more than what I was told. Just curiosity, I suppose. I was always digging around. Then Stuart – he was the librarian at university – I think he understood. We never openly talked about it at the beginning, but he just happened to give me access to material I should never have seen. In a way, I studied a lot more than engineering."

"Why *did* you come here?"

She pulled her shoulders in. "You'll laugh."

"Try me."

"Well, first of all, I wanted to find out for myself. What it's really like, on the outside. And beyond that… You know how I said nobody seemed to hear the music? Everything inside is like that. Nobody questions the status quo. I mean, maybe the odd person like Stuart, but even so, they keep quiet about it. And we're fed all these messages, but they keep the rest of the world so… so abstract. There is a monthly day of celebration for the workers out here. I'm not even kidding. You won't see a single worker at it, of course, but people attend it religiously. And some more important people make lovely speeches, and then everybody goes back to their lives without questioning whether they could change anything. Whether they even need to change anything. And the reality – whatever that actually is – it's glossed over with these lovely stories about these helpful people who live out here to make our lives beautiful. So I thought, maybe if I come here, and I collect some authentic stories, you know, unedited ones? Show people that people here are real people, what lives they have led, that they're just like them, then… then maybe it won't be so easy for them to shut their eyes to what's going on."

"Do you think that will work?"

"You've run out of questions," she said.

"I haven't."

"You have. You asked that one before I started. The one… that one."

"I did, didn't I?" His lip quirked as he got up. "Thanks for reminding me. I did like that one."

Had he genuinely forgotten? Or was he deliberately making her—

"It's ok, Maya," he said, clearly misinterpreting her expression. "Your secrets are safe with me. Apart from anything else, I have no interest in turning you into a target because people find out that you come from the land of milk and honey. I spent way too much effort keeping you alive just now."

"It's not all milk and honey."

"So I gather. It rarely is."

"Do you think it would work?" Maya asked. "My idea?"

"Are you looking for an honest answer?"

"Of course. Why else would I ask?"

Juan smiled, shaking his head. "The thing I've found is, people can't hear the music for all sorts of reasons. You can't assume that they're ready to hear it because you think you are. You also can't assume that you know all the reasons they don't. They might not be able to. They might even have heard it, but they disagree that dancing is the right response."

"You think I'm being naive. And presumptuous."

"Maybe a little. Doesn't mean it's not worth doing. It's a nice idea, and it will appeal to some. Your Stuarts. It's impossible to tell how many of those you've got to reach to make a difference. And I'm definitely not the person to tell you that because all I've got to go on are the bare bones of what you've told me."

Maya bit her lip.

"I'm sorry. I didn't mean to discourage you."

"No," she said, "it's ok. I asked for honesty."

"People ask for honesty all the time without really wanting it." He sank down beside her on the bed. "It's also a laudable goal, but a pretty tall order for one person, you know. Dismantling generations' worth of societal division."

Maya laughed. "I think I knew that one, secretly. And probably the other one, too." She shrugged. "I just want to help somehow."

"I know." He brushed a strand of hair back behind her ear with his thumb. "And you're full of youthful optimism. I've told you before, it's refreshing. Maybe I'm the one who's wrong. Too jaded. You should try either way. You never know where a path leads until you've walked it."

"Right," Maya said. He was suddenly very near. This close to him, the dark brown of his eyes shone, luminous against the black of his pupils, a near match for his skin. The warmth of his breath washed over her, leaving a faint echo in its wake. Her gaze flicked to his lips. The shape of them. The wide curve of their bow. Maybe if she just closed her eyes... Leant forward ever so slightly...

"I need to get to those accounts," he said, and the bed lurched with the abrupt withdrawal of his weight. By the time she had opened her eyes and brought herself back into the room, he was already striding out of the door.

CHAPTER TEN

She was washing glasses in the sink. The lights were low, the glow from the wall sconces mingling with the flickering embers from the candles on the tables.

They were alone.

The water ran warm over her hands. The glass within them smooth and solid.

He stepped behind her. She paused and breathed. And breathed.

She set the glasses down. Slowly.

His body was a palpable presence behind her, trickling liquid heat right down her spine. And lower. He stepped much closer, his arms encircling her. His palms splayed flat across her ribcage, then crept up further, thumbs skimming the sharp points of her nipples. He kissed her neck, his lips a ghost against her skin.

She could feel him there, hard against the small of her back.

"Juan…" she whispered.

His hands slid down, right there between her legs, and pulled her sharply into him.

She woke up very, very wet. Still in his bed.

Oh God. Was he in the room with her? On the sofa? She hadn't been making noises in her sleep, had she?

Maya pushed herself up on her elbows, heart thundering as she glanced around. No sign of Juan anywhere. But there, in the background: the steady splashing of the shower.

That image didn't really help.

She fell back onto the bed. Oh, damn it all to hell.

She was washing glasses in the sink. The lights were low, the glow from the wall sconces mingling with the flickering embers from the candles on the tables.

They were alone.

The water ran warm over her hands. The glass within them smooth and solid.

He stepped behind her.

She dropped the glass right in the sink with too much force. It cracked, a sharp pain slicing through her hand. She made a noise.

Damn it.

"Maya," he said, "are you all right?" He reached around her to turn the water off, then turned her lightly by the shoulders, enfolding her hand within his palm. Inspecting it.

In truth, the cut was not that bad. Some blood, but not too deep, by the look of things. Not painful enough for her to miss how warm his palm felt beneath her hand. How strong.

"You need to be more careful," he said, and something about the way he said it sent shivers trickling down her spine. He smiled a little. "I can't spend all my time fixing you up now, can I?"

He stood so close to her again. So close she could make out that he should probably shave quite soon.

She bit her lip. His eyes dropped down and caught the movement, then lingered. Lingered.

Then pulled away.

She hadn't been making noises in her sleep earlier that day. Had she? There was no way to know exactly when he'd left the room.

"I'll get a plaster," he said and turned towards the cupboards at the far side of the bar.

She thought of him that night, deliberately, for the first time. Back in her own bed in the shed. Not in a dream. And wondered if he'd ever done it, too. Perhaps that morning in the shower.

If only she could tell for sure. Damn it all to hell.

"So did you?" Rina asked.

"Did I what?"

They sat on the floor of the pub, surrounded by greenery, twisting branches and twigs into garlands and wreaths. Well, Rina was – Maya was doing a lot of twisting without much wreath to show for it. Lots of scratches on her hands, though.

"Maybe I should just help you with yours," she said, throwing her latest disaster back on the pile.

"Nah, keep at it. Takes practice, that's all." Rina began sticking berries between her ivy strands, securing them with metal pins. "Did you share the bed?"

"I thought you weren't interested."

"I think I lied. The mystery is too much. Even I can't contain my curiosity. It doesn't help that Beth keeps trying to gossip with me. I think she thinks I'm closest to the source, so I'll have more dirt to dish out."

"I'm not sure how I should feel about that, Rina."

"Oh, don't be stupid. Do you honestly think I'd pass anything on?"

"Fair enough. Well, there is no dirt. None. All squeaky clean here."

"Really?" Rina studied Maya for a long second. "I mean, sorry, I'm not trying to doubt you, of course. I just wouldn't have thought I was that far off with sensing the mood in the room."

"You're not," Maya admitted. "I don't really get it myself. I don't think I've been all that subtle. In fact, I know I haven't. I'm rubbish at subtle. There's a dictionary definition somewhere with an entry under 'subtle' which reads 'not Maya'."

"You're selling yourself short."

"Either way, I've definitely not been subtle with him. I've been awkwardly obvious. And there were a few moments where I thought he might… but then nothing happened. So he's probably just not interested."

"I doubt that's it," Rina said. "Maybe he's scared."

"You know what, I should fix these to the walls instead. I think that's more my skill set." Maya grabbed a completed wreath, climbed on a chair and held it against a supporting beam. "How's here?"

"That's great."

"Let me just grab some nails." She rummaged around in the toolbox. "I don't know, Rina, how could I possibly scare him? Look at me, I nearly died from a cold."

"It wasn't a cold."

"I know, but—you know what I mean. I'm hardly the one pulling the strings here."

"You must know it's not that simple. Haven't you ever been in this position before?"

"What position?" Maya said, setting the nail against the beam, hammer at the ready. "Helplessly trying to make sense of an enigma?" She hit it hard. "Frustrated with trying to work out if I'm imagining things?" She slammed the hammer into the nail. "Ready to let it all go one minute, and then he flutters his eyelashes and I can't even think straight?"

"I meant head over heels, yes." Rina grinned. "Love the fluttering eyelashes. You gotta call me next time he does that, sounds deserving of a witness."

Maya cracked a weary smile as she grabbed the wreath and balanced it on the nail. "I don't know. I mean, I've only had the one relationship. And, in hindsight, I don't think I was all that invested."

"How so?"

"I think I was just doing what was expected? Like I was meant to have someone because everyone did, and there are certain things you're meant to do to have a relationship, so I did them. You know, you go out, you have a date, you kiss. And so on. I didn't really have anything to compare it to."

"So you never felt nervous? Before you got together with your ex, I mean."

"No, I… I guess I didn't, not really. I thought I did at the time, but it wasn't the same. I was just worried about doing things the right way. Now I worry I'll… I don't know. Say something so spectacularly unsubtle that he can't pretend anymore that it didn't happen. And then he'll…"

"…reject you."

"Well, yes."

"Maybe he feels exactly the same way. And maybe because you're nervous, you're being just subtle enough to leave behind that seed of doubt."

"You think we're in some kind of stalemate."

Rina nodded.

"So what should I do about it?"

"Two options. You give it time. Patience. Often gets you further than you think."

"Or?"

"Or," Rina said, picking up a piece of mistletoe and holding it above her head with a broad smile, "you decide to be brave."

Maya tried to be brave. Every night as she packed up her notebook and wrapped her scarf tightly around her neck, as she watched Juan shrug into his coat from a safe distance, the mistletoe called to her. Rina, terrible meddler that she was, had insisted on fixing the damn thing right above the main door to the pub, blaming tradition. Every night, Maya told herself that she would slow down, linger, let the current drift them together at the door. And then she would find out, one way or the other.

Every night, some invisible force pushed her past the threshold, the currents turning to rapids which yanked her out of the room and away from all possibilities. If Juan noticed her haste, he never mentioned it. In fact, the quick-flowing conversations they had briefly dipped into after her recovery trickled to a stop, most of their walks back to her flat once again wrapped in silence, shrouded only by the icy mists their breaths left behind in the December air.

Perhaps she'd imagined the entire thing. Perhaps she'd misinterpreted his sheer relief at her survival. Hell, maybe he'd only been flirting with the idea. And now... now he had thought better of it. If only she could think better of it herself, once she was alone at night. She rarely succeeded, as if the stillness of their walks ramped up the tension inside her, as if not knowing made her want him all the more. And then, the moment that she lay in bed with no one near... Her head was far too full of him. So full of him. She couldn't help herself.

God only knew how she managed to look him in the eye on each and every following day. Somehow, she did, although the lingering awkwardness certainly blocked any casual chit-chat when they were alone as well. Why Juan wasn't talking... who knew. It was hardly out of the ordinary. And yet, there were those nights when he stuck around well past the point that she had shut the gate. Still watching her as she drifted off into the corridor between the houses, out of sight.

Christmas drew nearer. Even here, it still held some semblance of meaning with the pub due to close on the 25th, although Juan expressed some confusion at the idea of gift exchanges when Maya raised it in a quiet moment.

"It's more so you can rest," he explained. "I can't run the place without staff, and you all deserve a break, even if it's only a day. Wish it could be longer, but we have too many customers who are looking for somewhere to be. It's a little harsh to cut some of them off for that long, to be honest."

"You mean Christmas Day?" Rina joined in. "Eh. We throw enough of a bash for everyone the night before that most of them are still nursing their hangovers, anyway. You can't win them all. By the way, my friend with the band is passing through again, Juan. Should I tell her they're good to come?"

"Yes, do."

"Great." She turned to Maya. "We all get together on the day for a meal – mine and Ben's family, I mean. You're welcome to join if you'd like?"

"Thanks," Maya said. "I'll think about it." She cast a sidelong glance at Juan. "What are you doing?"

"I'm here," he said. "By myself. Where else would I be?"

And there they were again, suspended in time. He held her gaze and she held his, the silence stretching until the back of Maya's neck prickled uncomfortably and Rina slunk off to the side as if she had some very urgent business to attend to.

Of course, as ever, the moment broke.

Christmas drew near, and Maya had to admit that she missed a few traditions from home. Not the endless functions which stacked up in the weeks preceding the festive days. Not the pressure of hunting down the perfect little trinket from the art déco shop down the road, in the vain hope that her mother might approve this time round. Not even the anticipation of receiving a gift herself, because it inevitably had some invisible message wrapped inside it which spoiled its purpose. Only her mother could turn the finest imported chocolate into a conduit for disapproval.

No, she missed none of those. But she did miss the sway of the trees lining St James' Park, covered in shimmering pinpricks of lights on her way home from uni. She missed the illusion of the roaring fire which her mother projected on the living room wall throughout December. She missed the endless night outside her window, missed staring into it with her hands wrapped around a hot mug of cinnamon tea, spotting the streaks of ice which painted the glass silver.

More and more, winter crept into her shed, sneaking through the gaps and frosting her breath into plumes of white in the mornings. Maya spent several early afternoons hammering layers of thick cloth and additional wood to the inside of the walls. It meant she had to find a way of mending a rip in one of her skirts instead of buying a replacement, but the investment was worth it, softening the draught to a bearable level. She splurged the last of her money on a luxuriously thick sheepskin blanket and a second heater which Rina helped her to haggle down. They hardly transformed her flat into a cosy haven, but the combination made it liveable – Maya no longer dreaded waking up in the morning to find herself half human, half icicle.

Christmas Eve drew near, and then suddenly it had arrived as if the steady rhythm of the week had been cut in two with a knife. Maya had never seen the pub busier, or maybe it was all those tables pushed aside to make room for the band and a dance floor which made the rest of the place feel especially crammed. The musicians, nestled in the corner and playing peaceful carols, instantly transformed the mood, the strings of their instruments vibrating centuries of history into the air.

Either way, dinner was in high demand, as if everyone had been saving their appetite for this day alone. Maya flew from the kitchen and back with barely a break. She was taking a brief breather during service when she spotted Juan unfolding a thick piece of fabric behind the bar.

"Hey! You said nobody gave each other presents around here." She pursed her lips. "Such falsehoods. I'd forgotten all about Beth's jumpers."

"But that's just Beth's little tradition." Juan studied the jumper with a creased brow. "She's always been on the odd side. As this colour combination proves."

"You should put it on," Maya said. "Pay it the respect it deserves."

Juan sighed, then pulled the monstrosity over his head. "I normally wait to do this until it's the 25th and nobody can see me, you know."

Maya tilted her head to the side. At least the purple wasn't as hideous as it could have been. "It's surprisingly… understated?"

"The fact that you're having to phrase that as a question is not reassuring."

"Oh, fine." Maya grabbed Leroy by the sleeve as he wandered past her. "Hey, what do you think? We need a sartorial arbiter."

"Sartorial what, now?"

"Judge the jumper."

Leroy shook his head. "He's more of a single block colour man, but you don't need me to tell you that."

"Exactly," said Juan, jumper already halfway off his head again. "Knew I should have waited till the 25th."

"You're heartless," Maya said. "Do you have any idea how much it would make Beth's day to see you wear that? Especially if you've never done it before." She crossed her arms. "Besides, vanity isn't attractive."

"Nor is that jumper though, honey, you have to admit that," said Leroy. "Not unless you're a very strange one."

"Fine." Juan wrapped the jumper's arms around his waist with a big flourish. "I'm just too damn hot for it. How's this?"

"I—" Maya bit her lip, suddenly acutely aware of Leroy's presence. "I think that's a terrible joke, and you know it, so let's just leave that right there. I also think I left some people waiting for their pints."

Juan raised an eyebrow. Maya did her best not to squirm.

"You're way too tense for Christmas," said Leroy. "Go on, I'm going to buy you a drink, girl. Juan, can I buy the girl a drink?"

"Uh," Maya said. "Excuse me? Just who do you think he—"

"Your employer who has a vested interest in keeping you vertical enough to keep serving drinks to customers?" Leroy smiled. "Also, last I checked, the bartender."

"Right," Maya said. "Sure. We wouldn't want me horizontal with all the serving I've still got to do. I mean, to think of me being horizontal whilst serving—not being vertical or— Go on then, yes, please give me that drink."

Not that she needed it to make an idiot out of herself. Neither of them looked like it was all that easy to keep a straight face. Bloody Leroy wasn't even trying.

"Here you go." Juan set a shot glass on the bar beside her. "I thought you might go for efficiency right now."

"You thought right," Maya said and let the vodka melt the shame away into heat.

"And here are the pints." He pushed a tray towards her.

"Fantastic," Maya said. "You're a star. Thanks, boss."

And she grabbed the tray and let the noise of the room swallow her up.

It was many hours later that she returned for a proper break, leaning against the counter to take some weight off her back. She looked out into the room. The plates had been cleared from the tables, the music had changed to a livelier tempo and the conversations had turned raucous, filling the space with wave after wave of laughter.

At least people seemed to be having fun.

"Leroy bought you another drink," Juan said from behind her, pushing a glass across the bar. "Says you need to relax a bit."

Maya gave the glass a sidelong glance. "Do I need to be worried?"

"No," Juan said, rolling up his shirtsleeves. "He's a good one. Just wants you to enjoy the evening."

"I'm still working," Maya pointed out. He really did have lovely forearms. Lean and strong. "Someone needs to clean up the mess when all of this is done."

"I usually do that the day after. Plenty of time."

She turned to look at him fully. "You spend Christmas Day cleaning? That's a bit sad. I mean"—she replayed her last words—"not pathetic-sad. Disappointing-sad. I feel for you–sad."

"See it as a gift, if you'd like. To everyone who makes sure I don't need to clean every other day of the year." He smiled. "Trust me, I get the better end of the deal. Leroy's right, you should relax."

Maya grabbed the glass, inspecting the toffee-coloured liquid. "What is this?"

"Mead. Very nice if you sip it. Sweet."

"Well, I can hardly drink it without a proper toast. Not on Christmas Eve."

Juan sighed, but he turned to pour a glass for himself, clinking it against hers. "Chin-chin. To a new world."

"To new discoveries," Maya said.

The mead did taste sweet, layers of spices wrapping around honeyed notes which slipped down her throat like molten flames. She leant back against the bar, arms draped over the wood either side of her, soaking up the atmosphere. Tonight was everything the staid dinners she had attended with her mother had not been: lively, warm, just a touch chaotic. In the corner, the musicians picked up a new tune, a fast-paced beat, calling, inviting – demanding, almost – for people to join it. Across the room, one of the regulars pulled Rina's tray from her hand and dragged her to the dance floor against her laughing protests. Another couple joined them, then another, and suddenly there was a complete circle of them, melding into a group and then apart, fluidly switching from partner to partner, blending in new people as they joined. Maya watched the pattern build and unravel, build and unravel like a blossoming flower carried on the strains of the violins, echoing them, flowing with them. She couldn't have torn her eyes away if she'd wanted to.

"You should join them," Juan said, voice surprisingly close to her ear.

"I…" Maya hesitated. "I don't know. This isn't an empty square somewhere. I haven't the first clue what they're doing."

"You don't need to." There was a softness in his tone. Like something cracking open. "Nobody cares."

Maya watched the throng of people thicken. Not everyone in it was graceful, some already past their third pint. "All right, fine. But only if you—"

But before she could finish, Leroy was suddenly in front of her, outstretched hand grabbing her own. Maya yelped, stumbling her way through the first few steps, and then she was spinning, skipping, too focused on finding the flow to do much thinking. The more she let the music catch her, the more it filled her, moving her feet without her say so, without conscious thought. And the more it filled her, the more she could feel it, sweet like the lingering taste of mead on the back of her tongue, vibrant like all the Christmas lights she had ever longed for, bright fire which ran through her veins and lifted her higher.

She didn't know how long she danced for, one song morphing into the next, one partner rolling into another. She might have missed the moment amidst the maelstrom, but then there it was: her gaze catching on Juan out of the corner of her eye as she spun dizzily around her partner, their arms interlinked. For once, there was no doubt about it – he was watching her, elbows firmly set on the bar, cradling his face with both hands. And, for once, nothing masked his expression, everything about it open and warm, from the smile curving his lips and crinkling his eyes to the smoothed lines of his forehead, as if he was drinking in the very joy she felt pouring from her with each step. As if it was the only thing which mattered in the world.

Maya beamed back at him and lost herself in the reckless energy of the dance.

CHAPTER ELEVEN

"You totally chickened out tonight, you know," Maya said much later when they were nearly back at her flat. She had spent most of the way half-skipping and talking nonsense, passing on stories the musicians had told her during a break from their play. Juan probably wasn't all that interested in the deer the violinist's aunt had raised from birth, but she didn't care, too full of light and energy to shut up. Maybe she was a bit tipsy. Or maybe she was drunk on the music. Drunk on the vibe of the entire night.

Drunk on the way he'd looked at her earlier. She still felt the moment thrumming beneath her skin, as though his smile had sunk right into it.

"Excuse me?"

"You never danced," Maya said. "Don't think I didn't notice."

"It's a crime now, is it?"

"No. But I'm pretty sure you'll have to return your South American heritage card."

"You are, are you?" His voice was soaked in amusement. "Well, I had better get right on that. Do I need to get rid of the Spanish, too? Because I'm quite fond of it and it's been passed pretty solidly down the generations, even when a lot of other things drifted away. Or would you like to unravel my entire identity and decide which bits I get to keep?"

"Very funny." Maya nudged him in the side.

"It's a different kind of dancing," he said. "Maybe I just don't see the point of everyone and their horse throwing themselves into one pile. Maybe I think a dance should be between two people."

"Fantastic," Maya said before she could think better of it. If there was any moment to be brave, then surely this was it. "Because we both know I'm really only complaining because I'm disappointed that I didn't get to dance with you, and I'd much rather not share you either." She spread her arms wide, even as her pulse leapt. "So let's do it now."

"Now. Out in the cold. Without music."

No going back now. "I bet you can't," Maya challenged. "I bet you don't even know how to and you're just trying to wriggle your way out." They had reached the gate outside her flat. Maya turned to him, her breath misting into wispy clouds. "Or maybe you're just scared to dance with me?"

"I do," he said. "And I'm not scared of you."

"Great." Her heart was suddenly racing, drumming a heavy beat in her chest. "No time like the present, then."

He looked down at her for an eternity, the moonlight casting a blue tinge over his skin, throwing the angle of his cheekbone into sharp relief. Then he stepped towards her and pulled her close, arms encircling her waist even as her own folded around the back of his neck. "There's still no music, Maya."

"Just pretend there is. I have to follow you anyway, don't I?"

Juan made a soft noise, half laugh, half sigh, and fell into a sway. His leg slipped between hers as he drew her even closer until their bodies were flush, until she wrapped around him like the tangled leaves of a vine. It wasn't so much a dance as a gentle wave of motion, bare shifts of weight and minute steps which carried them in the ghost of a circle, but there was a kind of rhythm to it, the resonance of his own heartbeat, perhaps. For a few moments, Maya hung suspended in tension, and then she breathed and let go, their movements suddenly flowing like water. The wool of his coat scratched her cheek when she turned into it, remnants of warmth emanating from the places where their limbs intertwined. Everything around them seemed ashiver: the naked trees behind them in their bare rustles, the cool burn of the night air on the backs of her hands.

"Maybe it's not so bad," Maya said, a little breathlessly. "Plenty of things I've chickened out of myself as well."

"Like what?"

"I could have asked much better questions, that time we played twenty questions."

"Well, you only had ten. Why didn't you?"

"Maybe I wasn't sure I was ready for the answers."

"Are you now?"

"Are *you*?"

"Maya."

"This is nice," Maya murmured, resting her head against his chest. "Almost more like that memory I told you about than this evening was."

His hand cupped the back of her head, fingers trailing through her hair. "Even without music?"

"Even without music."

"I don't have fairy lights for you, either."

"They're overrated, anyway." She tilted her head. "Look up, there are the stars."

He looked down instead, straight at her, his face so close to hers now. His thumb brushed her cheek. "Maya."

"I totally chickened out about the mistletoe, too. Every damn night since we put it up. Should've brought—"

And he kissed her. The first touch of his lips was pure static, shooting through her body as though she were a live wire. Maya shivered with it, parting her lips on a sigh as his tongue traced their outline, stretching up on tiptoes so she could pull him closer. And then she didn't need to, because he was pushing her back against the gate, lifting her up, cold metal firm and stable behind her, keeping them pressed flush against one another. Then there was only the hot and wet of his mouth, over and over and over again, until they had to break apart to catch their breath.

He was looking at her like maybe she'd been right. Like she hadn't been the only one lost in thoughts at night.

"Would you"—Maya cleared her throat—"would you like to come in?"

"Yes. I would like that very much." He drew her near and kissed her again, long and slow and deep. She felt the curve of his lips against her temple when he withdrew. "Sorry, I'm making that harder right now, aren't I?"

"Uh, a bit." Maya wrangled the keys from her pocket and promptly dropped them. "Damn it. Sorry."

Juan stepped back, the gap between them like a gaping chasm while she fiddled with the lock. "I'm sorry," she said. "I didn't tidy earlier, I wasn't really expecting anyone to—"

"Honestly," he said, "your home decor's the last thing on my mind."

"Right." The gate clanged shut behind them, the lock better-behaved closing than opening. Still, Maya couldn't quite shake off the cloak of embarrassment which clung to her shoulders as she squeezed through the tight gap between the houses with Juan trailing close behind her. "There we go," she said, once they were past the door, flicking on the light. "Home sweet shed."

"It is rustic," he admitted. His eyes scanned the room quickly. "I'm glad I insisted on you staying after you were ill."

Maya switched on the first heater, then the second one. "Sorry." She kicked it twice with the back of her heel. "It only turns on with percussive maintenance. Real bargain. If I'd known this would happen, I'd have stayed at the pub."

Juan pulled her into a kiss, tongue darting lightly against her own, teasing, retreating. "We could always go back."

"That makes sense," Maya murmured between kisses. "I mean, it's the logical thing to do."

"Maya."

"Yes?"

"There's no way I'm walking back to the pub right now."

"Right," Maya said. His mouth was on her neck, his tongue tracing a hot line along her jugular. It seemed to be connected straight to the pit of her stomach, and lower, lower. "That makes sense, too. More sense. I mean—"

"Take this off," he said, already unbuttoning her coat. "And stop talking."

She tried to unbutton his coat in turn but only succeeded in tangling their fingers and hands into a confused mess. Damn it, she didn't remember this being so hard. "I don't seem to be doing much else that's of use."

"You're doing just fine." Both their coats landed swiftly on the floor. "You're perfect. Relax."

He dropped to his knees and then his mouth was on her breast, lips tracing her nipple through her dress. His right hand slid between her legs with a delicious press and all she could do was close her eyes and make a desperate little sound. "Just enjoy this," he said. He was unbuttoning her dress now, one button, then another, then another. "Tell me if it's nice."

"Oh, it's nice." Maya laughed breathlessly. The chill night air bit at her nipples as the dress joined their coats on the floor, but he soothed the sting away with his mouth moments later. She wanted to kiss him again, to pull him up by the shoulders and wrap him all around her, but she didn't get far past her fingers clinging to the back of his neck, thumbs tracing a line behind his ears. Her hips surged against his hand as if of their own accord, chasing the friction, trembling for more, and more, and more…

The friction vanished, his fingers hooking under the waistband of her tights, pulling them down with her underwear. They caught on the rim of her boots. He swore under his breath, loosening laces, but then she was kicking off her boots as well, and suddenly she was naked, flat against the wall with him kneeling before her. Somehow, with all the things she had imagined, this hadn't quite been on the list.

It didn't matter.

He kissed her hip. Ran two fingers over her like sharp, sweet lances. Whispered, "God, you're wet." And then his tongue followed, mouth opening as he pinned her to the wall by the hips with both hands, and Maya lost the ability to think entirely. He edged her onwards, neat circles alternating with light, slow licks until every part of her was thrumming, her legs shaking with the effort to hold herself up. Her hands scrambled against the wall, seeking purchase, but he held her steady somehow, redoubling his efforts. She was making lots of noise now, and maybe she shouldn't but she couldn't help it, she couldn't help it. There was only this, the spiralling tightness, the heat of his lips, and then the world broke itself apart around her and she shook with it.

Her legs folded beneath her, then. He caught her on the way down, wrapping his arms around her as she sank into his lap.

"Oh," Maya said when she could breathe again. "Oh wow."

"Mmmh." Juan nuzzled the nape of her neck, fingers teasing apart the unravelling strands of her braid. "Maya, do you have a bed, by any chance?"

"I— Oh. Yes, of course. Behind the curtain."

"Ah."

"Sorry, I—"

"It's ok. I didn't want to… break the momentum. But I have to admit, the floor is a bit cold."

God, she was being so selfish. "I'm sorry," she said, clambering to her feet. "I got a bit distracted." She extended her hand.

He took it, smoothly rising to stand. A grin spread wide across his lips. "Good." He pulled back the curtain to her bed. "I see… cosy. You're apologising rather a lot, you know."

"I know," Maya said. "Sorry." A peal of laughter burst from her. "I mean…"

Juan's smile softened. He grasped her elbow and brought her in close, kissing her. They sank into the alcove, Maya half on his lap. She could feel him, hard against her thigh.

"That was so lovely," he murmured, lips still brushing lightly over hers. His thumb edged into the space between them, dragging a slow path along her bottom lip. "Listening to you. Do you have any idea how much I want you right now?"

She felt a fresh rush of wetness between her legs, shivering with more than the cold. Why had it never been like this with Ren? So all-consuming, like she wanted everything at the same time but didn't have the first clue where to start. As if she'd mess it all up any damn second now and it would crumble apart like some fragile dream, some feverish imagining. She buried her face in his neck and kissed the skin there, his pulse a fast song against her tongue, his sigh as whisper-soft as his fingers trailing down the length of her spine.

"Why don't you show me," she said, rolling onto her back and pulling him with her. This was easier, somehow, all his strength above her. Like he became something solid to hang on to. Like he knew, like she didn't have to explain the faint tremble which still ran through her fingers. She slipped them beneath the edges of his jumper and the shirt underneath, sliding both past the ropes of muscles within his back. He shifted, pausing long enough to pull the jumper over his head and to unbutton his shirt. She brushed it the rest of the way off his shoulders. Learnt the line of his arms, feathering touches over the expanse of his chest.

If she'd been brave, she might have pushed him on his back and discovered him more slowly, more thoroughly. As it was, her breath tripped in her throat even as her fingers skimmed over his abs and lower, settling on his waistband. It was ridiculous, really, given the way his hips surged against her hand when she traced the outline of him – there was no doubt now that he wanted this, that he wanted her. So why was she all fumbling fingers, fiddling gracelessly with the button on his trousers as if she'd never handled one before? Whenever she'd dreamt of it, she'd been confident at this point. As if their first kiss would strip away any awkwardness, helping her to shed an invisible mantle she'd held on to for too long.

Yet here she was. Still herself.

The trousers came off anyway, albeit mostly with his help. Maya watched him roll to his back and skim the material over his hips beneath the too-dim light. She wanted to see more of him, all of him, every square inch of skin which was obscured by the shadows, but this would have to do right now, so she drank in the sight. She trailed her fingers along his collarbones, over his sternum, barely grazing his nipples. Watched the quickening rise and fall of his chest, licking her suddenly dry lips. He made a low noise in his throat which reverberated deep beneath her hand and her gaze flicked to his.

His eyes were darker than the shadows, holding hers. He raised his hand, fingers tangling in her hair with a slow, rhythmical push and pull, and she couldn't bear it any longer then, just looking at him, couldn't not kiss him, the slick glide of tongue against tongue carving a space in her chest which thundered with want. She sank down on him, moulding herself to him from top to toe, his cock a brand against her hip, his thigh damp with her slickness where she pushed against him. She tried to coax him into her arms and on top of her, but he seemed to be resisting, like an invisible tether was holding him in place, elastic yet firm. After the second attempt, Maya pulled back, confused. "Don't you want— I mean…"

He grasped her hand, kissing her fingers, her knuckles. "It's ok. I wasn't planning on this. I don't have anything with me." His fingers guided hers, lower, lower, until he was pressing against her palm. "This is fine."

"Oh," Maya said. She couldn't resist giving him a long, slow stroke, watching the way his eyes fluttered closed, even as her brain was still stumbling over the meaning of his words. "It's fine, you don't need to worry. I've got a chip."

He blinked. "Sorry?"

"They take population control pretty seriously. Everyone has one, a permanent hormonal implant. You have to apply, if you get married, want to start a family. They deactivate it once you're approved."

He frowned.

"Don't think about that too closely," she said. "Not now. Please."

"No," he agreed after a long moment. "Not now."

"Sorry," she said. "I didn't mean to kill the mood."

"Maya. Stop apologising for things which aren't your fault."

"Ok. I'm just… I'm probably just nervous. This isn't like I— You make me feel so…"

"I know," he said with a sharp-edged laugh. "I know."

This time, when she urged him on top of her, parting her legs, he flowed with her like water. She lay beneath him, feeling the way he fit himself to her shape, the warm kiss of skin on skin, his thighs pressing hers wider.

"So you do want to, then," she whispered.

"Don't be ridiculous," he murmured, brushing the hair out of her face with one hand, the other coming to rest at her hip.

And then he was pushing inside her, one slick, sweet slide and then another, and then another, almost as if he couldn't help himself. Maya shifted her hips, finding the edge, knee slipping against his side, hands gripping his buttocks to pull him in tight until that bright, blinding spark burst through her each time they came together.

Juan bit his lip. His breaths were uneven, his eyes heavy-lidded. She could feel the strain in his muscles, the tight control of his movements fraying around the edges. "Are you ok?" he asked. "Because I'm not sure…"

She pulled him close, burying his face against her neck, her lips skimming over his earlobe. Her heart was a thunder inside her chest, or maybe that was his. "Keep going. Right there."

And then he was no longer controlling anything, surging into her with deep thrusts, and all Maya could do was close her eyes and ride the wave of it, the push and the pull, the tension building all over again. All she could do was cling to him, heels digging against skin, palms flat to his shoulder blades, and lose herself in the rhythm. She pressed her face into his neck, feeling the echo of his breaths, the tightness in her belly building, building, and when he finally shuddered, shaking himself apart in her arms with a helpless moan, that was her done, too. The rush was softer this time but no less deep, unspooling every last inch in her body which had been holding on.

Juan's weight rested on her for long moments before he began to pull away.

"No," Maya murmured against his neck. "Stay."

"I'll crush you."

"You're not that heavy."

He was, actually, but it soothed her to lie buried beneath him like this, as though she could stretch the moment into infinity and make believe that they were still one tangled mess of limbs. In the end, they settled for a middle ground: his head pillowed on her shoulder and one leg thrown over her hips, supporting most of his weight on his side.

She kissed his temple, running her fingertips over his head, following the smooth curves of his scalp beneath a hint of stubble.

"Why do you shave your head?"

"To abide by an ancient religious ritual that has been carried through my family for generations."

Maya paused. "Really?"

"No. Because I started going grey prematurely. But who wants to admit to being vain. Much easier to remain mysterious."

"Thanks for your honesty, then."

"You're welcome."

"I think you'd still look good with grey hair."

"Thank you. I don't."

"Well, I probably wouldn't like myself going grey either."

His fingers traced slow patterns over her side. "You'll always be beautiful."

Maya drew a deep breath.

"Is this you opening up the last ten questions, by the way?" he continued. "Because I'm probably as defenceless right now as you'll ever get me."

"That's what you'd say if you wanted me to believe your answers."

He lifted his head, looking at her. "Trust me on this." His thumb parted her lips, his tongue an insistent flicker against hers for a long moment. "You are so, so beautiful. I would do anything for you right now."

Maya swallowed against the sudden lump in her throat. "No," she murmured. "No questions. That would be taking advantage."

"And that is why," he said quietly.

Maya let her thumb flow along the arch of his eyebrow. "To be honest, I couldn't think of anything decent, anyway. I don't even have the energy to turn the light off right now."

His eyebrow lifted beneath her finger. "Neither will your battery, at this rate."

Maya sighed. "Spoilsport." She pulled from his grasp and rolled to her feet, turning off the light. Only silver streaks of moonlight danced through the small window in the corner, illuminating the room and the bed until she pulled the curtain closed when she returned. He drew her back inside his arms and wrapped them in the blanket, the gaps between them dark and silent spaces beneath its cover. Her fingers settled at the nape of his neck. Drew circles there in a drowsy caress. Everything was as it should always have been.

"Juan?"

"Yes?"

The words pressed against her lips, insistent, urgent. She could almost taste their shape, feel their melodic flow.

"Nothing," she said. "Good night."

"Good night, Maya."

Maya closed her eyes and let the steady rhythm of his inhales and exhales lull her to sleep.

She woke up needing the loo some time later. All around them was still soaked in black. Juan didn't wake when she stole her way out of bed and into the garden, but he shifted as she slithered back beneath the blanket. Eyelids fluttering.

"Shh," Maya murmured. "It's ok. Go back to sleep."

He blinked. Then grasped her chin, his kiss languid with lassitude and sleep. She burrowed into his arms when she withdrew, turning, the length of him flush against her back.

His hands trailed up her thighs and all across her belly and her breasts. Soft, slow movements. She was already wet again, and when he nudged her leg forward and slipped inside her, he fit. The way he moulded to her, like they were merging into a single body. Like they were wrapped tight inside one skin.

She made a little noise. Pushed back against him.

"God, I've wanted this." His voice was deeper than the night and just as quiet. "So much."

She smiled against the pillow. "You did?"

Juan feathered a laugh over the nape of her neck. "Every damn day. For weeks."

He'd kept that hidden. Very well.

Not now, though. Now it was inside her, all around her, was in his fingertips as they slid between her legs and painted sweetness into her. She let it fill her, let him fill her, cresting like a wave and washing her away until there was nothing else left.

Nothing else left.

CHAPTER TWELVE

She woke up to an empty alcove and a dim light trickling through the curtain. Behind it, her flat was just as bare, not a lingering sign that anyone else had ever shared her space.

For a dizzying second, Maya wondered if she'd imagined it all. Too drunk, too tired, just one of those astoundingly vivid dreams which—but no. Her body told the story, sticky and sore in all the right places. She could still smell the sex on the sheets.

No, she hadn't imagined a thing.

Maybe he'd needed the loo. A couple of minutes from now and the door would open and he'd stroll right through it. He wouldn't vanish like this. He would at least have left her a note.

She slid from the alcove, found the basin of water she stored indoors to keep it from freezing, washed herself. Wrangled her long, tangled hair into a bun. Found a change of clothes and got dressed. Turned off the heaters, the shed warm enough now that it would carry the heat for a while.

She stared at the door. On closer examination, something glinted near its wooden edge, right there on the floor. Her keys. Like they'd been pushed through underneath the gap.

She picked them up.

Maybe the note had slipped behind the desk. She sank to her knees, looked beneath it, behind it, in the other corner. On all remaining surfaces. Rifled through the bed.

There was no note.

It didn't make sense. She flung on her coat, fingers shaking as she fastened the buttons. The door slammed shut behind her.

The toilet at the end of the garden was unoccupied. She used it, washed her hands in the bucket of rainwater outside after cracking the thin sheet of its ice and stood beside the overgrown hedge. She hadn't checked the clock, but to judge by the sun it was morning still, the bright white winter light casting the world around her in stark contrasts, draping everything in an ethereal glow.

It didn't make sense. There would be a logical explanation. There had to be. She knew now that she hadn't imagined the attraction between them. She knew that he wanted her. He wouldn't just leave, like it meant nothing. Like she meant nothing. She'd worried about all sorts of stupid stuff last night as well, hadn't she? This was just… just her mind running away with things. There had to be a good explanation.

The walk to the pub had never felt longer. The roads seemed to stretch endlessly, bare tree after bare tree after bare tree. The cold stone reverberated with the echoes of her footsteps, hollow and grey.

The pub stood silent, steady and indifferent, as it always did. The front door was closed. She rapped it once with her knuckles. Again. Maybe he was upstairs. She hammered it with her fist. And again. Maybe he wasn't even at the pub. She pummelled the door with both fists, hard enough to make it shake on its hinges.

It opened, Juan on the other side.

"Were you trying to break that?"

"Excuse me?" she said. "What are you— What the hell is going on?"

She tried to step inside but he blocked her, putting his foot in her way. "Would you let me in, please? It's freezing out here."

"No," he said, "I don't think that's a good idea. Maya, what are you doing here?"

"What am I—what am *I* doing here?"

"Was I not clear?"

"Clear?" She took a steadying breath which steadied nothing. "What, you mean fucking someone's brains out and then disappearing without a word of explanation the next morning? You think that's clear?"

"Let me be clear, then." His face was stripped clean of emotion. Bare as the trees. "It was a mistake."

"A mistake," Maya said. "I don't understand."

Last night he'd been so open. Now there was nothing there. A wall.

"What is there to understand? It shouldn't have happened."

"But… why? It was everything I ever—" Something like hysterical laughter was bubbling up in her throat. She pushed it down. "I don't understand. Give me one good reason why that was a mistake because I don't see it."

"I don't have to justify myself to you."

"Like hell you don't! It's not like I'm some random you just picked up at a bar."

"All the more reason to finish this now."

"That doesn't even make sense! We've been building up to this for months. You can't just… erase all of that because you're getting cold feet!"

"You have been building up, you mean. How could you possibly know what went through my head? Maybe you were a nice distraction. Pretty. Just a little bit too tempting."

"No," Maya said, shaking her head. "Please don't do this. Listen, I get that it was intense. If you're scared—"

"Don't presume to know me. You're a clever girl, so think about it, hard, for a good long moment. You don't."

She wanted him to be wrong. But she'd also never dreamt this could happen. That he'd be capable of putting her through this. The world seemed to be slowly tilting on its axis, as though it were losing solidity. Or maybe it was her who was dizzy.

"No," she heard herself say, as if from a distance. "I guess I don't."

He stared at her, jaw set. A long moment unspooled, sliding away into nothingness.

"You're still here," he said. "What will it take to make you go away?"

Maya stared back at him. This was the moment, the moment where she wrapped her dignity around her and turned away, head held high.

Instead, this was the moment where the tears rose, unbidden, gathering thick in the corner of her eyes and slipping down her cheeks. One, another, then a flow. Maya clenched her teeth to keep her lips from trembling, to stop any sound from escaping. But she couldn't stop the tears.

He didn't blink. Just watched her for a little while. "Do you need me to apologise? I'm sorry. I'm a very selfish man. I took advantage of you and I knew better. It should never have happened."

Maya shook her head.

"I'm sorry it wasn't clear to you why I left, either. I assumed it would be obvious. That we could avoid this conversation."

"Right!" Maya burst out. "But I was just too stupid, was I?"

"Maya…"

"You said"—her breath hitched—"last night you said—"

"Men say a lot of things straight after they've come. And right before. Haven't you learnt that yet?"

Maya gritted her teeth. She wouldn't look away. She wouldn't.

"Go home. Or go to Rina's. Take the day, get your mind off this. Take a couple of days, if you need them, I won't count. Come back when you feel ready. I'll do my best to give you the space you'll undoubtedly need."

"Oh, so I still have a job?"

"Of course you still have a job."

"There's no fucking of course about it! How can you possibly think there is?"

"As I've said, this is on me. So yes, you do still have a job, if you need it. If you want it."

"So you can tell yourself you're doing the magnanimous thing? You— You're a complete fucking arsehole!"

"Yes," he said, unflinching. "Finally, you get it."

And he shut the door in her face.

She didn't go to Rina's. There was no way she could have spoiled Christmas for her, not after everything she'd done for Maya, after all the times she'd included her. She deserved a carefree day with her family, deserved every last ounce of happiness which Maya clearly wasn't supposed to have right now.

Besides, how would it have helped? To sit among them, with Ben's quiet affection palpable any time he handed Rina a bowl of food, with Solace's calls for cuddles a steady refrain throughout the day? With Ben's parents and Rina's mother and grandmother – a stark reminder of everything Maya had never really had?

No, Maya was better off on her own.

The shed echoed with its earlier warmth, the sheets still stained with his scent. Maya should have torn them off and chucked them into the corner. She buried her face in them instead, breathed them in, and let the tears come.

It still didn't make sense. The memories came thick and fast, flooding her in a rush of images. Every time he had ever smiled at her. Every time she'd caught him watching her, that ghost of contemplation lingering in his eyes before they flicked away. Every time he'd expressed concern, looked out for her, all the sleep he'd lost when she'd been unwell. All those nights he'd walked beside her quietly. Nobody had asked him to.

The way he'd looked at her when she'd been dancing. As if there had been only her in the entire world. The way he had held her in the circle of his arms last night, the way he had kissed her, as though he wanted to crawl beneath her very skin. Like he was utterly lost in it. None of it fit with a selfish man chasing purely physical pleasure.

Then again, people did things for strange reasons. It felt good to be wanted, didn't it? Flattering. Why else had she let Ren pursue her, dated him, stayed with him for months even though her own feelings had been lukewarm at best? Hell, if he hadn't started talking about marriage, she might never have considered if their worldviews aligned, whether she actually wanted him. She might never have left him. She might never have left the Zone, either.

And it felt good to be doing the right thing, didn't it? She wanted to tell herself that it didn't add up – the way Juan was taking the blame, the fact that he'd apologised. That he'd been cold but not cruel, when cruel had hung within easy reach. That he could have flayed her right down to the bone with some choice words, but he hadn't. He hadn't. That meant he cared, didn't it? Somewhere. Deep down.

Or maybe her parting words had hit to the core of it: it had nothing to do with his feelings for her, only with his desire to feel magnanimous. He was just someone who needed to know that he was doing the right thing. That he was being decent. Had she not told Ren that she was the problem, as well? And hadn't that felt like the right thing, the kind thing to do, when he was so clearly, clearly besotted with her?

After all, if Juan felt remotely like Maya, how could he have stayed so composed when she cried? Not a muscle in his face had moved. How could he have left in the first place? If she reversed their positions, the thought of waking, wrapped all around him, skin blood-warm against hers, breaths peaceful and even… The thought of sneaking away, of just leaving him there…

She could never have done it.

Maybe he was only being truthful. That he fancied her enough to fuck her, but that it would never become more than that. That if he let them get started, he would string her along until, in time, he would get bored. Maybe that was why he'd sidestepped all their previous opportunities to connect. Because there'd been another Maya at some point in the past who'd got all tangled up in him. Because he'd learnt from it.

Maybe Maya had even worn her underwear.

And if that wasn't cruel, if it was kind, then why did it hurt so much? If he was just being honest, then really, the problem was

Maya, wasn't it? Because she was already all tangled up. Hopelessly besotted. He'd never made her a promise, had never acted like more than a very good friend before last night, and yet here she was, crying into her pillow, lost.

Overinvested. Overemotional. Pathetic.

All her life she'd lost herself in people like this. Not men, certainly not Ren – today was new in that sense, a different flavour to a familiar ache. But all those times when she'd been younger, when she'd thought she had found a group of friends, that she would finally fit in – only to discover that she'd got it wrong again, that she wasn't wanted, didn't belong at all…

It wasn't so different, was it? The grief tasted the same.

There had been that one time – after the school ceremony, perhaps? Or maybe after the birthday party? The detail of the who and the what had already blurred, the actual conflict a smudged photograph at the back of her mind. But the aftermath still sang loud and clear: the way she had sobbed into her pillow. The door creeping ajar and the soft thud of heels on carpet. The way her mother's hand had run over her hair, teasing apart the strands with long nails. So foreign. So familiar.

"Oh Maya," she had said, a sincerity in her voice which Maya had later searched all other memories for in vain. "It's all just a show. Haven't you learnt it yet? When will you learn…"

She'd sounded sad. Hadn't she? Some days, Maya was convinced of it. On others, the melody of her voice distorted, impossible to place.

Right now, Maya didn't even care. She just wanted it back: the soft cotton thread. The promise of comfort. The cold shiver of love.

She just wanted him back.

CHAPTER THIRTEEN

The next day came too quickly, howling winds shaking her awake in the early hours of the morning. Maya forced herself to do all those things she hadn't done yesterday: throw the sheets in the washing pile and swap them for fresh ones; bathe in the large tub she had recently bought for winter; eat a few slices of bread, although they stuck in her throat like nuggets of lead.

All she wanted to do was crawl back into bed, pull the blankets over her head and make the world go away. But she couldn't, she wouldn't let herself do that.

For one, whatever Juan's reasons, she wasn't going to make this easy on him. She wouldn't give him the satisfaction of hiding away to lick her wounds so he could avoid the consequences of his actions. No, if he wanted to push her away like this, then he would have to face her, every damn day. And if she looked like crap because she'd been crying all night, if people asked awkward questions, well, he'd have to face that, too. If he had any shred of decency left in him, then any guilt he'd feel as a result was only right. He deserved to feel it.

He deserved to feel it, just like Maya was feeling the gaping void which he'd cracked open inside of her.

Still, the closer six o'clock drew, the more appealing her bed looked. When it was time to leave, she caught herself hovering at the door. First, she'd forgotten her gloves, but then… did she really need them? Was this the right scarf, or was it warmer than yesterday and the light one would do? When was the last time she'd been to the loo? And why was she stalling for time when she only had herself to answer to?

Some unnamable force propelled her into leaving, in the end. It wasn't warmer outside. The trees on the way to the pub were no less bare, groaning with the wind in the vestiges of twilight. The pub was still covered in the ivy and fir branches which Maya and Rina had pinned to it weeks ago. They would need to take them down soon, if the wind didn't get to them first. Remove the last traces of the night.

Maya pressed her palms against the rough grain of the door. She could do this. She could. She wasn't soft. Not anymore.

The pub was the opposite of the raucous celebration on Christmas Eve, only a couple of regulars dotted around the edges of the room, nursing their hair of the dog. There was no sign of Juan anywhere. Rina stood by the bar, polishing a long line of glasses.

"Hey stranger," she greeted Maya. "You're a bit later than usual." She waited until Maya had come close, then dropped her voice. "Was half expecting you round mine yesterday, but you never showed. Anything you want to tell me?" She raised her eyebrows, the corners of her lips lifting. "You didn't get… tied up anywhere else, did you?"

If it had been anyone other than Rina, Maya might have succeeded. She'd have smiled politely, said she'd just wanted a quiet day and moved on. But it was Rina. It was Rina, and how had Maya not even thought of this – of course she'd be paying attention. Of course she'd ask all the wrong questions.

She opened her mouth, unsure what she meant to say, and it rose in her like a wave, dark and ugly and raw, strangling the breath from her lungs. Of course, Juan chose precisely that moment to step around the corner, face still as a pool in winter.

"Sorry," Maya rasped, spun on her heel and fled the pub.

The door clanged shut behind her, the echo of her boots a cacophony until she came to a stop by the canal. She breathed in deeply. And again. She needed to get a grip. And again.

She sank to the ground, leaning into the solid strength of the cobblestones. The tears were a block of ice somewhere inside her, pushing at her throat, threatening to crack and spill forth in a flood of shards.

She couldn't let herself cry again. She'd only just stopped.

"Maya? Maya, are you he—hey. There you are. Are you ok?"

Maya shook her head, listening to the thud of Rina's approaching footsteps. Should she be relieved? Embarrassed? How on earth was she going to step foot over the threshold again, after her amateur dramatics? She'd been so determined to look him straight in the face.

Maybe her mother had been right. Maybe Maya should have gone into acting. Except for how shit she seemed to be at hiding her true emotions.

"What on earth happened?" Rina asked. "This— It's about Juan, isn't it."

Maya swallowed thickly. The hem of her coat was beginning to fray. She picked at it, nails catching on the thread. If she wound it tight enough, maybe she could snap it…

"Come on, talk to me. Help me understand."

Maya drew a breath. "He stayed the night. It was amazing. And then he… left."

"Left."

"Poof. Gone the next morning. I had to hunt him down, come all the way here. Apparently it was all a mistake. Selfish little indulgence on his part. Should never have happened."

"Bullshit."

Maya laughed. The canal echoed the sound back at her, lending it a metallic edge.

"I mean," Rina said, "I've seriously never seen him like this with anyone. I'm not buying that for one second."

"I'm a nice distraction, apparently." Maya chucked a stone into the canal. "Do you think he means 'easy to play'?"

"Oh, Maya. I don't think… that doesn't ring right."

"You want to tell him that? I've been over and over it, but I'm not the one who's insisting." Maya shrugged. "I don't even know anymore. Maybe I just got carried away. Wanted him too much. Didn't realise how much until—"

She bit her lip, burying her face in her hands.

"Hey." Rina sank down beside her, arms wrapping around Maya.

"You should have seen him. He was just so damn cold. Like it didn't affect him at all. Like none of it mattered." She shook her head. "Sorry. You still have to work with him, too. I shouldn't be putting you in an awkward position."

"Don't you worry about me," Rina said. "If he's been an arse, then he can deal with the consequences. And you know me, I can stay professional whatever. Although, to be honest, I have half a mind to have words with him."

"No, don't," Maya said. "It's not between you two. Besides, he even apologised. Can't even fault him, see? Squeaky clean."

Rina frowned. "Well, apology or not, it's still a shitty way to treat you. He's got extra influence, being your boss and all. He should really have thought it through first."

Maya stared out at the canal. The moonlight was refracting off its waters, rippling white waves cutting through inky black. She breathed with them for a moment. And another.

"What am I going to do?"

"If he was that definite, I guess you can only respect it."

"Right," Maya said. "Right."

"I'm sorry," Rina said. "I wish I'd never encouraged you now. I must have got it so wrong somehow. Should've let you trust your instincts."

"It's ok. It's hardly your fault, you're not a mindreader. And my instincts were all over the place, anyway."

"No, but I'm your friend. And I'm here for you. You hear me?" She drew Maya close. "I'm here for you." She kissed the top of Maya's head. "It's his loss, anyway. You had better remember that."

"Thanks," Maya said, daring to lean into the touch. Something inside her had loosened, some indefinable thing she couldn't quite name. "I… thanks. You're a good friend. Not quite sure I deserve you."

"Oh, don't be rotten!" Rina ruffled her hair, a gesture which had Solace ringing all through it. "That was my whole point. Of course you do."

"There's a lot I haven't told you about myself, you know."

"Of course there is. We all have those things. Keep them, they're yours. Or share them, if you feel ready. Who am I to say when that should be."

She pushed to her feet, her hand stretching out towards Maya. "Come on. You can get through this."

Maya took it and rose, brushing the tear tracks off her cheeks, eyeing the pub in the near distance. "I don't know if I can."

"You came here, didn't you? Could've stayed home. Nobody but you made you do that. Not me. Sure as hell not him. Just you."

Well. There was that.

"Come on," Rina repeated, taking Maya by the arm. "I'd say you've got me, but the important thing really is, you've got you. Let's go."

She survived her shift, against all reason. The ache in her chest remained, transmuting into a dark weight which she dragged along with her. It slowed her movements and thoughts, turning the simplest tasks into a challenge, whispering and mocking every time she caught herself drifting off into reminiscing. Juan stayed true to his word, keeping out of her way and never once addressing her directly, but even so, it was impossible to ignore him entirely. Every so often Maya's gaze would catch on him like flypaper, and despite the sickening lurch to her stomach it seemed an impossible task, then, to tear her eyes away from him, to focus on what she was doing.

She succeeded. Barely.

It was near the end of her shift when Leroy stopped her while she was clearing the tables.

"Evening, darling. You've barely said a word tonight."

"Tired," Maya said. "Ready to head home."

"Just what I wanted to chat to you about. Figured you might fancy some company."

Maya looked up from her tray. "Excuse me?"

"It's a long walk, isn't it? Better shared than alone."

Oh. Oh, that son of a—

"So I figured we might as well share it."

Maya pressed her lips together. "How thoughtful," she managed after a moment. "But I wouldn't want to put you out."

"Well, I happen to be walking your way anyway. I live nearby."

"What a coincidence," Maya said.

"Isn't it? And I just happen to feel like hanging around a bit longer today, so I'll probably be trailing you either way when we go. And that'll just feel uncomfortably like stalking, won't it?"

Maya glared at him. Leroy shrugged.

"Or we could just decide to walk together."

"Sure," Maya said. She took the tray of dirties behind the bar, stepping closer to Juan than she had been all night. The glasses rattled and clanged as she slammed it down on the surface. "Let's do that. I'll be grateful for the company. And I won't wonder at all how you even know where I live, seeing how I never shared that little piece of private information."

"You didn't? Must have overheard it at some point, then."

"Well, whoever you overheard it from needs to mind their own business." She could sense his presence, solid like an invisible wall beside her. She kept her eyes fixed on Leroy. "Because they're overreaching."

"Probably something to that." Leroy gave a small shrug. "See you in a bit, then, darling."

"See you in a bit," Maya said and began to scrub the glasses to within an inch of their life.

She was still seething by the time she exited the pub, Leroy in tow. "Go on, then," she said, pulling her collar up against the bite of the night air. "Let's get on with this farce."

"I'm not the one you've got beef with, sweetheart."

Maya shot him a look. "No. You're just playing along with him. Doing him a favour. He's good at that, isn't he? Getting people to do him favours." She picked up the pace, feet swallowing the pavement beneath her.

"Maybe I'm doing you a favour instead. How would you know?"

"I don't," Maya admitted through gritted teeth. "Doesn't mean I have to like it. You're very welcome to leave if you think I'm not being appreciative enough."

Leroy chuckled, shaking his head. "Headstrong, you are. Ready to run through a wall, huh?"

Maya crossed her arms to the wind and kept walking. Leroy's shadow rose beside hers, taunting her with Juan's absence. If she squinted just right, stretched the shape of it a bit, made it slightly taller…

She would have felt less alone walking by herself.

"You know," Leroy said, after long, silent minutes. "I'd trust him with my life."

"More fool you," Maya said bitterly.

"I'd trust him with my life," Leroy repeated, "but I don't, for one second, kid myself into thinking that the feeling is mutual. Now, I don't know what went on between you two, and I know it's none of my business, but I do know this, he's not someone who trusts easily, Juan. He's good at pretending when he needs to, but I don't think he really knows how to handle it when anybody gets close."

"Great," Maya said. "Well, clearly I was the one who made the mistake, then."

"Don't be too harsh on yourself, is what I'm saying. It's probably him, not you."

"Thanks." Maya pulled her coat more tightly around herself. "I think I knew that already."

"Did you really? Do we ever?"

The air had a different edge to it tonight. More biting. Maybe it was going to snow.

She cast a glance at him. "So why are you telling me this? What am I meant to do with it?"

"I can't tell you that." Leroy smiled wryly. "Look at me, fifty-five and I never worked it out. Or would I be sitting in a pub every night, with my best friend a commitment-phobe bartender? All I know is that you were brave to try. And that matters."

"That's pretty cold comfort right now."

"I know, darling. I know. What? Don't look at me like that. You gals don't hold a monopoly on heartbreak, you know. Even if you like to act like it, sometimes."

Maya sighed. No, it wasn't that simple, was it? Never that bloody simple.

They walked in silence for a good while, but something kept itching at her. "Has he ever called you that?" Maya asked.

"Sorry? Called me what?"

"Friend. You called him your friend. Has he ever called you that?"

Leroy thought about it for a moment. "Not that I recall. No."

"Then how do you… Why do you trust him so much?"

Leroy shrugged. "He's always had my back. Listened when I needed an ear. Pulled some strings when I was in dire straits a couple of times. He didn't need to."

"But you still wouldn't say you're close. That you know him."

"Not in the way that you mean, no. As I said, he plays his cards close to his chest. But that's fine by me." He studied Maya for several breaths. "You're different, though. I don't think that's what you're looking for."

"No," Maya said. No, it wasn't. She'd always wanted to know. Know things. Know people. Know them down to the raw marrow of their bones, the messy, tangled knots inside.

Really, she only had herself to blame.

"Don't be who you're not," Leroy said. "I have learnt that much. Anyway. That's where my wisdom ends." He stopped outside a row of houses, tracking numbers on facades. "Is this where you're at? I don't mind walking you, by the way. For you. Not for him."

"Is it not weird?" Maya pulled out her keys. A snowflake drifted from the sky, melting against her palm. "What with you being his friend."

"Only if you make it so."

"Ok," Maya said and attempted a smile. "I'll try not to, then. I'll try."

CHAPTER
FOURTEEN

She did try. She succeeded at not feeling bitter about Leroy's company during the late-night walks home, learning instead about the drudgery of his days in the factory, the incessant dramas in his extended family. But she also tried to let go of the rest, to let Rina's advice sink in, to respect Juan's wishes, however absurd they seemed. If he wasn't prepared to give what she wanted, then they were both better off this way, separate and whole in their own rights. And why had she left the Zone in the first place? A man had been nowhere near the list of her reasons. She just needed to remind herself of that. She needed a distraction. A focus.

She explored the surrounding area, sat in the market square observing people, jotting down notes which painted pictures. Had it always looked so bleak before? The piles of rubbish around every other street corner, abandoned by the overstretched maintenance services. That man with the limp, that woman with the bright criss-cross of scars all down her neck. The girl trying to make away with a loaf of bread from the market stall, only to get slapped round the face for her efforts.

She should be grateful. She was healthy. Fed and relatively safe.

And still, everything ached.

She wrote up everything which Beth had told her until the words were no longer a jumbled mess but the story of a girl growing up and growing old amidst deprivation. She spent some days with Rina and her family, allowing Solace's vibrant joy to cut through the heaviness which clung to her like a second skin.

It might have been easier if Juan hadn't started staring at her again.

She wasn't aware of it at first, too keen on avoiding eye contact wherever possible to soften the ache which was becoming a familiar companion throughout her days. They barely spoke now, and when they did it was perfunctory, the least amount of syllables to convey the necessary information. They ducked around each other in the cramped space behind the bar, never touching. The whole thing had become some elaborate dance, invisible yet obvious at the same time. Even Beth didn't ask Maya about what had happened, clearly dissuaded by the tension which hung between them. She drew Maya into her booth more often, though, cracking jokes about other customers. And she started knitting Maya some handwarmers.

It was January – only a week and a lifetime later – when Maya first noticed it, glancing up at the right moment by pure chance. The way he was looking across the room at her, as though he'd been looking for a while. The raw edge to his eyes which resonated with everything she cradled inside her like some precious wound. Then his eyes darted away, fast enough that she might have imagined it all.

She tried to let it go. She was seeing what she wanted to see. That was all. That was all. She couldn't get her hopes up again. It would be a harder fall, the second time around.

But it kept happening. And the more it happened, the less Maya stuck to her own promise, catching herself watching him in turn, being the one caught watching. Getting lost all over again in the lines of his arms as he poured drinks, knowing their strength now; in the delicate movements of his fingers as he fixed a loose bolt on a cupboard, knowing how precisely they'd played her and brought her to the brink. It was madness, and Maya knew it, but some days it was gravity, and she was helpless, helpless to resist.

Sometimes Rina joined in the game, too, shooting concerned glances at Maya as if she wanted to say something but had thought better of it. Beth was undoubtedly watching the whole damn thing, too. And Leroy. Hell, there was probably a bloody betting pool.

It was all getting rather ridiculous.

The nights were the worst. Her head was full of him, all the what-ifs spinning webs around her thoughts until they were a tangled net of interlocked chains. Maya tried, but there was no disentangling herself. He was her first thought when she woke, her last thought when she went to sleep. Sometimes she woke from dreams, hazy images of them wrapped into a seamless loop, limb to limb, skin to skin. Sometimes she woke from half-whispered promises, too frail to catch, from disorienting stumbles through endless houses with locked doors, her only guide a faint reverberation in the ground beneath her bare feet.

Her pillow was always wet.

Some days she no longer knew if he was watching her or she was watching him or if they were watching each other. What had started as a dance was now one giant, twisted mess.

She lasted until late January. Then, hard on the heels of catching him staring at her again, something inside her, some shapeless resolve, finally cracked. There was nothing special about the moment otherwise, except for this sudden knowledge: she couldn't take another damn day of this.

She told Leroy she didn't need a chaperone that night. He took one look at her, shrugged, and turned back to his drink. She waited until the evening thinned out the crowd. Grabbed the heavy-set keys to the front door from the lockbox when she was alone at the bar for a moment. Lingered, trailing behind the last couple of customers, including Leroy, and ushered them out of the door. Locked it behind them.

Juan looked up from the logbook, genuine surprise washing over his features when she placed the key in front of him on the counter.

"Maya," he said. "What are you still doing here?"

"I'm not playing this game anymore."

"Excuse me?"

"I keep going over it. Over and over, going in circles. It's driving me crazy."

He pushed himself off the counter, straightening to full height. "We've talked about this. You know what I—"

"No. No, actually we haven't. You threw a whole bunch of patronising stuff at me when I was shell-shocked and off-balance. That doesn't count as a conversation."

"And you're in a better position to have one after a month of obsessing about it all?"

"Who says I'm obsessing?"

"It's been a month and you want to dig it all up again? Forgive me if that doesn't sound like someone who has let go to me."

"You're right. I haven't let go."

Juan frowned. "This isn't healthy."

"You're damn right it isn't. Neither is whatever it is you think you're doing, though."

"Excuse me? I'm giving you space. I'm giving you room so you can—"

"Stop it. You're still watching me. You think I'm too stupid to notice? And before you start, you don't watch me like someone who's feeling a little or even a lot guilty, and who's checking to see if the person they're watching is ok. No, you watch me like you're missing me. Like you're pining."

"Don't be absurd. I don't pine."

"No? Well, you won't mind it if I come closer, then, will you? It won't bother you." She stepped up to him. "After all, it won't mean anything, will it?"

"Maya."

"It won't bother you if I touch you, either," she said, flattening her palm against his chest. "Because it means nothing, right?"

"Maya, stop it." He grabbed her hand and pulled it off him. But he didn't let go, their palms floating, fingers intertwining, in the space between them.

"And it won't bother you that you're feeling my skin against yours right now, will it?" She took another step closer, barely shifting her fingers, stroking them against his own. "It won't be tempting at all. Because you haven't thought about this, have you, when you're lying alone in your bed at night. What it was like, to touch me, to kiss me, to feel me come. What it would be like to do it again. That the only thing standing between you and me right now is this bullshit line which you've drawn in the sand."

There was barely a hand's breadth between their faces. His pupils were black, black, black, blown wide. She turned her hand in his, feeling his pulse thrum against her fingers. Her own had quickened the moment she touched him, as if the contact alone was enough to make her come alive.

"You're a clever man," she said. "If you honestly think you're doing us a favour here, you really need to think again."

"Go away, Maya." She could hear the deep breath he drew, his nostrils flaring ever so slightly. "I'm trying to do the right thing."

A peal of laughter shook through Maya. "In what universe?"

"Maya, please. Leave me alone."

She raised her chin. "Or what?"

And then his hand was in her hair, his lips on hers, tongue parting them, and she had her answer.

It was different from their first kiss. Harsh. Punishing. Like he was angry with her. Good – she was angry with him, too. She bit at his lips, their teeth clicking together as her nails dug into the nape of his neck and Juan made a soft noise, tilting her head back further, opening her up. His tongue was wet-hot fire, setting her alight from the inside, and Maya met it with her own, unleashing every shred of fury she had felt over the past month. Not that Juan seemed to mind, kissing her just as furiously, pushing her back in three stumbling steps until her back hit the wall.

She wanted to sink into him. She wanted to pull him closer, closer, crawl beneath his skin, but all she had were her lips, her mouth, her hands, inadequate tools to bridge the gap between them. At least he seemed to feel the same because his hands slid behind the back of her thighs and hiked her up against the wall.

Her legs wrapped around him, and then they were flush, fusing even as his tongue sliced her open, deep down to her back teeth. On the next kiss, his hips surged and if Maya hadn't been wet already, she would have been now: feeling him hard against her, friction only heightened by the layers of their clothes. They fell into a rhythm, or maybe the rhythm fell into them because Maya sure as fuck didn't seem to be controlling her own movements anymore, clinging to him as he ground against her, tension building low in her belly, there, there, just out of reach.

He swallowed all the desperate little noises she made until there was no more air, until they had to break apart, gasping. Maya sucked in deep breaths, dizzy with the cool air flooding her lungs, dizzy with how much she wanted him.

"Tell me to stop," Juan said, his voice a rasp near her ear. "You should tell me to stop."

Like hell. Maya rolled her hips, pressing against him in one sinuous arc, and Juan groaned, fingers digging into her hips. And then Maya wasn't up against the wall anymore, suddenly slamming face-first into the nearest table, barely catching herself on her elbows. Something crashed to the floor, the sound of shattering glass ringing in her ears. She scrambled against the wooden surface, but his hands were already beneath her skirt, pushing it up, pulling at the waistband of her tights, her underwear, and it was easiest, then, to let him, to relax into the cool wood, to rest her cheek against its coarse grain, to close her eyes. The weight of his hand lay heavy between her shoulder blades, the other on her hip, and then he was sliding into her, hard and rough and deep, and Maya sobbed with the intensity of it. He made a noise, too, a small, helpless sounding thing somewhere between a moan and a gasp, and then he was fucking her into the table and there was nothing that felt helpless about that.

She couldn't move much in this position, could only give herself over to the force of his thrusts, split open and raw, aching in the sweetest way. She could only ride the wave of his laboured breaths which seared the nape of her neck as he folded himself over her to find a better angle, to go deeper. But it wasn't enough, all the perfect friction withdrawn in an instant, the occasional press of the table too random to build a pattern which could take her over the edge. Oh God, it wasn't enough. She tried to lift herself up, to inch a hand underneath so she could touch herself, but he was too heavy, too far gone already to notice, his hands getting in the way, and Maya… Maya was lost, too. Her throat caught on small sounds, refusing to shape them into words, so she let herself go limp, let him drive her to the brink and away again. Surrendered to the push and pull, let him fill her, over and over and over. It was all there was, now. All there was. When his thrusts grew uneven, when he finally stiffened against her on a low moan, forehead pressed to the back of her head, she shook with it, squirming as he pulsed inside her.

Fuck, but she wanted to follow him. She needed to come.

For a second, there was only his shaky breath, like liquid glass on her skin. The tightly wound knot deep inside her. Then he shuddered and withdrew. Maya whimpered, bracing herself. Any second now, he'd flip her over and finish the job…

Instead she heard a rustle of cloth – and then the dull sound of footsteps rushing away. By the time she'd cut through the daze of arousal and confusion, pushing herself up on trembling arms and looking around, she was alone in the room.

Oh no, he didn't. He wasn't actually doing this again. The bastard.

She wouldn't let him get away with it. Not this time.

CHAPTER FIFTEEN

She slid off the table, stumbling as her tights and underwear tangled around her ankles. She tried to pull them back up, but her thighs were slick with the both of them, the fabric sticking to her skin and refusing to budge. In the end, she peeled off her boots and dropped them to the floor, tearing off tights and underwear in one fell swoop. Sod it. Both were a sodden mess and wouldn't do much good anymore, anyway. Her skirt was long and who was here to see?

The door to the stairwell still stood ajar. Her bare feet swallowed the steps two at a time as she ascended into the darkness. What if he'd locked himself in his room? But no – past the empty corridor, another open door beckoned. Maya burst through it, pausing as her eyes adjusted to the gloom. There was no sign of Juan, not until her gaze tracked left, catching on the spill of light beneath the bathroom door. The faint sound of trickling water drew Maya nearer, even as goosebumps trickled up her spine. This door was not closed, either, swinging lightly on its hinges at her touch.

He sat on the floor, not far from where she had collapsed some months ago, knees to his chest as though he was trying to fold the bulk of his body into the smallest space possible. An ache bloomed beneath Maya's sternum at the sight of him, and suddenly she couldn't hold on to her anger anymore, all the heat

161

of it feathering apart into wisps of smoke. Because there was something else written in the lines of his limbs, something which ate up all the space in the room.

The water in the sink was running, a steady pitter-patter of droplets against porcelain. Maya bent forward reflexively to turn off the tap and Juan startled, looking up at her.

"Maya," he said, in a toneless voice. "What on earth are you still doing—why can't you just go away?" He shut his eyes, head sinking back against the wall. "Haven't I done enough?"

And something slotted in place inside her, a puzzle piece which hadn't quite connected before. Shards of the mosaic coalescing. How early he'd left home. Because his father had been unwise. His mother's wrist, broken. Him looking after her. A child. Him – not his father. How crucial it seemed to be to him, in everything. To be decent to people.

How he kept running from Maya. Like something terrifying was right there at his heels. Like maybe if he pushed her far enough away, he wouldn't have to look at it.

It wasn't her, though. It wasn't him, either.

She sank to her knees beside him. "What exactly do you think happened down there just now?"

Juan made a small noise, not quite a laugh, not quite a sigh. It had an edge to it, though, bleeding with quiet despair.

"You know I wanted that, right?"

His hands curled into fists at his sides. Maya could almost feel the imprint of fingernails against her own skin, little crescent moons digging into palms. His voice scratched low over his words when he answered. "You were trying to get away."

"I was trying to touch myself! To come!"

162

An endless moment stretched before he looked at her, his lips a thin line cutting his face in two.

"Did you think that at the time?" she asked. "That I was trying to get away?"

He shook his head. "I wasn't thinking at all. I was just…"

"…feeling."

He barked a laugh. "Always so polite. For want of a better word, let's run with that."

"Fucking, then. Is that better? You were fucking me, and all you could think about was fucking me. Which was fine by me, by the way, because I enjoyed you fucking me. The only thing I didn't enjoy was when you fucking stopped and left me high and dry because you—"

She swallowed the rest of that sentence. She wanted to tell him that he was being an idiot, but it wasn't that simple, was it? None of this was simple. None of it, and maybe she needed to keep her mouth shut right now.

"It's like I can't stop with you." His voice was low, barely there, almost as if he were talking to himself more than to her. "It's like I can't stop."

"Don't be stupid. Of course you'd stop."

"You don't understand. I've never felt this way before. You're not like any other woman I've been with. It's different, this… this…" His hands painted empty shapes in the air. "Maya, I'm no good at this."

"Yes, I can see that." She reached out and drew him towards her until his temple came to rest against her collarbone, her fingertips trailing over his smooth scalp. "You're letting your head run away with you." She paused for a long moment, searching for words. "You'd never hurt me. You're not your father, you know."

A deep shudder ran through him, then, and Maya's heart ached a little. A lot.

"Is this why you left? After Christmas? Because you felt… out of control?"

"I just knew you deserved better."

"You're right, in a sense. I deserve someone who respects my right to make my own choices. Don't you think so?"

"I… Yes, of course you do."

"Well, what if I choose you?"

He gave a breathless little laugh. "Then I'd question your judgement."

"That's not very nice. Maybe my judgement is excellent. Maybe I see some things more clearly than you do."

He sighed. Raised his head to look at her, drawing his thumb over her lower lip. "Maya, please be sure. If we do this, I don't think I can… Sending you away the first time was already too hard."

"You're great at not showing it."

"I've had to be."

"Yes," Maya said, "I do get that. Well, I'm not going anywhere, so it looks like you're stuck with me." She pressed her forehead to his. "I know it's scary. I'm scared, too. But I'm here with you."

He kissed her, then. Less harshly than he had downstairs, but no less deep, like all the anger had evaporated, leaving behind only yearning. His hand cupped her head, and she sank into the touch, leaning into him. When he withdrew, his lips feathered over her cheekbone, up to her temple, ghosting over her ear. The tenderness snicked a place in her open, memories trickling into its space.

"Just tell me," she murmured, "everything you said when you sent me away. Was that—that was the lie, right?"

Juan sighed. "It didn't even need to be a lie. You take the truth, you bend it just right… it becomes something else." He kissed her hair. "I've always wanted you, if that's what you're asking. I've always known I shouldn't."

"Well, that's debatable." She grasped his hand, threading her fingers through his own. "Who taught you that? About lying? Your father?"

"Yes. No. In a way. He reserved the right to lie for himself, of course. But when someone expects the truth of you without accepting it, you learn to walk the line. We find ways to please, don't we. We always find ways to please." His thumb rubbed against hers, a rhythmic, hypnotic glide. "I shouldn't be telling you this."

"You should tell me more of this. But maybe in good time. When you're ready."

He inhaled deeply, burying his nose in her hair. For the longest time, they sat like this, leaning into each other until the cold tile began to pull at Maya's bones, leaching the warmth from her thighs.

"I need to get my clothes," she said, disentangling herself from his embrace. "I left them downstairs. Couldn't get my tights back on."

"Right." He withdrew and looked at her legs. "You're barefoot."

"I'm also not wearing underwear. It was ruined."

"Right," he said again, licking his lips.

She cast him a sidelong glance. "You'll always see that table and remember fucking me over it, you know."

"Yes, thank you. I'm aware."

"So we had better make this round work because I'm not sure how we'd get through looking at it every day if we didn't. You know, given how last month went. I don't think I have it in me."

"No pressure, then."

"No pressure."

She pushed herself to her feet. He didn't follow immediately, gazing at her from the floor with a frown. He looked smaller like this: too-long limbs squashed into a restricted space, an awkward fit.

"You looked at your bed every day for the last month," he said softly. "Slept in it, too."

"Yes. It wasn't great."

"I'm sorry. I never meant to… I never wanted to hurt you. You must know that."

"I think I do," Maya said. "You were doing your best. We both are."

"I've missed you." He turned his face away. "God, don't tell anyone."

She should have told him that was a ludicrous thing for him to say. Who on earth would she tell? And even if she did, what would have been the harm?

"It's ok," she said instead. "I'm here. I'm not going anywhere. Come on." She extended her hand, nudging him slightly. "It's cold down there. I'm so done with cold spaces. You know I was never properly cold until I came to this godforsaken place? Do you have any idea how much I'm looking forward to your bed tonight?"

His lips twitched. He flowed upwards with a smoothness which belied his bulk, barely putting any weight on her hand. "Is that where you'll be then? My bed?"

"Yes," Maya said. "Unless you'd prefer I sleep on the couch, of course."

He trailed his fingertips along the side of her face. Over her shoulder, down her arm. Over her hip, coaxing her skirt up in a circular motion.

"I left you high and dry, you said."

"Yes," Maya breathed.

"I should fix that. Not very polite of me."

"No. It wasn't." She stretched up on tiptoes, brushing her lips over his. "Was it nice, though?"

"Was what nice?"

Her heart thundered, whether with arousal or a lingering trace of embarrassment she wasn't quite sure. "Coming inside me."

He laughed, a rich, dark sound. "It's all I want to do. But that's not very realistic, is it?" His hand wandered from her hip to the V of her thighs. "Or very kind, when you need some of this." He ground the heel of his palm into her and she made a sound, swaying a little where she stood.

"Come on." He stepped away. "I think you deserve somewhere more comfortable than a wall this time."

"The wall wasn't so bad," she said, but she followed him into the shadowy bedroom anyway. He switched on the lights, their bulbs glowing awake into a warm golden hue which washed over the room. Maya watched him from beside the bed, shaking her hair from its braid, and began to unbutton the long neckline of her blouse.

He joined her, fingers covering her own. "Let me do that."

She let her hands drop at her sides, feeling the rise and fall of her ribcage as he flicked the buttons open, one by one. His palm drew a long line down the open gap of skin he revealed, and she shivered.

"It's absurd how much I want you," she whispered.

"I know," he said and brushed the blouse off her shoulders. The backs of his hands painted lines along her collarbones, moving outwards and taking her bra straps with them. His thumbs hooked under, pulling them over her shoulders, one hand sneaking to her back and undoing the fastening with deft ease. This was not, Maya reflected in a corner of her mind, a man who didn't know what he was doing. And yet, he was somehow just as overwhelmed as she was.

The bra fell to a puddle on the floor. His hands continued to shower her in light touches, feathery movements back up her shoulders, over her collarbones, along her arms, the faintest caress to her belly and the swell of her breasts. Maya closed her eyes and vibrated with anticipation, fighting the urge to pull him close and hurry him up.

He was watching her intently when she opened her eyes again, like he was studying the smallest shifts of muscle within her face. Their gazes locked, holding, and then he drew both thumbs over her nipples – still gently, the barest of touches – and Maya whimpered as heat shot through her, all the way between her thighs, making her clench tightly around nothing.

The corner of his mouth quirked. "You like that?" He repeated the motion. "So sensitive." He bent forwards, licking a long line up her neck, lips near her ear. "I bet you're even wetter now than you were earlier." Another brush. "Shall I check?"

"Please," Maya said, not caring one whit if she sounded desperate.

His fingers travelled along her back, still unhurried, maddeningly slow. She wasn't sure what she'd do if he kept up this pace – completely embarrass herself with ridiculous noises, or spontaneously combust, perhaps – but then he was unzipping her skirt and it joined the rest of her clothes on the floor, leaving her naked before him.

He massaged the base of her spine, winding circles which meandered around to her hipbone, into the divot of her pelvis, over coarse hair, and then he was parting her with two fingers, sliding inside her, and Maya had to grip on to his shoulder for purchase.

He hummed against her temple. "I think you are," he murmured. Two fingers became three, curving, crooking towards him. Maya swayed and tried to work out how to grind down and stay standing while her legs turned to liquid. Thankfully, she didn't need to: he grabbed her waist with his other arm and lifted her on the bed like she weighed nothing, laying her down on the sheets as he crawled over her. The heel of his hand pressed against her, finally, finally, all that delicious friction which she'd been missing for so long.

She gasped, arching her hips into his touch, and he smiled. "This what you needed? Right"—another press—"here?"

Maya bit her lips, her hips seeking a rhythm.

"You do that a lot, you know," he said and gave it to her: a slow, slick withdrawal followed by a smooth, deep push inside her. And another.

"Do… do what?"

"Bite your lips. And then all I can think about is how I want them red and glistening and… it's absolutely maddening. Here, let me do it for you."

And he bent down, teeth catching on Maya's bottom lip and drawing it between his own, worrying at it until it felt sweetly raw and swollen, the sting of his teeth a counterpoint to the slip-slide of his fingers inside her.

"That's better," he murmured when he withdrew. Maya stared at him, lost in the inexorable pace of his hand, riding the rise and fall of it, breathing, breathing.

She wanted to close her eyes, but she couldn't. Not when he was looking at her like this, gaze swallowing her every movement, pupils blown wide, like he couldn't tear his eyes away. Like he wanted to undo her and watch it all, bit by bit, and yes, that was actually what was happening, wasn't it – he was taking her to pieces, one thrust of his fingers at a time, he was taking her apart and she wasn't going to last long, was she, she was right there, right there, right there and—

The pressure relented, his fingers suddenly slack and unmoving, and Maya sobbed with the loss of sensation.

"Oh God," she managed, "why on earth did you stop?"

He kissed her temple. "I owe you, don't I?"

"So you stop? You bastard, you—"

"Shhh." He kissed her silent. She felt the curve of his lips against hers when he withdrew. "Trust me." His hand fell into motion again, resuming its rhythm. "This is going to be so good."

She couldn't remember, later, how many times he did it, bringing her right to the edge before stopping, watching her squirm and starting again. She didn't know at what point her eyes fell shut, either. Maybe when the heat of his gaze became too much. Or when he bent his head over her chest, alternating light flicks to her nipples with his tongue until one long, connected line of fire ran through her body, his fingers and mouth stabbing bolts of ecstasy through her which burned low in her belly. She scrambled against the bed, grasped at him, nails digging in the gap between his shoulder blades and then she was finally, finally there, only this time he let her, pushing her through the wave as she shook with it, and then another, and another and, oh fuck, what if it never stopped?

He was whispering words into her ear which didn't make sense and Maya gasped for air, laughter bubbling up in her chest like champagne, flooding her, spilling over. She couldn't control it, couldn't even try, and then suddenly her eyes were flooding, too, and it wasn't laughter pouring through her anymore but tears, great heaving sobs she couldn't get a hold on.

"Sorry," she managed between shudders. "Sorry. Not hurt. I just—just—"

"It's ok," Juan said. His fingers slipped from her, gently stroking across her belly. "I know. I've got you."

And Maya buried her face into the crook of his neck and sobbed it all out. The intensity of the orgasm, the last month, the yearning, the loss, the hope, the despair. And somehow it was ok, here in his arms, in a way that it hadn't been in her own bed, in the flat, in the Zone. Like the tears were filling a fissure she hadn't known existed, molten silver settling and fusing a crack into a whole.

"Sorry," she said when she could speak again. "I don't want you to think you did something wrong. That was just—just—"

"—intense." He brushed the hair out of her face, strand by strand. There was something endlessly tender about the gesture. "Too much?"

"Yes," she said. "No. I mean"—she shifted to face him as he settled in bed beside her—"feel free to do that again sometime. Just not anytime soon. Give me a couple of hours at least."

He laughed. "I'm sure I can wait."

She nestled close for a kiss. "Are you? Because it feels like you could go again."

"I can wait." His hand painted a line up and down her side, tracing her curves. "This is nice."

"It could be nicer," she said, playing with the buttons on his shirt. He'd never taken it off. How unfair. "If you wanted it to be. I don't mind if you do. I just don't think I could come again."

He chuckled, the sound dancing into the corners of his eyes. "Where did you hide this part of yourself, Maya?"

"I didn't hide anything," Maya said distractedly. He wasn't stopping her from pushing open his shirt – in fact, he shrugged out of it to help her. It had been too dark last time to see much of him; now she explored the dips and slants of his chest, the firm edges of his muscles, the contrast of smooth skin and sparse coils of hair. She ran her fingers over the dusk of his nipples, along the faint scars running here and there. He sighed beneath her hand.

"You did. All that coy embarrassment before at the slightest double entendre? Very demure. Very captivating as well, I'll admit."

"I was just worried you'd find me out." Maya slid her hands down the taut line of his stomach. "Probably pointlessly. You knew all along, didn't you?"

"Fairly early on in, yes. The build-up was pretty noticeable. Especially all that lip-biting."

Maya sighed, too. So much for that dictionary entry not listing 'Maya' under 'obvious'.

"Am I ruining it?" she asked, finger halting over the button of his trousers. "The captivation?"

His tongue darted over his lips. "Hardly. Please feel free to continue expressing this side of your personality. If you'd like to, of course."

"All right." She flicked the button open. Wrestled the cloth over his hips until they were both as naked as each other, until she could drape herself over every inch of him and feel the warmth radiating from his body. He was definitely hard again, hot skin like silk in her grip when she stroked him, her pulse quickening a little with his moan. "Then I think you should fuck me again."

There was no urgency to it this time, a different desire driving her as she slung one leg over him and brought them together. Just the sweetness of knowing he wanted this, enjoyed this, that she could make him surge against her with such abandon, that he could lose himself in her. They fell into a soft sway and stayed there for a long while, both of them on their sides and his hands in the arch of her back holding her close, his nose buried in her neck, her hair. Then he rolled her onto her back, moving with her and she felt wide, wide open like this, warm and full and brimming with a curious tenderness. Maybe it was for the effort she sensed in him, now, the strain of his muscles as he worked through the rolling waves which brought them together and apart, together and apart. Without being lost in her own pleasure, she could feel it all: she could tell he was getting closer from his gasps and the way he worried at his lip, the way his forehead sunk to her collarbone. She ran her fingers over the back of his neck.

"Juan," she said. "Wait."

He froze in perfect stillness for a beat, breathing heavily, before lifting his head. His heart was pounding hard against her chest. "Is it… are you…"

"I'm fine," she said softly. "See? You stopped." And she drew him in for a kiss. "I knew I could trust you."

He shook his head and laughed, a thready sound. Buried his face in the crook of her neck. "God, Maya…" Her fingertips chased the tremble of his muscles into the hollow of his back, slickening with the sheen of sweat which pooled there. "I can't…"

"Then don't," she whispered. His next thrust was rough and unchecked, but she didn't mind. So was the next and the next and she lifted her hips, pulling him in deeper with her heels, urging him on until his hips lost the rhythm and he shook himself apart around her, inside her, clutching her as though he might never let go.

It was easier to fold themselves into a comfortable whole without him crushing her in this bed than it has been in hers. They lay in silence for a long time, his head pillowed on her breasts as he drew small circles on her belly. Long enough that the silence began to press at her, empty space gathering the weight of uncertainty as the seconds trickled past.

"Are you ok?" she asked, eventually.

"I'm fine." He pushed himself up on one elbow, studying her. "Maya…"

"Yes?"

He hesitated. Licked his lips. Brought her palm to them, ghosting over the fleshy skin at the base of her thumb where her chip slumbered, then over each fingertip in turn. "You're something else."

"Thank you. You, too."

The invisible weight lingered. Warmer, though.

"I think I'm too tired to get my clothes," Maya admitted.

"Downstairs is a far place," Juan agreed.

"Is it ever permissible to leave a pair of underwear on a pub floor when it's also your workplace?"

"I don't know. Maybe you should take that up with your boss."

"Very funny."

"I'll let it go just the once. Right now the worse crime is not having you in this bed." He paused. "I mean, when you think about it, is it permissible to leave your underwear on any pub floor?"

Maya nudged him in the side. "Are the lights a far place as well?"

He shot her a look, but he rolled out of bed anyway, extinguishing the light across the room and then the ones nearby while Maya nestled her way under the blankets.

"It is a lovely bed," she said when he joined her.

He hummed, wrapping his arms around her as he moulded himself to her back, chest warm against the length of her spine. "Much lovelier like this."

CHAPTER SIXTEEN

The next morning sped past in a blur, long, liquid hours in bed broken only by a shared shower, and a much-needed trip to her flat for extra clothes. Juan convinced her to have some lunch before they hid under the sheets again, stretching out the minutes until opening time as far as they could.

Sadly, he also insisted that keeping the doors shut to spend the evening in bed as well was not an option. Maya couldn't really argue – though she tried, laughingly hindering his attempts at getting dressed until the clock on the set of drawers ticked too close for comfort even for her sake.

If she'd been conscious to avoid looking at him before, now the reverse was suddenly true. From the moment they opened up, she was acutely aware of every eye on her and her utter inability to keep the smiles from cracking her face. Sure, she felt tired and sore, but a lightness suffused her which she couldn't contain, her movements quicker, her fingers more nimble than they had been in a long time. Every task before her seemed effortless.

Leroy took one look at her, accepted the drink she was holding out for him and said, "Great. I get my extra half hour of sleep back."

Beth didn't say a thing, but Maya could have sworn she heard her mutter, "Knew you'd work it out," when she walked past her with a full tray of drinks.

Rina did a double-take when Maya inched past Juan to reach a bottle on a shelf. Odd – how naturally they'd shared space before, how strained and artificial it had been not to, for the past month. And how easy it was now, even though Maya itched to extend any moment they touched for longer than strictly necessary. When Rina raised her eyebrows in a silent question, Maya could only shrug and burst into a smile, overflowing with giddiness until she cast her eyes down and focused on scrubbing the counter instead.

It was mid-shift when Maya nipped to the kitchen with some orders, vaguely aware that the bar was deserted. Neither Juan nor Rina was anywhere to be seen. Probably gone to the loo. She had better be quick—

She ground to a halt a few paces into the corridor. They stood nestled in a dark corner near the stairwell, swallowed by shadows. Maya fell back instinctively, dropping out of their line of sight when Rina's voice wafted across to her.

"I know it's none of my business, but—"

"You're right," Juan interrupted her. "It isn't."

Rina sighed. "She loves you, you know. She really loves you. She was utterly cut up about it when you dropped her."

"I know. You honestly think I don't?"

"I… ok. Fine. At least we're on the same page."

"Would you like me to sign a waiver as well? Some impossible commitment to never hurt her, perhaps?"

"Ok, that was fair. I'll butt out now."

"Rina. I'm glad she has a friend in you. I've always been glad of it."

"Well, as long as you know that I'm not cleaning up any more of your messes. I already have one child to tidy up after."

Ouch. Maya could picture her: hands on her hips, that stance she slid into whenever Solace was doing something particularly obnoxious. She could also picture Juan: arms crossing over his breastbone like armour, the only sign that the sour twist to his lips came from a soft place, not one of strength.

"Sometimes I wonder where I've gone wrong," he said, an edge to his voice, "to have my staff speak to me like this."

"Have I ever done it before?" Rina's tone was gentler now. "Well, maybe consider instead where you've gone right, then. Maybe I expected better from you. Trusted you to treat her well. And it was trust you were after, wasn't it?"

The seconds stretched.

"Or is the real issue that I'm expressing concern for her and not for you?"

"Oh, for heaven's sake. Don't be ridiculous."

"Because I gladly would, but I never got the impression you'd be all that keen to hear it."

"I'm not."

"Great. Well, I'm doubly glad then that you've finally decided to hear it from her at least." There was a rustling sound. "That's me done, I reckon."

"Fantastic," Juan said, and before Maya could turn on her heel, he'd stepped out of the shadow of the stairwell and stood right in front of her. "Maya."

"Hi," Maya said. She fought the urge to beat a hasty retreat, encouraging her lips into a smile instead. "Less than twenty-four hours and I'm already catching you in dark corners with other women. I can see why she's worried."

The corner of Juan's mouth twitched. He took another step towards her and smoothed his palm over her hair.

"I'll keep an eye on the bar," Rina said. "Maya, I'm happy for you both. Genuinely."

"Thanks," Maya murmured, only half-aware of her walking past. Then they were alone. "Sorry," she said.

"What for?"

"Listening in?"

"I would have done the same if I were you," said Juan.

"I don't know if that's reassuring or not."

"It's honest."

"Yes." And she knew now what that meant to him, didn't she? She grasped his hand, enveloping it in both of hers. "What she said, about how I feel about you…"

"It's ok."

"No. I mean, I'd sort of hoped to be the one to tell you, but then I was working up to it and what with everything, I wasn't quite sure how… if…"

"Maya, it's fine." His other hand covered hers, holding on tight. "I know."

Maya looked down at the knot of their hands, some silent thing inside her heart curling and uncurling. "You said you were no good at this. Maybe I'm not, either."

"Then don't overthink it. Let's just… let it be. For now."

"All right," she said and kissed him.

"Juan? Dónde estás— Hello."

Maya startled at the noise. "Oh," she said. "Hi."

She was sitting on Juan's bed in a puddle of blankets, wearing nothing but one of his thick cotton shirts and reading a book whilst he was taking a shower. The last thing she'd expected was for her lazy morning to be interrupted by someone walking straight into the room.

"This is an unexpected surprise," said Don.

"Likewise." Maya cast about for her skirt only to spot it halfway across the room, draped over the back of the sofa. Right where Juan had draped her across its edge, not long ago. Damn it. A pair of jogging bottoms caught her eye – definitely not hers, but within reach – yes, they'd do.

"Perhaps I should come back at a better time?"

"No, no, that's fine." Maya wrestled with the fabric, slithering into the trousers without flashing too much skin. "I just wasn't expecting company."

"I can see that." Don smiled, the same easy smile he had smiled on the night Maya had met him. Now if only he had the decency to look away…

"Sorry." She finally slid off the bed. The trousers pooled around her legs, absurdly long, would probably have fallen down if not for the drawstring. "He's just in the bathroom. Should be out any minute." Hopefully not naked. "Juan! You've got a guest!"

"Well, I'm glad to see you've found such a good home here." Maya flushed.

"Though not quite what I was anticipating when I said you'd get on just fine."

"Right. It's been a while," Maya said, injecting extra brightness into her voice. "To be honest, I thought I'd see you before today, but you've been elusive."

"Oh, I've dropped by. We must have just missed each other before." He tilted his head. "I don't suppose Juan's mentioned the times I've stopped in?"

"No," Maya said. He hadn't, had he? To be fair, it hadn't been that long since she'd stopped sleeping at her flat. A month, maybe? God, where had the weeks gone?

Don's eyes narrowed. "So I take it this is a recent development I'm walking in on?"

"Yes," Maya said. "No. I mean— Would you like some tea?"

"That's ok, Maya," Juan said, from somewhere over her shoulder. She turned around to see him cut straight across the room, only a towel wrapped around his hips. "I'm sure Don doesn't mind waiting in the office while I get dressed?"

Maya watched them lock hands in greeting, palm to wrist, forearm to palm.

"Of course not," said Don, eyebrow lifting. "I'm so sorry to have disturbed your privacy."

"No te preocupes."

"And yours," Don said, with a nod at Maya. His smile was all warmth again, but for some reason, it left her skin tingling unpleasantly. "I'm pleased you've settled in well."

"Thanks," Maya said, crossing her arms.

She waited until the door had shut behind him before she approached Juan.

"He knows nothing about us?" she questioned, while he dug out a jumper and some clean boxers from the dresser.

"It's none of his business." Juan dropped the towel. "So I didn't see the point in telling him."

"Right."

"Is there a problem?"

"No. Just… don't you think it's a bit weird that someone who has the keys to waltz into your bedroom whenever he pleases doesn't even know that he might encounter a half-naked woman there?"

"Yes, I'm sorry about that." He'd just buttoned his trousers and was reaching for a shirt. The sharp definition of his muscles vanished beneath the fabric as he shrugged it on. "I'll see to it that doesn't happen again."

"It's not even about that! This isn't about me feeling awkward because he saw a bare leg. I'll live."

Juan turned to look at her. "What is it about, then?"

"I… It just feels… feels…"

"…yes?"

Maya's shoulders slumped. "I don't know."

"Fine. Feel free to enlighten me when you figure it out."

She pressed her lips together. "There's really no need for that tone."

Juan exhaled, closing his eyes. Opened them again and grasped Maya's face with both hands. "Maya. Do I look like I'm ashamed of you?"

"No. I wasn't trying to say you—"

"Because I'm not. I'm not. But I need you to… can you please let me go out there to talk to my boss right now and let it be?"

"Of course." She swallowed against the sudden heavy weight in her throat. "I'm sorry."

"No need." He fastened the last few buttons on his shirt before pressing a kiss to her forehead. "I'll see you in a bit."

And he strode from the room, leaving Maya to drown in grotesquely oversized clothes, alone.

He was right. She was being ridiculous. They'd spent the last few weeks in this bubble, half of it in bed, barely a moment apart, and it was doing weird things to her head. Sure, he wasn't exactly demonstrative with her during working hours, but then he was only being professional, wasn't he?

She grabbed some fresh clothes and rid herself of Juan's, though a trace of his scent still clung to her skin. Maybe a shower would clear her head.

But her mind kept catching on thoughts, swirling back to unease. Juan was right, he didn't act like he was ashamed of her. He could easily have asked her to keep their relationship quiet, private as he was, but he hadn't, not once. He hadn't asked her not to share details of their days – or even their nights – with Rina. And he hadn't pulled her up on the moments when her hand lingered too long over his at the bar, when she squeezed past too closely. In fact, he usually smiled when it happened, as if he welcomed the brief moment of reconnection. He wasn't parading their intimacy in front of others, but he also wasn't obscuring it. Their relationship had to be the worst kept secret inside the pub by now.

So why should it rattle her so, that Don hadn't known? Why couldn't she rest easy in the knowledge that Juan had handled this exactly as he had with his staff and his customers? That the opportunity to share simply hadn't come up because Don and Maya hadn't crossed paths?

It wasn't really about Don knowing about her at all, was it? It was about her not knowing anything about Don. About Juan keeping things from her. Was this why he'd been so at ease with her cover story, back when they weren't anything to one another yet? He hadn't dug because he didn't want her digging?

She was combing her hair on the sofa, dressed in a clean skirt and camisole, when Juan returned.

"Everything ok?" Maya asked.

"Yes, fine. I've got to head out in a little bit."

She set the comb down. "To do what?"

"Run some errands."

"Right."

Their gazes locked for a long moment.

"Hopefully I won't be too long," Juan said, a gentle note softening his voice.

"That's not what I…" Maya fiddled with the comb in her lap, her eyes fixing on its plain surface. His mother's. Now she used it nearly every day. "Ok."

His footsteps drew close. Then his fingers slid beneath her chin, lifting it so she was looking at him. "You still upset with me?"

Maya took a deep breath. "Intimate."

"Excuse me?"

"Intimate. That's what it feels like. Like you're in this strangely intimate relationship with him and somehow I know nothing about it."

"Well, I have known him for considerably longer than I've known you."

"I know."

His hand slipped away. "Would you like me to erase any relationships I've had before you?"

She turned the comb over in her hands. The tiniest hairline fracture ran along its length, too subtle to impair its integrity. "No, of course not. I— It's just like there's this whole side to you I'm in the dark about."

"Does it matter? Isn't the important thing what we are when we're here? Together?"

"Yes, of course. But… I'm curious. I want to know you."

He crouched before her, grabbing both of her hands, his forearms resting against her knees. The comb fell from her grip and onto the sofa, forgotten. "You do. More than most people. Probably even more than him."

"If that's the case, then why can't you tell me where you're going?"

"Maya, please, let it go." He squeezed her hands, frown carving deep lines into his forehead, thin like his smile. "Can we—can this stay good?"

An ache bloomed beneath her sternum. "Sometimes I feel like you don't trust me."

"I do. Just because I can't share everything with you doesn't mean that I don't. Can you believe that?"

"All right," she said, the words dropping heavily in her throat. "I'll try."

"Thank you." He drew her close and kissed her, thumbs tracing all the way up her cheekbones to her temples, palms wrapping around the oval of her face. Maya let the flow of it pull her along, let it wash away the doubt and the hurt. He was right – she should let it stay good. Let them stay good. There was no need to question anything. Not when she could feel him like this, sinking under her very skin.

He brushed his lips over her cheek when the kiss ended. Pulled her into a hug. "You're the most…"

"…yes?"

Juan shook his head. "The most." He kissed her head, nuzzling her curls. "I love it when you wear your hair down. You should do it more often."

"All right," Maya said again. "I'll see yours, too, eventually, you know. You can't always be ahead with a razor."

He laughed and flowed to his feet. "Not a chance. You underestimate my vanity." He headed for the door, grabbing his coat along the way. "I'll see you later. Should be back before opening, but if I'm not, are you ok to handle it?"

"Yes, sure. Stay safe."

The flash of his smile lingered in her even as his footsteps echoed away through the hall.

CHAPTER SEVENTEEN

"How tired are you?"

Maya paused, damp cloth halfway along the bar counter. The last person had just trickled out of the pub, and Juan had locked the door behind them.

"I've been worse." She shrugged. "I mean, it's late, but we did have a lie-in."

"Leave that, then, we can get to it tomorrow. Get your coat on. I've got a surprise."

It was a cold, clear night, the first balmy days of March no match for the endless darkness which drank any accumulated heat back up the moment the sun set. Maya huddled into her coat, stealing glances at Juan as he directed them away from the pub.

"This is all very mysterious," she said.

"Good. Got to keep you guessing, don't I?"

"Do you?" Maya asked. Hard on the heels of this morning's disagreement, the teasing tone in his voice gained a cutting edge.

"A pleasant surprise." He squeezed her hand. "Promise."

Soon, they stopped before a heavy metal gate. Juan fiddled with a key, wrestling its creaking bolts open to reveal an empty yard beyond, one of the few bare pieces of land which wasn't already covered in old and crumbling housing stock. Once upon a time, it must have been a building site, the concrete skeleton of a block of flats still rising eerily into the pitch-black sky.

Before it, not nearly as broken-boned but perhaps almost as ancient, stood an old-fashioned car.

"Oh, wow." Maya stepped closer to it, running her hand up the navy bodywork. It was covered in scratches and dents, war wounds from times long past, but it seemed to possess all its parts. "It still works?"

Juan nodded.

She spotted the fuel tank. "It's a hybrid? I thought those were illegal."

"Not quite, but very hard to find."

That made sense. Barely anyone drove out here, anyway. If you wanted to head beyond the old ring road demarcating London from the Counties, you had to catch expensive bullet trains between substations or find a traditional horse and cart. The occasional car which rolled up on these roads immediately spoke of someone who had money. Or who was on official business from the Zone.

Even so, one of the most striking features of the Ring had always been the carcasses of cars which littered the streets. Most had been long stripped for scrap metal and parts, but every so often a more recognisable one would loom, its gaping rusty mouth and mangled innards testament to a different time.

This one was definitely alive.

Juan ambled over to the door and opened it wide. "I've only got it for tonight. Thought you might like to see something more than the same five square miles of grey streets." He sketched an exaggerated bow. "Milady?"

"Hell yes," Maya said, beaming as she sank into the passenger seat. The leather squeaked beneath her weight but gave way, hugging her close. She watched Juan walk around the car and slide into the driver's seat. "How on earth do you know how to drive, anyway?"

"One of my first jobs was with the rubbish collection. You need some basic skills even for those vehicles. Can't do everything on autopilot when you've got kids whizzing round your legs." He jerked his chin in Maya's direction. "Seatbelt."

"Seat-what?"

He pointed up over her shoulder. Maya stared in confusion.

"Oh, for heaven's sake. Did they teach you nothing inside your little bubble?" He reached over her, pulling a long strap from the door and across her body, clicking it into place. "There."

Maya ran her fingers over the fabric. How odd.

"Don't look at me like that," Juan said. "It's a safety device. The whole car beeps at me non-stop if you don't use it."

He nimbly fastened his own before sticking the key in the dashboard.

"It beeps?"

"It beeps. Screeches. Has a tantrum."

"Right," Maya said. "Who decided to program that in?"

"I don't know."

"Do you ever think people must have been very strange? Back in the day?"

Juan lifted both eyebrows. "Have you read any history books?"

"Yes," Maya said. "Exactly my point."

"We can't go as far as I'd like," he said apologetically as the car hummed into life. "I've got some spare fuel in the boot, but I need to be sensible."

"Where would you go if you had the choice?"

"Give me a minute." They had rolled past the open gate, the car moving like a silent ghost. He unlatched his seatbelt and ran to close it, and Maya understood now: the car suddenly seemed to believe it was a late-night advertisement for the latest VR dance-off. Only more aggressive.

"Very strange," she repeated when he was sitting next to her again in sweet silence.

"You should respect your ancestors," he said with a quirk of the lip.

"Well, you're not, so I don't see why I should, either." She crossed her arms. The air was growing warm, the contrast in temperatures prickling goosebumps up her spine. "Where would you go?"

"The sea. I've always wanted to see the sea."

"That sounds nice," Maya said. "I only ever saw a VR version of it. But it's not the same."

"Tell me more about that."

"VR?"

"Yes. I've heard rumours, but that's all you get here. Rumours trickling out with the odd person who crosses the lines. The people who luck into a service job in the Zone rarely come back."

"Do you think it's luck?"

"That's debatable, I suppose. All I know is that half the population here would give their right hand to get in."

"They get to keep their hand, but they all seem to lose their voices. It's a bit creepy."

"What do you mean?"

"None of them speak to you. I tried for a while because I was so curious. Approached street sweepers and the like and struck up a conversation. They all just looked at me and turned away." Maya shivered. "It must be part of their contract not to interact. All about controlling the information flow."

"They get stability in return."

"Yes." Maya gazed out the window. They'd left the tight streets with buildings looming on either side, cutting out onto a broader connecting road. It must once have been an artery for commuters heading into the city. Larger assemblies of trees ran alongside it, the first outcroppings of Epping Forest.

"VR," she said. "I guess it's a way to keep people occupied. Keep them sane. Work. Daydream. Work. Daydream. Connect, but at a distance. Just real enough that you can imagine you're not stuck in the same ten square miles forever. You get the goggles which tune straight into your retina. The earbuds which block out all ambient sound. The haptic suit which gives you sensory feedback so you can feel like you're interacting with the simulation around you, but…"

She shook her head.

"But it always felt really shallow to me. Like we're playing at something that we've got some base code to, you know. But the devil is in the details. That sea looked beautiful, and I could hear and see the waves. But I bet you if I touched the sand, it would be nothing like the real thing. Each grain would be the same size, just that touch too perfect. You lose all the nuance. All the grit."

"You want things to be real."

"Yes."

"But reality isn't just the beauty of your simulated beach every day. Or a sunset, or—"

"—riding extinct species through the jungle in a timed race."

"Really?"

"Really. People get bored."

"Well, that's about as far from my life as I can imagine. My point was, reality is also the ankle you break when you don't notice the hole on the beach after you've touched all that sand."

"You better watch where you're going, then."

Juan shot her a fond, exasperated look.

"I know," Maya said. "Maybe I didn't fully get that before I came here, but I think I've got a much better grasp on it now."

"You would still take what's real."

"I would still take what's real." She reached across and dropped her hand on his thigh. "Any day."

They drove on in silence for a good long while, Maya staring out of the window into the darkness. There was something oddly comforting about travelling like this, so close to the outside, yet cocooned from the world, neither leaving nor arriving but suspended somewhere in between. She had no place to be. No place but here.

Eventually, though, the car came to a stop.

Maya took a long look at Juan, then flung open the door. The night air greeted her, crisp as a fresh blanket of snow. They were at the bottom of a hillside, on a tarmac path which had long since cracked with the strength of plants and grass forcing their way through. Behind them, a lonely magnolia was trying to welcome spring early, the pale shadows of its bloom quivering in the chill. The full moon cast a white, wet glow over the landscape and the grass running up the slope before her. At its top, leafless oak trees groaned in a murky crowd, marking the edges of a forest which absorbed all remaining light.

Above them, the sky stretched, endless velvet studded with stars.

"Oh wow," Maya said and strode towards the hill. "This is stunning."

"I hoped it might be." He sounded quite pleased with himself. "I wasn't sure I remembered it right."

She waited for him to catch up. "You've been here before?"

He nodded. "A long time ago. A cousin's wedding. As big a family event as I've ever been to. They had enough money to drive everyone out to put on a show." He frowned. "Or maybe they didn't, but they found it somewhere. Come to think of it, this is where I first learnt to drive. My uncle showed me. Down there, obviously." He pointed at the flat plains they were heading away from. "But the ceremony was up near the woods."

"How old were you?"

"Young. Ten. Maybe eleven? I struggled to reach the pedals even though I was tall for my age."

"You must have been excited."

"I don't think I got all that excited as a rule. But yes, it was definitely a break from the routine. It looked very different in summer. Imagine all those trees, full of leaves, in bright sunshine. It was incredibly windy that day, they were threshing about like they might come down any minute. None of the food would stay put. The bride's veil wouldn't stay put, either."

Maya laughed. "I bet she was pissed."

"Probably. I admit, she wasn't really my main focus."

No, she wouldn't have been. "Why take me here?" Maya asked.

"You remember that night outside the museum you told me about?"

"Of course. Nobody else knows about it, you know."

He shot her a sideways glance, the subtlest curve to his lip. "This might be my equivalent," he said. "The wedding itself was boring, but it also meant both my parents were distracted. So many people milling about that it was easy to sneak away. So I sneaked away. Found a little path that cut into the forest. Kept walking and their voices grew fainter and fainter. Until there was only me and the woods and the trees. I still remember looking up and seeing the sunlight filtering through all those leaves. Green and gold. The scent of the moss. You're right, VR could never replace that."

"You weren't afraid?"

"No. Not then. Never then."

"Not even that you might get lost?"

"But I wasn't lost by myself. I was free."

Maya swallowed against a sudden heaviness in her throat. She reached out, the back of her fingers skimming along his arm.

"I mean, there was hell to pay later." He smiled, the moonlight cutting his lips into shadow and light. "But it was so worth it. I would always have done it again."

They had nearly reached the top of the hill. Maya turned around to take in the vista, the slopes of grass rolling into the plain, the shimmer of a lake in the distance. The gloomy border of trees encircling it all.

"Why did you stay in London when you left home?" she asked. "Why not leave completely, head out to the Counties? Try somewhere new, find somewhere else you could feel this free?"

"It was what I knew. And my mother… I still saw her sometimes. In the market. She always asked me to come back. Join the next family gathering. Make amends."

Maya shivered a little, but it wasn't from the cold.

"You didn't."

"No."

"What happened to her? Did he—"

"No. She just got sick. Very sick. I found out from an old family friend I ran into. The funeral had already happened."

"I'm sorry."

"Don't be. Not your fault."

"Is he around, still?"

"I don't know. I don't want to know. Is that terrible, Maya?"

She studied his face. Not a muscle was moving. "Do you think it is?"

"Sometimes. Sometimes not. At the end of the day, there are many things more terrible than thoughts."

"Yes," Maya said. "And many more beautiful." She let herself fall backwards on the grass. "Look at the stars."

He hadn't the last time she had asked him to. Even now he hesitated, only joining her when she stretched out her hand and coaxed him to the ground. They shone brighter here than they had in the Zone, sharpened diamonds undulled by a layer of gold cloth. Maya's eyes tracked the North Star, the Great Bear, Orion's belt. The shimmering echo of a billion exploded stars in its nebula.

They were far more beautiful than in any VR.

"It's pretty cold down here, you know."

"And such heat above us," she said. "Did you know that just one of them contains enough energy to sort out this whole sorry mess we're in?"

"We as in you and me? Or we as a species?"

She nudged his side. "Stop being an arse. The latter, obviously."

"I didn't, actually."

"And here we are, scrambling about still trying to make fusion happen, getting nowhere. Feeding on the sun's crumbs."

"Maybe we're not ready."

"Ready for what?"

"Ready to hold that much power."

Maya sighed. "I wish that weren't true."

"Or maybe sometimes the stars are just the stars."

"Maybe. I often wonder if people have stopped looking up at them. If that's half the problem."

He shook his head. "I think people look up. But they see how far away they are. So they reach as high as they're able."

"We touched them once, didn't we? At least we went to the moon. We could do it again."

"That's a nice dream."

Something about the words stung. And the bright pinpricks in the sky – suddenly they'd drifted farther away. Maybe this was how they'd lost them.

Juan looked over at her. "Oh Maya, I didn't—you know I like your dreams. They're just…"

He fell silent for a long while. So long that Maya wasn't sure he would ever finish the sentence.

"Just…?" she prompted.

"…just hard to hold on to when you're down in the mud."

A veil passed between them. Ethereal. Invisible. Why did he have the car? What had he needed it for? Had he taken the gun?

Curiosity pushed the bitter tang of questions at her lips. A deeper emotion swallowed them back down.

"I won't go rushing up without you, then," she said, threading her fingers through his. "It'll take me some time to build that spaceship, anyway."

"I'd offer you the car as a starting point, but I think I need to return it."

"Shame."

"Indeed."

She rolled towards him, nestling into his side. It was cold, the earth hard as rock beneath her hip. Their breath misted clouds into the air. But his hand was blood-warm in hers, skin against skin igniting a slow burn carried by their pulses.

"Thank you," she said. "For taking me here. It's beautiful."

"You're welcome. I wish I could give you more."

"Is that what you think? That you're not giving me enough?"

"I'm realistic. I know I can't possibly match what you're used to from the land of milk and honey."

She clambered on top of him, straddling him, her hands grasping either side of his face. "You're giving me this," she said, their lips inches apart. "Nobody there ever did. I wouldn't go back for the world. Not even if they told me they had a spaceship."

He bridged the gap between them, lips sliding whisper-soft over her own and then they were kissing. If it hadn't been so cold, Maya might have let it build, stoking the pooling heat in her belly by bringing them closer. But here they were, and it was freezing, and they were being dreadfully, dreadfully serious for such a perfect moment, weren't they?

The curve of the hill beckoned. A quick calculation of their trajectory – yes, if she shifted them a little, adjusting the angle just so…

He yelped when she first flipped them, arms reaching out to the side for purchase, but Maya didn't let him get a hold on anything, using her own weight and momentum to cling to him and propel them sideways. And then gravity joined her, and they were tumbling down the hill in a tangle of limbs, messy and awkward, and Juan was sputtering in her ear and Maya was laughing, and all the world was a dizzying spin.

"What the hell?" he said when they finally came to a stop. "Have you totally lost it?"

But he was smiling even as he shook his head.

Maya laughed. "I've always wanted to do that."

"Risk being crushed against a hillside?" He unravelled his limbs from hers. "Get your hair covered in soil and grass?"

"Oh dear," Maya said, picking at her open curls. "Does it totally ruin my look?"

He brushed some grass out of her hair. "Hardly. Makes you look like you've just had a roll in the hay, which is rather appealing."

"You're filthy."

"And you're just a touch crazy."

"You love it," Maya said with a sudden burst of confidence.

His lips curved in a wry smile, the moonlight refracting off his face as his thumb skimmed along her bottom lip. He'd looked at her like this before, like he was brimming with things he wasn't saying, full of guarded, unspoken truths.

He had better never stop.

"Can you take me there?" she asked.

"Where? The hay?"

"You undoubtedly will. No, I mean the Zone. The edge of it. I've never seen it from the outside."

"I… we can head close to the perimeter, yes. If you're sure."

"Is it silly that I want to?"

"No sillier than rolling down a hill. Come on." He rose, pulling her to her feet with him. "I'll need to take a look at the maps for a route, but I'm sure I can work it out."

Strictly speaking, it wasn't true, of course, that she hadn't seen it: the Zone was a constant presence, the faint glow of its energy field stretching across a far distance. On clear nights, Maya could guess at it even from outside the pub. This hill in the middle of nowhere was the first time she'd ever stepped beyond its reach. The empty sky, clear of pollution, whispered that her previous life was only a dream.

He took them in via the main artery, past the reservoir substations and the allotments of Tottenham. As they approached Dalston, he turned into the sidestreets so the cover of buildings could wrap around them and shield them from prying eyes. Maya had never been as far as Regent's Canal. The area beyond it was a no-man's-land, Rina had explained, and only a madman would be brave enough to scale the tall walls which had been erected on both sides of the waterway. Nobody sane would ever pass into Shoreditch.

So it was a surprise to find stairs hewn into the concrete once they reached the north wall. Who had built them? Surely they hadn't been part of the original construction when its job was to keep people out. Maya raised her head to take in the structure towering above them. It was everything the hill had not been. Ugly. Unnatural. Stripped of all life.

"Don't they patrol it?"

Juan shook his head. "They don't need to. Not this side."

"How can you be sure?"

"Trust me," he said.

She climbed ahead of him, groping her way up the steep and uneven steps. On a windy day, she might have blown straight off, would never have attempted the ascent. But even with a mere breeze caressing her face, her stomach filled with butterflies the higher she rose. Almost near the top, and she made the mistake of looking down, suddenly swaying perilously.

"Dizzy?" Juan grasped her elbow and guided her up the last step. "It's ok. I've got you."

"Silly, isn't it? The number of times I went up the Shard…"

And then she could see it, still one of the tallest buildings in the skyline more than a hundred years after it had been built. It rose angular and tall in the distance, blurred by a golden shimmer, half-obscured. She could see, too, what Juan meant about the need for patrol. Before them, the canal dropped like a gorge, the wall on the other side reinforced by a barbed wire fence at its top. Undoubtedly riddled with sensors. It would have taken a spectacularly dry day and a lot of effort to even attempt the climb. How many had tried it? How many had managed?

"Sit down," Juan said. "You should feel more stable."

She eased herself to a cross-legged position, still leaning into him when he joined her. He was right – the world stopped tilting on its edges, solidifying the more she cast her gaze into the distance. This close, she could almost hear the hum of the glittering sphere, taste the ozone wafting across to them. It crackled with static, brilliant and impenetrable.

"It's beautiful, isn't it," Maya said quietly. "Somehow I always knew it was a prison."

Juan kissed the top of her head and rested his chin in her hair as he pulled her closer. For long moments they sat in silence, absorbing the sight.

"You never mentioned how you got out," he said eventually.

"I found a way to deactivate the tracking features on my chip. Took some time, they're fairly intricate. But then I didn't want to just... dig it out." She shuddered at the thought. "Stuart got me on a supply train to the substation near Edmonton. Don't ask me how he managed it. It's all automated, so as long as you know the right codes you can sneak your way in. I hid between boxes of electrical cables. Crept past the guards when I arrived and waited near a landmark for Mike." She rubbed her face. "Could've gone terribly wrong, in hindsight. I didn't even know Mike. Hell, he might never have turned up."

"But it was worth it."

"Of course." Maya beamed. "It got me to you, didn't it?"

He stroked her arm. "Where is it?"

"Where's what?"

"The chip."

"Oh." She stretched out her hand before him, open palm facing the sky. "Right here."

"Here?" His fingers traced the curve of flesh at the bottom of her thumb.

"Yes. There."

"Invisible," he said.

"They're tiny." She shrugged. "Like many things which have an impact, I suppose."

Juan folded her fingers into a fist, wrapping his hands around them. She shimmied closer, nestling into the silk of his neck. The late night was beginning to sink into her now, lack of sleep weighing her eyelids down.

She liked how he held her. His arms always felt so strong and comfortable around her.

"Do you not miss anyone?" he asked. "Not even your mother?"

"I don't think she ever really wanted me," Maya said. "How can you miss someone who doesn't want you?"

"Oh, easily." He laughed, a dry, rough sound. "Easily."

"Maybe I do, then," Maya admitted. "But it's no use chasing what doesn't want you, is it?"

He looked at her for a long moment. "Well, it's her loss, either way." His fingers combed through her hair, separating the strands. "Though I can't bring myself to be very angry with her if she brought me you."

"I guess everything has its place."

"It does. Come on, you're yawning. Let's go home."

"Yes." Maya drank in the sight of the glimmering hues before them one last time. "Let's go home."

CHAPTER EIGHTEEN

"Hello, stranger. Long time, no see."

Maya looked up at the voice spilling over the far end of the bar where Juan was closing the cash register. The woman leaning on the counter was, in a word, a bombshell: everything that Maya had secretly longed to be in any shallow moment which had ever possessed her. Tall and lithe, with perfectly coiled, black hair, she wore a form-fitting dress which clung to every curve like sugar to a caramel apple. Her teeth flashed white between crimson lips, sculpting into a wide smile.

And she was eyeing Juan as if he was the dessert on offer.

Maya bit her lip. Her not-at-all-crimson, slightly dry lip.

"Sophia," said Juan. "It's been a while."

"I know, I know. Been busy. Rarely hang out round these parts anymore, to be honest." She peered at him from under her lashes. "But I was passing through, so I thought"—her equally crimson fingernails tripped up Juan's chest in slow motion—"I'd make a special effort to stop by. Just for you."

Maya's stomach churned. She had spent several months when she was fifteen trying to perfect coy glances from under her lashes, practising in the mirror daily. It had been a ridiculous phase, but not nearly as ridiculous as her attempts had made her look. How did this woman achieve sultry instead?

"That's very thoughtful," Juan said, taking Sophia's hand and setting it down on the counter. "I don't believe you've met Maya?" And he turned his head, extending his other arm in Maya's direction.

Maybe the floor would swallow her up. What a stupid thought – why should she be the one to scamper away into a corner? She let Juan reel her in, leaning into the solid weight of his hand against her back.

"Hi," she said.

Sophia's eyes narrowed, flicking from Maya to Juan, then back again. "I see," she said after a long pause. "I take it congratulations are in order? Who knew someone would make an honest man out of him one day?"

"Uhm…" Maya said. "I'm not—"

"It's ok, Maya," said Juan.

Sophia laughed. "Who needs a ring these days, anyway. More trouble than they're worth, right? You only melt them down for cash in the end. Believe me"—she dropped her voice to a conspiratorial whisper, looking straight at Maya—"you're better off without one."

"Right," Maya said, barely stopping herself from gripping the counter. The muscles in her arms coiled, tight and tense. But Juan was drawing little circles in the small of her back, and that was sort of nice.

"Well," Sophia said, straightening. "Much less entertaining visit than I'd hoped for, then." She paused, cast her eyes down, then back across at them, a speculative glint shimmering in their grey tones. "Unless you have room for one more?"

"Sophia," said Juan.

"Fine, fine." Sophia pushed off from the counter with both hands. "Why doesn't one of you bring a large glass of your nicest red to that table over there so I can drown my sorrows appropriately. And maybe look tragically beautiful enough to attract some mildly entertaining company."

And she sauntered off, hips swinging from side to side.

"Are you ok?" Juan asked once she was out of earshot.

"Sure," Maya said. Did her voice sound higher than usual? It no longer seemed entirely in her control. "Fine. Let me just bring her that wine."

"Is that what you'd prefer?"

"Yes," Maya said. "Yep. I think that sounds great."

"All right. But let me know if you change your mind."

"Juan!" Rina was waving from the door. "Can you come to the kitchen for a second?"

For a moment, Juan hovered, as if suspended on a string. Maya had never seen him hesitate this overtly.

"It's ok," she said. There. That sounded more like her. "I've got it."

"All right," he said again, planting a faint kiss on her forehead as he rushed off.

She took a deep breath, then found a large glass and liberated the more expensive of their vintages from the locked shelf – wine itself was a rarity, like other imported goods. The deep red liquid nearly matched Sophia's lipstick, pouring slick into the glass. It was ok. Maya had always known that he had a past, hadn't she? This was bound to happen. She just needed to stay professional.

Still, she couldn't help but run her fingers through her tousled hair before she carried the wine over to Sophia. Not that it made much of a difference.

"Thank you," said Sophia. "Why don't you join me for a second. Sit down."

Was this a good idea? Who knew. Maya sat.

"I'll admit, I'm surprised," Sophia said.

"And why would that be?"

"Oh, sweetheart. You still worried? Come on, he couldn't have been clearer."

"I'm not worried," Maya said.

"But you are. It's written all over you." Sophia flashed another wide smile. "That's ok, I'm used to it. Most women react to me like this." She drummed her nails on the table. "Most men don't reject me, though. Half of them would be pestering their wife for that threesome I offered just there."

"You must be very disappointed, then." Sophia's perfume wafted across the table, enfolding her in an intoxicating blend of blossoms and musk. It made Maya's stomach turn.

"Disappointed? Of course. I could really have done with a good... release, you know? But to be honest, right now my curiosity is overshadowing all that."

"Clearly. You still haven't explained what's so curious about us."

"Honey. So terse. You think I'm insulting you?" Sophia laughed. "Not at all. I just never saw him as the type to settle for earth."

"Earth." Maya frowned. "What, like earth, fire, wind or water?"

"Precisely."

"And what are you? Fire?"

"Nah. Water. I fit myself into all the right places. Or I fit them into me, as the case may be." She took a long sip of her wine, somehow turning the simple motion into an artistic performance. "See?"

Despite herself, Maya's lip quirked. "What makes me earth, then?"

"I don't know. You seem so… solid. Dependable."

Dependable. Did she mean boring? The nerve of the woman. "You've only just met me!" Maya set her jaw. "For all you know I could be earth, fire, wind and water combined. Or none of them."

"Ah. I'm beginning to see the appeal. You've got layers."

"And you just take them off and leave them in other people's drawers, is that it?" She narrowed her eyes. "I've worn your underwear, you know."

"Oh, really?" Sophia leant forwards. "Pray tell. That sounds delicious. Was there roleplaying?"

In hindsight, maybe that hadn't been the smartest thing to say. Or the kindest. Maya dug her nails into the wood of the table. "You're awful."

"Am I really?" And there was the flutter again. This time distinctly directed at Maya. "Tell me, am I bad?"

"Well," Maya conceded, "everything does have its place. Not," she hastened to add, "that this place is right here, right now. Because it really isn't."

"Spoilsport. Let's face it, you're benefiting indirectly from all the places I've been."

"I'm sure I'm very grateful."

"So you should be. It takes a lot longer to train some men than you might believe."

Maya frowned, a heavy weight tugging at her chest. "Now that *is* awful. What on earth happened to you to—"

"Can I get some service around here?" a man called from the table beside them. "Or are you just chatting tonight?"

"Well," Sophia said. "I believe that is your cue. Do enjoy him, my sweetheart. No hard feelings from my side." She reached into a pocket – where it fit on her dress was anybody's guess – and handed over a crisp banknote. "This should cover the wine. So lovely to meet you."

"Enjoy your evening," Maya said and got to her feet.

She ran into Juan mere moments later, on her way to drop the food order to the kitchen.

"Hey." He stopped her by her elbow. "Are we ok?"

"Sure," Maya said. "Why wouldn't we be?"

"You don't look so sure."

"I…" Maya looked down at her hands, then shook her head, facing him again. "It's fine. As you said, I can't expect you to not have had a life before me. It was just a surprise, that's all."

He studied her for a long moment. "You spoke to her. What did she say?"

"Nothing. Nothing."

"Maya."

"Nothing of importance, anyway."

He pinched the bridge of his nose. "Then why do I get the sense you've let her get into your head?"

"It's not even about what she said. She wasn't unpleasant. She's just so… so…"

"Yes?"

"…so totally unlike me."

"Is that what scares you?"

His eyes were dark. Why wouldn't he stop looking at her like that? Maya dropped her own gaze, picking at her thumbnail. "She said it surprised her. I guess it surprised me, too. I mean, it's not every day you suddenly find yourself up against every man's wet dream. And I know it's not a competition and I really appreciate the way you handled it, but I can't help but feel like I'm not—"

"You're right," Juan interrupted her. "You're nothing like her."

He stepped close and closer, gently backing Maya into the wall. One hand smoothed down the side of her face, thumb skimming her jaw and lifting her chin.

"She was always a very safe option. I could never have… I've never felt about her the way I feel about you. She wouldn't have let me, and I wouldn't have let her, and that was always very clear from the beginning. Do you understand?"

Maya swallowed thickly.

"I've never felt this way about anyone, if I'm honest," he said. "From where I'm standing, you're so far from safe it's not even funny. So if you somehow think you're not enough, then please stop it. I…" He paused, breathing deeply for a long second and then another, and then he made a low, frustrated noise in the back of his throat and leant in to kiss her.

Maya melted into the touch. Perhaps it was stupid. Ludicrous to compare when she had all the proof right in front of her. She knew it; she knew it, and maybe she just needed it confirmed, seared into her with the heat of his tongue. Maybe this was just what they were, this dance, the uncertainty, her uncertainties, the places where she was bendable and he wouldn't break. But what did it even matter that he couldn't say the words when his fingers wrote it into the skin of her hip, when his lips painted the knowledge onto hers with each sweet slide and retreat. She stretched up on her toes so she could pull him closer, their bodies moulding together with ease, and of course she believed him. She believed him. She believed him.

A cough nearby disrupted the spell. Rina's voice followed suit. "Any chance you could move this away from the main thoroughfare, maybe? Some of us are trying to work."

Juan broke away from Maya. In profile, she could see his pulse thudding rapidly in his neck. "Of course," he said and cleared his throat. "Thanks for being professional."

Rina's eyebrows shot up. "Someone has to be. Honestly, you guys, if I wasn't rooting for you…"

The door to the bar area clanged shut behind her.

Juan pushed himself off the wall, carving out space between them. "See?" He laughed. "Ready to humiliate myself for you, and I don't even care." He shook his head. "I spent years building up a reputation."

"Juan," Maya said. Her own heartbeat resounded deep in her chest. "I love you, too."

He parted his lips. Closed them again. His fingers squeezed hers for a long, suspended moment. "We should get back to work."

"Yes," Maya said. "Let's."

Despite her better impulses, it nagged at her. Not Sophia, not truly, although the flashes of her came like ghosts when he undressed Maya later that night, visions of Juan unwrapping her in the same spot, laying her down on the same bed. Maya shook them off, rooting into his touch, leaning into the way his hands skimmed her curves when she lay bare before him, as though she were all he could see.

Maybe she was.

But something had hooked into a space deep inside her, the space which held all those questions he refused to answer. She had tried to shut it after each moment which trickled inside: the transistor, the gun, the car, Don's silent presence. Now it gaped like a wound, leaking doubt.

How different had he been with Sophia, that she'd been so surprised at their match? And if he had been different with her, then who was he in those places he held Maya at arm's length from? Who was he with Don? Did it matter? Was it not part of what had attracted her to him, the contrast of who he was with the crowd and herself? The mystery? The unknowns?

He was the same now, his breath a song against her neck as he moved inside her, so why did it feel like he was evaporating through her fingers, his skin solid but something immaterial wafting away? Why was she grasping at shadows as though she could weave them around him and twine them into a whole?

"Are you all right?" he asked, once they were finished, and he was lying on his back beside her, breaths still short and shallow. "You seem very far away."

"I'm fine," Maya said, scooting close to bury her face against his chest. She should be. She could be. "Just tired. Go to sleep."

But it took her a long time to drift off herself, to soothe to the beat of his heart.

CHAPTER
NINETEEN

Night still wrapped around them, its ebony blanket lifted mere inches by the first hints of dawn when Maya woke. Beside her, Juan was fast asleep, the soft susurration of his breaths the only noise which cut through the silence. Maya pushed herself up on her elbow and watched him, the shape of him sharpening against the sheets as her eyes adjusted to the gloom.

He looked younger like this. Sleep smoothed out the lines between his brows, painting ease over his features, slackening his jaw. The dark smudges of his eyelashes stained the top edge of his cheeks. The blankets shivered with the steady rise and fall of his chest.

Was he dreaming? Maya reached out a hand, then hovered.

She had. She had been dreaming. She'd been in the park again, digging. This time, there had been no echo, nobody calling for her, but the sand still clung to her fingers, wet and red.

She brought her hand to her face. Clean, dry skin. Of course.

She was losing her mind. She should close her eyes and snuggle into him and go back to sleep. It was too early for this.

The bed creaked a little when she slipped to the floor, but Juan didn't move, the metronome of his breath undisturbed. Goosebumps prickled over Maya's skin as her feet padded across the wooden floor. She grabbed the robe slung over the back of the sofa and shimmied into it, holding her breath at the rustle of cloth.

Silence fell.

She tiptoed towards the door, each step taking her further away from his warmth. She shouldn't be doing this. She should. If he woke now, she could still pretend she was on her way to the loo, could flow back into his arms afterwards, wrap them into one body beneath the covers. This wasn't like her.

This was exactly like her.

The door scraped open with a low groan of its hinges and Juan sighed, shifting onto his other side. Maya's heart thundered in her throat, but he didn't move again.

And then she was past the door and in the corridor, past the office door and shut in and with a single lamp lit, and she didn't have a lot of time, and what was she even looking for? She fell to her knees behind the desk, pulling open its drawers. So many papers. No getting sidetracked by details, just skim them, she just needed to skim them. Food orders. Drink orders. Supplier forms. No. Employment contracts. Yes, maybe. No.

Her hands were shaking. They had never shaken when she was a child. Why had it become harder instead of easier? How long had she been here?

Rental agreements for the pub. Correspondence. More correspondence. Annual energy consumption certificates. More supplier contracts.

"You're looking in the wrong place."

Maya's heart sank. "Juan," she said, scrambling to her feet. "I wasn't—"

"Of course you were." He stood by the door, half in the light, half blending into the murky depths of the corridor. "Let's not do this. Sit down."

He walked over to her. He was only wearing his jeans, black material slung low enough to expose his hip bones. What an odd thing to notice.

"Sit down," he said again, and this time the edge in his voice had Maya sinking into the chair behind the desk as though pulled by strings. Where had her own voice gone? She couldn't find it.

He pulled a large folder from the shelf beside her. Threw it on the desk. Another one followed with a thump. And a third.

"I believe this is what you're looking for."

She met his eyes. His gaze was shuttered, his features bare, stripped, empty. He was miles, miles away. And more.

"Juan…" she said.

"Please." He crossed his arms. "Take your time."

Maya opened the first folder. Rows upon rows of numbers greeted her. She looked at him, tilting her head.

"I'm sure you can work it out."

Maya turned back to the accounts. Daily takings. Monthly summaries. Outgoings. Expenses. Tax. She flicked through the first folder, then moved on to the second. At first glance, it all looked innocuous. Tidy. Well-kept. Everything matched.

Except…

"There's no way those numbers are right. We don't sell anywhere near enough to be close to those margins."

"No, we don't, do we."

"You're fudging the accounts."

"I must be."

"Why?"

A smile played about his lips. "What do you think?"

"Well, it's not to withhold taxes. You must be ten times worse off this way. At least."

"Quite."

The truth seeped from the pages, soaked up by her greedy fingers. "You're… you're laundering money? I… do they even check this kind of detail out here? Nothing is electronic."

"They might. If they suspected someone of being unusually affluent given their circumstances. The governmental inspectors don't just work in the Zone, you know. Someone needs to keep us low-lifes in check. Prevent total anarchy. Ensure we actually pay our dues."

"So anybody smart would arrange for a back-up. A reasonable explanation."

"Of course."

"And Don isn't a stupid man."

"No. He is not."

"I…" Maya's voice broke. So many possibilities. Her head spun. "What is it you're covering, Juan? Tell me it's coffee. Coffee and cigarettes, right? They must be a bomb on the black market."

He laughed. It was a broken sound. "It's not coffee."

Maya's stomach churned.

"It could be far worse, of course," he said, a note of levity creeping into his tone. "It's not prostitution. It's not hard drugs."

"Is it not?"

"I'm fairly certain. But of course you're right. There is never an absolute guarantee."

"Well if it's neither of those two, what is it, then?"

"You know all those lovely hospitals you have in the Zone? All those shiny, bright buildings with that sweet medicine that makes you all better?" The levity had vanished, replaced by bite. "See, we don't have that here. There's the odd one dotted about, but none of them have enough capacity to be of much use."

"I know. I know that already."

"I wasn't finished. Because you're right again, some things are tremendously profitable on the black market. Especially—"

"Drugs," she said. "As in, medicines?"

"See? I knew you'd get there."

"It's—it's how you had all that stuff to treat me when I got ill."

"Yes."

"And he sells them. At a profit."

"Oh yes. A very tidy one. Completely unaffordable, for some. Tough luck, if you're one of them."

"I—how do they even get them? Where do you source something like that?"

"They skim off the labs. They skim off the shipments to the hospitals. Ours and yours. Yours are riskier, obviously, but they probably offer much greater variety." He shrugged. "I'm a bit far from that point of the chain to do more than speculate, really. All I know is that he stands firm on quality, so it's not cooked up in some backyard somewhere. No, best get it straight from the source. Who cares if there's even less to go round for everyone else, that way?"

Maya brushed down the paper in front of her. Her fingers were trembling again. The numbers blurred before her eyes, then refocused.

"You wanted to know why Don has such influence?" he continued. "Well, tell me, why would anyone cut themselves off from a guaranteed route to look after their family if they ever needed to? Even if it leaves them penniless."

"But that's wrong. It's extortion."

"It's power. Besides"—bitterness dripped from his words—"he can be so generous and charitable when the mood strikes him. He even gives me room to be charitable without seeking permission as long as I don't go overboard. So long as the bottom line isn't affected. But you're right. It's a conscious play. Makes people like him. Look the other way. And at the end of the day, people will part with anything to keep the ones they love healthy and alive, won't they? Even their last transistor."

"You swapped it," Maya said, another puzzle piece slotting in place. "For something you had stockpiled here."

"Steroids. A brief break for an asthmatic child. And all for the small price of risking your job by stealing technology from your workplace. Bargain." He huffed a laugh, lips twisting. There was no humour in the gesture. "That child will probably die anyway, if it hasn't yet. Needs ongoing treatment, not a one-off."

Maya's stomach twisted, too. "Do you do that often? Actually… distribute stuff?"

"I can't always avoid it. It's not really part of my agreement with Don, no. But sometimes he needs me to do jobs that fall outside the norm."

"Like when you had the car. You needed to shift something for him."

"Yes. Big shipment. Some supply lines broke. He needed to fill the gap to have it arrive in a safe place."

"He needed someone else to take the risk, you mean."

"Yes."

"So that's your job. To be the fall guy."

Juan's lip quirked. "When you put it like that. Yes. Yes, that's me, Maya. The fall guy."

A long silence fell.

"Maya. Say something."

"I can't believe you didn't tell me about this."

"And what would you have wanted me to say?" His voice rose on the words, a harsh note creeping into its timbre which Maya hadn't heard before. "I cook the books for a dodgy outfit that is likely far bigger than even I know? I choose to close my eyes to the collateral damage that comes with that because it's allowed me to set myself up with a relatively comfortable life and I find the personal risk acceptable? I justify it away by telling myself that at least I can do good for some of the people immediately around me? That I can play the system here and there, maybe help the odd person or two? That if it's not me, it'll be someone else who benefits from it? Someone who won't do those things?"

He leant forward, both hands slamming down hard on the table, either side of hers. "Was I supposed to just tell you that — when? When I first kissed you? When I told you we were a bad idea? Or when you came back and you insisted that you knew what you wanted, without really knowing anything? Did you ever *really* want to hear who I am, Maya?"

She had, hadn't she? That's what she had wanted. To know all of him. Except when she looked at him now, which part was she seeing? How could she reconcile them? This anger. His gentleness. His kindness. All the people who must have suffered because of his choices. Collateral damage.

"I need some space," Maya whispered. Her voice seemed to be coming from far away. "I need time to think."

"Yes, of course." He stepped back, shoulders collapsing in on themselves. "By all means."

She fled the room. The first rays of sunlight were spilling over the horizon, drenching the bedroom in a golden glow. Maya threw off the robe, dressing mechanically. Tights, skirt, bra, shirt. Coat. Where was her coat?

She had told him she loved him. Less than twelve hours ago, she had told him she loved him.

She grabbed the bag with her phone which she'd stowed under the bed when she'd moved in. Chucked in some clothes. Any clothes. Some food. What else?

A crash echoed across from the other room. Shattering glass.

Maya slung the bag over her shoulder and strode through the hallway towards the front door. She wasn't going to look. She wasn't going to look.

Juan sat at the table, head in his hands. The floor was covered in shards, the remains of a water carafe which usually rested on the shelf. He looked up at her when she stopped, their eyes catching. There was something raw in his gaze, not anger now, no, more like something had been cut open, like the blanched pallor of exposed bone.

Maya's vision blurred, and then her feet were carrying her through the corridor and down the steps, taking them two at a time. The front door slammed shut behind her, and she was running, running even though the morning air was prickling cold damp into her lungs, even though she had nothing truly to run from. She ran until her legs protested as much as her lungs, until her body forced her to stop, until she was panting, hands on her thighs and heaving against the waves of sickness which swelled beneath her sternum.

Before her, the trees swayed in the wind. White cherry blossoms wafted the first embers of spring into the light of dawn, glowing like the lonely magnolia on the hillside that night.

Maya couldn't tear her eyes away from them.

She sank to the ground. It wasn't fair. It wasn't fair. Why couldn't she have listened to Rina for once and let it go, stopped digging, let it be? Here she was, trying to race away from the truth she had invited, trying to race home, but where was home? Who was home? Had he not been the closest to knowing, the closest she'd ever been?

Her flat reeked of emptiness, a shell which hadn't been visited in months. Maya sat at the desk for long minutes, for half an hour. Then she wrapped herself in thicker layers and headed back outside.

She walked past the crumbling houses, their facades green with moss. Past the children playing ball behind overfilled garbage cans, no parent in sight. Past the skeletons of cars and the stray cats chasing the birds from their nests on a wall, into the din of the market. She walked through the swathes of people and bought herself a fresh roll with egg, giving half to the woman huddled in a pile by the gate. She watched the people. Really watched the people.

She walked. Through the park, past the remnants of a different time. Past the ruins of a Japanese pagoda, more memory than structure now. All the way to the wall and alongside it, trailing its line until she reached the steps which she and Juan had climbed that day.

They weren't empty now: a handful of teenagers were scrambling up and down, nudging each other and roughhousing, daring each other to jump, telling tall tales of the day they would pass into the Zone and make it big. She should scramble right up there with them and shake them, tell them the truth, make them see, make them understand. Instead, she watched from the sidelines until they became wise to her presence. Then she slunk back off into the grey streets.

She found a pub. It reeked of tobacco and rank beer and claimed to stay open until the following morning. She sat at the bar, sipping her drink as she brushed off one guy, and another, and another, until she found a dark corner to huddle in, face obscured and sheltered from unwanted advances. She wolfed down some soggy chips which had barely been fried.

She watched through the curls of smoke which curdled the air in the room. Really watched. The men and the women and the inevitable brawl which broke out shortly after midnight. She listened to the crunch of knuckles meeting bones. To the steady tide of anger which rose and swelled in people's voices, even after the fighters had been expelled.

She watched. She listened.

The pub held true to its word. At some point, she dozed off, jerked awake again, clutching her bag. Many hours later, she unfolded her locked limbs, stepping out into a new dawn alongside swaying stragglers, darting away from the guy who was sick in the gutter. A bone-deep tiredness buzzed through her, a strange sort of energy.

Juan looked like he hadn't slept, either, when the side door crept open. Dark circles smudged ink beneath his eyes.

"You came back," he said.

"Of course I did," Maya said. "Can't leave you staring at that table by your lonesome for the rest of your days, can I."

He took a breath. Then another. Then he backed away, sitting heavily on the stairs.

Maya caught the door with her foot, levering herself inside. She dropped her bag on the floor and sank down beside him. Juan watched her all the while, deep grooves carved into his forehead. But when she turned to look at him, hand feathering over the nape of his neck, a shudder ran up his back and he buried his face in his hands.

Maya stroked the skin beneath her fingers. Further up, the faint scratch of stubble greeted her. His breath hitched and she drew him close, pulling him down to rest his head in her lap. It was an awkward fold until she scooted up a step and even then – a tangle of long limbs in a small space. It didn't matter. She listened to the rise and fall of his breath, watching it steady, slow, grow even. Beneath her ribs, an ache bloomed, bursting bright like cherry blossoms cascading to the floor in a rush.

"You're right," he said eventually, so quietly that she could hardly hear him. "I should have told you. I didn't know how to. I didn't want you to leave."

"Well, I haven't."

"I know." He shivered beneath her touch. "I don't know why."

"You try, don't you? You try and make it more than it is. Better than it is."

He made a small sound. "It's not enough, Maya. It's never enough."

"No," she agreed. "It isn't."

The scratch of stubble prickled her palm. It felt longer than she was used to.

"I had a look around while I was gone," she said. "I mean, it's funny, I've been here almost a year now, so you'd think I've had plenty of time to look, wouldn't you? But I don't think I've really been seeing. How people live. What it must be like to live like this day in and day out, with no chance of escape. What it must be like to grow up around here. I thought I did, but I didn't. I was just like every other person inside the Zone, seeing what I wanted to see."

She took a deep breath.

"The truth is, I've only touched the surface, haven't I? I've gone on a wild ride, experienced some kind of highlights reel, like the VR tour to long-lost sights across the world that my friend once got for Christmas. But I've always been shielded from what's underneath. By Stuart. By Rina. Most of all by you. So how can I possibly judge? I mean, who was there to shield you?"

"I've had myself. It's enough."

"Is it?"

"I thought so. Before you."

"Maybe it is. If you never look for the stars."

They sat for a long moment. An inch of sunshine crept past the rim of the door, stringing dust motes into golden filigrees.

"He could stop it by now, you know," Juan said. "Stop doing it for the money. Turn it into something that helps people. If he wanted to. Maybe not at the beginning, when he first set up. But he could, now. He could easily afford it. I know it. He knows it."

"You're not him, though," Maya said. "And you weren't wrong. If not you, he would find someone else. Probably someone who blinds themselves completely to what they're doing. Someone who doesn't even want to know. Or someone far worse."

"But it is worse. That I'm aware and I still don't change it."

"Maybe you can't. Maybe you're not that powerful."

"No." His laugh scraped the air as he lifted his head. His smile didn't reach his eyes. "I'm not, am I? I'm not at all."

She cupped his face. "I can't ever really understand. But I do understand that, in spite of it all, you're still trying. Maybe that's what matters."

"Maya," he said, voice cracking on her name, and he kissed her.

His face was unshaven, too, scratching against her chin when she leant into the caress. She raked a fingernail along the rough grain of his cheek, bending down, and then bending down wasn't enough anymore and she slid off her step, flowing onto his lap. Her limbs twinged with the movement, sluggish from lack of sleep, and the wooden steps dug into her knees, unforgiving. Everything about this was awkward, but it didn't matter, it didn't matter. She could feel him respond to her the longer they kissed, and despite her exhaustion her body responded as well, wet heat gathering between her thighs. Maybe she couldn't understand, but maybe she could give him this at least: a moment where he could forget, some place where he could just feel. And maybe in some strange way that mattered, too.

She broke away long enough to wrestle with their clothes, cursing – who had ever thought tights were a good idea anyway – but in the end, impatience won, and she was sinking onto him and he was sinking into her, deep, deep, deep. He sighed and melted against the stairs, drinking her in. She found her balance with both hands, found a rhythm and a pace, hard and close and perfect, and then she rode him, watching, watching, following the minute shifts in his face, every tiny agony which soaked into the corners of his eyes. She rode him until he came undone, head thrown back and throat exposed, and then she buried her face against his neck and kept going until she sobbed her pleasure into his skin, shaking, breathing.

"I'm too old for this," he murmured, while her heart was still racing a helpless gallop in her chest. "This has to be one of the worst places I've ever had sex."

"Charmer," she said, unpeeling herself from him.

"Places," he emphasised. "Good God, my back."

"I've not broken you, have I?" She scrambled off his lap, trying to convince her clothes back into some sort of functional arrangement.

"It's fine." He straightened. "You look terrible, by the way."

Maya raised an eyebrow. "Did you want me to stay or did you want me to head back off?"

"Exhausted. You look exhausted."

"I didn't really sleep."

"Great. Me neither." He pushed himself to his feet, belt clicking as it snapped closed. "You won't mind, then, if that's the next thing we do?"

"Let's," Maya said. "But first, could you help me with these bloody tights?"

CHAPTER TWENTY

The days lengthened. The trees shed their blossoms and burst into greens. Maya cancelled the rental agreement on her flat and lugged what little remained of her belongings to the *Hope and Anchor*. She took her notebooks out some days, scribbling lines, but she always set them back aside. Who would she show them to? And for what purpose? He had been right. She wasn't one to start a revolution.

They had left their bubble, but they still hung suspended, the edges of their togetherness bleeding together and apart in their daily flows. Some mornings they woke in a tangle of limbs, and Maya knew she wanted this, always. Some days, especially when Juan locked himself in the office with Don, she had to reach deep inside herself to find a piece of calm, the reminder that their lives were built on shifting sands pushing sharp words to her tongue. She took to sitting by the side of the canal until Don had left, watching the ducks and the waves and waiting for Juan to join her.

They never spoke of it again, but the knowledge remained: a low hum beneath her skin, just like the static of the sphere which had accompanied every day of her former life.

The notebooks crept towards the far edge of the dresser, nestling right up against the wall.

"You've stopped reading again," Juan said to her one day.

He was working out on the far side of the room, shirtless. Doing push-ups while she was reading aloud to him. They'd fallen into a routine, somehow, not that she could remember how it had started.

"Have I?" Distinctly possible. It was distracting. The way the sunlight dappled patches of gold over his bare skin. The ripples of his muscles.

"That"—he didn't stop as he turned his head to look at her, smile flashing wide—"was not the deal."

Maya laughed. Cheeky sod. "No, the deal was that you get physical and mental exercise all at once, right?"

"Right."

"Whilst I read myself hoarse and try to translate diagrams into narration."

"Welcome—" He sank down low. Rose up again. "To join. In."

She liked this stage, when he got all out of breath. Probably the lead up to it which had distracted her from the benefits of certain solar circuits over others.

"No, thanks," she said. "I'd rather drape artistically."

His laughter brought him to the floor. He rested there for one long beat, then flowed up to his feet. To be fair, she wasn't really draping. More huddling in his shirt, her hair a mess around her face, her curls in desperate need of detangling.

Juan's gaze skimmed over her. "At least both of us are multitasking, hmm?"

She picked up her mug and took a sip of tea. "Exactly."

"And we'd just reached the good bit, too."

"I know," she said, emphasising the word. "But then you stopped."

She liked that fondness as well, the way it started in his eyes, then spread all across his face like the morning light's first warm glow.

For one second she thought he might come over, but he stepped towards the dresser instead, reaching for his water bottle. His eyes fell on the notebooks. He picked one up and waved it at her. "You haven't touched these in weeks."

Maya frowned. "Haven't I?" He was right. She hadn't.

"Why not?" he asked.

She shrugged. A trickle of unease was inching up her spine, like something she had buried rising from beneath. "It didn't seem to matter all that much. You know, anymore."

"It mattered hugely to you not that long ago." His brows drew close. "Maya, is this because of what I said?"

She bit her lip.

"Is it?"

"I don't know. Maybe." She shrugged again. "Thing is, you were right. It was a ridiculous idea to start with."

"I never said that, in fairness."

"No." Maya smiled a little. "You were much more diplomatic than that. You're pretty good at being diplomatic."

He walked across the room, dropping the notebook near her legs, then sank on the bed beside her. She could smell the sharp scent of fresh sweat. "I'm also great at being cynical. I definitely remember telling you that as well. And that I loved your optimism. And that you should do it, anyway."

"Like I said, you're very diplomatic."

"Maya…"

"Ok," she said. "Fine. Maybe I'm being cynical right now. But"—she raised her hand, gesturing at the space around them—

"it's all changed, hasn't it? It's not like I'm going to go back, am I? This is… I'm here now. With you."

His lips curved downwards as they pinched. "I don't like this."

An ache was growing in her chest. She looked down at her hands, caught between its pull and the edge of laughter. "I'm just trying to make you happy."

"You do." He cupped her face, nudging it upwards until their eyes met. "By being you. Not by letting go of… what drives you."

"And also, I don't want to go back now. I'd miss you far too much."

"Well, that one, I get." He kissed her once, a sweet and lingering caress. Then he rose to his feet. "Clearly you'll have to find another way."

"Excuse me?"

"Find another way." He jerked his chin in the direction of the notebook. "To do something with that, without leaving. You're clever, you'll work it out."

She watched him head towards the bathroom door. Why hadn't she even thought of that? It seemed so obvious, the minute that he said it.

The solution was obvious as well once she dug into it. Still, she thought about it for some more days before she took the risk. She hadn't turned her phone on once since leaving the Zone, the possibility of being tracked looming like a heavy cloud.

It still loomed now. But then again… someone would need to be actively scanning for the signal. This wasn't like the constant drip-feed of the chip. If she was quick, it would only be a blip amidst a sea of data.

She dashed her message out, then hit send and switched it off again. Her heart echoed inside her chest with the fierceness of drums.

That night, her shift dragged on, slow as molasses. Her nails drummed on the counter one too many times, often enough that both Juan and Rina shot her questioning looks. Maya ignored them. Where was her patience? The less frequently she checked, the better, the lower the chance of being detected. Besides, he wouldn't even see it straight away. He might want to think about it, as well. Patience...

Still, by the time Juan was in the bathroom, getting ready for bed, her fingers itched too much to keep the phone inside its drawer. She switched it on, breaths loud within the stillness of the darkened room.

The screen glared at her. Stuart had messaged back.

> *It's good to hear from you. You sound well. Was a bit concerned, nothing more from M's side once you left, but thought perhaps for the best. Wish you could say more about what your life looks like now, but you're right, best keep it simple. Some people asking after you in first few months, but then all quiet.*

Who had asked? Her friends? Ren? Her mum? Surely not her mum.

> *I like your idea. I'll do it. I can do them as pamphlets. Trusted eyes only, first. A trickle.*

Then maybe spread out further. Let's see how it lands. One step at a time.

Absurd to think her portrait of Beth might be sent to someone she had never met. It was so rough still. Flawed. Imperfect. What if it made things worse? And what if—

Send them in batches. Maybe once a month. Minimise contact. Keep you safe out there. As can be. I'm glad you're well. Please look after yourself.

Look after herself. And what about him? What if—

Her fingers flew over the screen.

I don't want you to put yourself in danger.

She hit send. Switched the phone off. She should have thought about this more.

"Are you ok?"

Maya looked up, watching Juan come towards her, a towel wrapped low around his hips. The way he walked, the way the darkness kissed him. Everything flowed so easily, right now, right here. Why was she endangering this, again?

"I think I've found a way," she said and stared down at the phone. "But I'm not sure I like it."

He sat next to her. His skin was still damp from the shower, a faint sheen glistening on it. "Why not? And what is it?"

"I'll send them to Stuart. The stories. Short profiles of people, snapshots of what things are like out here. He'll publish them, underground. Find the people who want to read them. Have them passed around."

Juan ran his hand over his scalp. "That sounds workable."

She frowned. "I'm worried that I'll put you all at risk. You and him and everybody else. They could easily track the phone, each time I send him something."

"True. I'm already doing that, though, aren't I? Putting everyone here at risk?" He smiled. "I thought we'd had that conversation. Someone once told me it matters when we try. I figured they were probably wiser than me, at the time."

Her lips curved up despite herself. She leant against his shoulder. As though she could absorb it, the solidity of his posture beneath the softness of his skin. "You have too much faith in me."

"No." He kissed her brow. "Just the right amount."

"It's him as well, though. Stuart. He's safe and sound in there. Set up for life."

"But he agreed to do it? To take the risk?"

"Obviously," she said. "Or I wouldn't be worrying about whether I should go ahead with it."

"Well." Juan let go of her and sank onto the covers, splayed out beside her. It wasn't right, how relaxed he seemed. "Then someone also told me once you needed to let others decide for themselves. Whether something is worth it."

"It isn't fair when you use my own words against me like that."

"Isn't it?" His smile was stretching wide now, warm suns melting against the sky. "But I've learned from you. So much. Shame if I can't pass it on, isn't it?"

And then he drew her into his arms and kissed her, and how on earth was Maya meant to argue with him when he was right there, lips warm and smooth, fingers winding in her hair? It wasn't fair. It wasn't fair.

The phone dropped off the side of the bed, at some point. Not lost. Only temporarily forgotten.

When Maya switched it on again the following day, journal at the ready to take pictures of all the pages she had written, a message blinked into existence like it had been waiting.

> *To be honest, the older I get, the less it all makes sense, what I do here. This does. Let's do it.*

And what more could she say to that? She set to work.

CHAPTER
TWENTY-ONE

May's batch was well-received, according to Stuart. People found the stories fascinating. Unexpected. He'd teamed up with some trusted friends to explore possibilities for wider distribution, ways of tapping into the network.

So Maya sent him more. She tried to strike a balance. More than grim tales about the latest wave of illness which swept through the population. Maya herself was spared it, as it mainly hit the elderly, but every bloody day she worried about Beth. No, she wanted them to see more than that. Like how the people here banded together to deal with the fallout. How they arranged for burials for those who could not afford them, so their loved ones wouldn't simply be collected by the clearing teams of Enforcers who took them… somewhere. Someone even set up a fundraiser to collect the necessary money in dribs and drabs.

Don donated generously once it had taken off. Of course he did.

She didn't write about that.

She wrote about small moments which cut apart the darkness: the jokes, the laughs, the music in the square. There was always music, once you paid attention, always music hidden away somewhere.

She wrote about the trees threshing in full grown thickness during bright summer days, the luscious sweetness of the first strawberries harvested by hand. The way the earth crumbled between her fingers when she picked them.

It was mid-June when Rina called her to the kitchen one evening, right at the beginning of their shift.

"Can you make sure Juan doesn't come in here for the next few hours?" she asked.

"Sure." Maya's forehead wrinkled. "But why?"

Rina gestured at a small springform pan in the corner. "To bake the cake without him cottoning on to it."

"Cake," Maya said. "For what?"

Rina crossed her arms and pursed her lips. "He didn't even tell you? Today's his birthday."

He hadn't. Then again, she'd never asked.

"I made him one last year," Rina continued. "Figured it would be a nice tradition to start, given how quiet he keeps the whole thing. Nothing big and flashy, you know, just a little touch. I would've brought you in on it earlier, but I thought you might have your own traditions you'd want to start."

"Right," Maya said. "Well, I might have, had I known. But I guess he doesn't want a fuss made, or he'd have mentioned it."

Rina frowned at the cake tin. "You think it's too much?"

Maya shrugged. "It's hardly trumpets and fanfares, is it? As long as you wait until people are gone, I don't see the harm."

"That was the plan, yes."

"I'll keep him busy, then."

Juan stood behind the bar, bent low over it and chatting to Leroy when Maya approached. She studied him for a moment, eyes trailing his shape, the outline of his muscles beneath his shirt, the casual tilt of his lips. The ease which painted all his movements with a subtle grace.

He hadn't said a thing. A bit odd, wasn't it? Not hurtful, per se. But strange.

He turned towards her, like he'd felt her gaze. "Yes?"

Nobody else within their vicinity. If Rina knew, then so must Leroy. It probably wouldn't hurt…

"I hear it's your birthday today?" she asked. "And you didn't tell me?"

Leroy promptly shook his head. "Bro…"

Juan plonked a glass on the bar in front of him. "Oh, don't you start. You haven't got a leg to stand on."

"Harsh. But true. I still don't know how old you are, you know."

Juan ignored him. "It's just another day," he said to Maya. "As far as I'm concerned." He held her eyes. "Good chance I would have forgotten all about it myself, if it wasn't for this joker here." He thrust a thumb in Leroy's direction. "Every damn year he likes to remind me I'll soon be helping him push up the daisies."

"I'm just a lightening rod today, aren't I?" Leroy said. "That's what you get for trying to teach the next generation not to repeat your hard-earned mistakes."

"All right," Maya said. "I get it, there's nothing to it. Although I do still think that you deserve a celebration."

Juan's expression softened a touch. "That's very sweet of you," he said. "But completely unnecessary."

Their gazes held. And held.

"Just me," Leroy muttered beside them. "Just me and you, dear whisky. Together on this lonesome stretch of night."

Juan's lips twitched as he turned to him. "You start singing it rhapsodies, I'm cutting you off."

Leroy lifted his glass. "Speaking of legs you can no longer stand on, I swear last year somebody was accusing me of robbing cradles."

Juan's voice dropped into a low, emphatic tone. "I'm thirty-bloody-seven, all right?" He straightened. "Satisfied?"

"There, now," Leroy said, eyes crinkling. "That wasn't all that hard, was it? Spring chicken in your prime."

"I still love you," Maya said and picked up a tray of pints. "I value your experience."

She pretended not to hear Leroy splutter as she walked off.

Even Leroy had left when Rina finally emerged from the kitchen and joined them at the counter.

"Happy birthday!" She whipped her hand out from behind her back with a flourish.

Juan stared at the cake for a long, suspended moment. "You should take that home," he said eventually. "Give it to Solace."

That was… a little rude. Not like him, not within this setting. He normally made a point of recognising effort, didn't he?

Clearly, Rina thought so as well. Her eyebrows lifted as she set the plate down. "You're welcome," she said, and although she hid it well, Maya heard the edge which swelled beneath her placid tones, cutting them through with hurt.

"What he means to say," Maya said, "is thank you. For the effort. And the expense." She nudged him lightly in the side. "Right?"

Juan sighed. "Thank you," he said. "For the effort. And the expense." He looked Rina in the eye. "I don't like chocolate. I should have told you last year, so you wouldn't have wasted all your time and money again. I'm sorry that I didn't. But I never dreamt you'd try and turn it into a tradition."

"Never mind," Rina said, still sounding like she minded a fair bit. "Maybe Maya will. Don't worry, I'll know better in future. Can't win them all." She shrugged and grabbed her coat off the hook. "Enjoy the rest of the night, guys."

Maya watched her walk through the door. Then she turned towards Juan. "I don't like chocolate?" she echoed.

He sighed again and turned away towards the shelves. Began rearranging bottles.

The shelf was perfectly tidy.

"Juan…?"

"It doesn't have pleasant memories attached to it," he said. "That's all." The silence stretched. "I probably should have just accepted it. No way she could've known."

Ah. That made more sense. Maya stepped close to him, resting her hand on his upper back. His muscles tensed beneath her touch, then began to relax in stages beneath the weight of her palm. He inhaled deeply. Exhaled again.

"My mother made me one, once," he added. "He didn't like that she did. I can't even remember why. Probably the money. Or maybe because it was for me."

Maya glanced at the cake. The candle's flame was still dancing merrily atop it. "You want me to get rid of it?"

He turned around, her hand slipping away. Stared at it for a trickle of seconds, then shook his head. "It's only a cake. I'm giving it way too much power. This is ridiculous."

238

"It isn't," Maya said. She smiled a little. "But maybe you need to make new memories. Or blow that candle out and make a wish for something better."

He looked at her like that was utterly ridiculous as well.

"Fine. I'll make one, then," she said. She blew the candle out, a thin trail of smoke rising and vanishing into the dusk of the room. "I wish I'll always get to keep you with me. No matter what else happens."

Juan's lips curved. "I thought that if you say them out loud, they won't come true?"

"Says who? How would you even know the rules of wishing, if you refuse to make one?"

The smile was growing wider, though he was evidently making some attempt to subdue it. "Fair point. Between us, you're the authority."

Maya clambered on the countertop and grabbed the fork. "You don't mind if I try it? I used to love this kind of stuff."

"Be my guest."

She took a bite. All of it tasted luscious, the sweet explosion of its flavours wide and gorgeous across her tongue. The fine-crumbed texture. The depth of it, that raw and bitter edge. She closed her eyes and let it flood her senses. God, she'd missed chocolate.

When she emerged from her rapture, Juan was watching her. Eyes dark and pupils wide. He stepped towards her, hand sinking inside her hair.

"I'll probably taste of it," she whispered against his lips when he drew her in.

"I don't care," he said and licked her mouth open like he didn't.

It was a tad filthy, maybe, right here on the counter. As if the table hadn't been enough. Then again, desperate situations called for desperate measures. If there was anything she'd learnt out here, then surely it was that.

June had triple the pamphlet distribution compared to May, Stuart said. That they were exploring ways of cutting into VR systems on the sly. Maya wrote more and sent them. Anonymous, no names and no locations. But always real.

She hadn't wished for it to grow like this. She hadn't even hoped. In hindsight, maybe she should have done. Although the bigger that it grew, the more she felt the precipice of risk.

Maybe she should have wished for something else entirely.

June spun into July. July ran into August. And then, one balmy evening late in August, it all came tumbling down.

CHAPTER
TWENTY-TWO

The end walked into the pub with a quiet click of heels on wooden floors. Maya was absorbed in drying the glasses so she didn't pay the sound any heed at first, only looking up when the woman before her cleared her throat loudly.

"How can I help—" She swallowed, barely whispering the next word, a faint exhalation vanishing like dust motes in the air. "Mother?"

People were looking. Of course. Even Sophia had blended into the background, dark to the dark. Nothing about her mother blended: her pristine, white dress, her tightly coiled, blonde hair – and definitely not the two bodyguards which flanked her either side. Everything about her screamed money. Everything screamed that she belonged somewhere else.

"It's true." Her clipped tones rang clear as always. "I didn't want to believe it, but it's true."

Maya stared at her. Oh God. It was happening. What was the last she'd heard from Stuart? She'd messaged him two days ago.

He'd not responded at the time, but then, he rarely did.

"Over a year I've been searching for you. A year. I was giving up hope. Thinking you might have died. And here you are, playing barmaid in this hovel. And doing—God knows what you'd even call it."

"It's not a hovel," Maya said. "It's my home."

"Home!" Her mother scoffed. "What, this, your home? Surrounded by these, these"—she raised her arm with a sweeping movement, lip curling—"people?"

"Yes," Maya said. A heat was beginning to simmer inside her veins, a sharp counterpoint to the rapid thrumming of her heart. "You're quite right. They are people."

"Oh, don't be facetious. I was being polite."

"Funny, because that's not what it looks like from here." Out of the corner of her eye, she noticed Juan set down a bottle at the other end of the bar. The dull thud of his footsteps carried him closer.

"Well?" her mother said, crossing her arms as if Maya hadn't spoken. "Are you going to explain yourself?"

"Can I help you, Miss?" Juan cut in gently. He was using his most affable voice, the one he normally reserved to dissipate an escalating argument between customers.

"I doubt it," Maya's mother said, gaze fixed on Maya. "Well? I'm waiting."

The knife of a hundred eyes pierced against Maya. She dropped her towel. "I think we should take this somewhere quieter."

"Fine. You know I have absolutely no interest in turning myself into a spectacle."

"Right." Maya bit her lip against the laugh which threatened. She mouthed an apology at Juan, navigating around the bar and exiting the pub in the straightest possible line. Really, she should be mouthing apologies at everyone she passed – how many of them had heard every word just now? How many of them had sensed the derision which poured off her mother in waves? More importantly, what had Maya dragged them into? Could they sense it, the edge they suddenly all balanced on?

The hush which draped itself over the normally lively room trailed her as much as her mother's footsteps.

Outside, the sunset was bleeding reds and pinks into the sky. Beneath its grandeur, her mother looked all the more a statue, drenched in warm colour which seemed to slide right off her skin. An ache echoed inside Maya's chest, her fingers itching with the urge to reach out. Perhaps she had missed her, after all.

"Well? You've got your peace and quiet." Her mother wrinkled her nose, turning briefly towards the canal. "And the stench of sewage. What on earth possessed you to come to this place?"

Maya crossed her arms. "Do you actually care?"

"What a thing to say! Of course I do."

"Are you sure? Because last I check—"

"I was going frantic with worry, Maya!"

Maya bit her lip. Before her, a spill of sun bathed the cobblestones in a golden glow.

"I looked everywhere. At first, I thought you'd had an accident, so I checked all the hospitals. But you weren't there. So I kept looking. I spoke to all of your friends from university, but nobody had the slightest idea where you might have gone."

"That's because they're not my friends," Maya mumbled.

"I even spoke to your little boyfriend, but he was none the wiser. Apparently, he wasn't even your boyfriend anymore?"

"Which you might have known, had you bothered to ask."

"And I really didn't want to involve the Enforcers, but in the end, I had to. You left me no choice."

Her heart was still a thunder, now threatening to split her ribs.

"Except they couldn't trace you. Your chip seemed to have gone dead."

"Yes." Maya pressed the word between her lips. "I hacked it."

"But naturally, that didn't stop me. You know me, I'm not the one who gives up easily. That little trait was always yours. So I kept at it. Escalated matters, went up the chain when people were clearly just incompetent. Building… the *right* kind of relationships until I finally found the ear of someone who appreciated the seriousness of the situation. Who promised me they wouldn't rest until we had you back."

That sounded like… a whole host of things Maya didn't want more detail on. Somewhere far beneath the fear and anger, tendrils of guilt were winding up her bones.

"And then all of a sudden, these digital pamphlets began appearing. Files popping up on people's screens when they should be clean. Not even routing through the central system. Spreading like some kind of… disease. I read one, even. Utterly absurd nonsense. I immediately knew that it was you. They found the source quite swiftly. So efficient, the system."

"Stuart," Maya finally said. Her voice was shaking. "What's happened to Stuart? Is he ok?"

"Who? Oh. That librarian?" Her mother waved her hand in the air. "I don't know. They took him somewhere."

Took him somewhere. Took him somewhere. The earth was tilting. She wanted to be sick.

"So now I've finally found you, I have to ask myself, Maya: Why? Why would you do this to me? How could you?"

"It wasn't about you," Maya said. Her voice seemed to be coming from far away.

"Wasn't it? Because you've always had this side, this stroppy, childish need to fight me on everything that makes sense. Purely to spite me. Tell me, dear daughter, how is this any different? This little rebellion of yours, played out on some grander stage?"

"It had nothing to do with you!" Maya took a deep breath and another, but it did nothing to slow the rapid thrum of her pulse. "It was about me, ok? I was curious. I wanted to understand. All my life I've been lied to, and I just wanted to know the truth!"

A long moment stretched. But her mother's voice, when it came again, was unchanged, the same steel wrapped in a thin layer of contempt. "Do you have any idea how many strings I had to pull to even be here right now? What I've had to do?"

"I don't," Maya said. "But I suppose I should be grateful?"

"That they didn't just pick you up as well? Of course! I'm here to offer you a pardon! They were always going to trace you after what you did, but I got in there just in time. I've given you life twice over now, and you can't even see it! Where would you be, if not for me?"

Their eyes locked. Maya's teeth clenched so tightly that she felt like her jaw might crack.

Her mother's shoulders slumped. "Why, Maya? Why couldn't you have been more like me?"

"Excuse me?"

"It would have made things so much easier. I'd so hoped you might be. That the fact that you only had my influence to go on would make a difference. That it would give you the opportunities you needed. Allow you to blend in, to become a success. By all rights, you shouldn't even remember him."

"Remember who – you mean Dad?"

"Oh, don't be dense, Maya! You were never many other things and we both know it, but one thing I always thought you were at least was sharp. Accepting or graceful would have been a long sight better, but if that's not what you were blessed with, at least make use of what you have." Her mother shook her head. "Of course I'm talking about your father. You had to be just like him, didn't you? Always asking questions. Leaving no stone unturned, finding all the answers. Never for one second wondering what it might do to me if I lost you, too. If they took you away. And now look at this." She spread her palms wide. "Look at where we are."

"Is that what happened?" Maya asked. "They took him away?" Like Stuart. Like they would her.

"Always so proud. Always doing the right thing." Her mother laughed, a hollow sound. "Tell me, how is it the right thing, to leave your wife and your only child so you can throw yourself on the sword of some ideal? Do you think anyone even remembered?"

And Maya was suddenly awash in a flood of emotions: a sadness and a loneliness which weren't solely hers, and a desire which was – to make it better, to make it right. For whom, though? For Stuart? Her father? Her mother? How much of this was old and how much new? She couldn't quite sort through it. Could only let it sink within her, into her skin and flesh and bone.

Her mother straightened, wrapping composure around herself like a cloak. "Has your little escapade given you the answers you were looking for?"

"It's not an escapade," Maya said. "It's my life."

"Don't be ridiculous. Your life is inside. It's with me. You've got a degree to finish, a job to start. A family, someday, if they'll let you after all this. You've had your little insurrection, but it's over now. You're coming back with me."

Maya shook her head. "You honestly believe that? That they will pardon me? After what I've done?"

"Of course." Her mother crossed her arms. "They rightly shouldn't, but I'm terribly convincing. And like I said, I've found my way up to the highest places. They wouldn't lie to me. I'm here, aren't I? Why else would they give me twenty-four hours to get you to come willingly?"

Maya opened her mouth, but the words stuck in her throat, heavy as lead. Her eyes stung.

"To keep you where they want you?" Juan's voice drifted past her, his tone quite mild.

Her mother's eyes narrowed. "Excuse me?"

"To keep you where they want you," he repeated. His eyes skimmed over the men at her side, then back to her. "They sound very confident in their ability to still pick her up, even if you fail, perhaps? Maybe they're well aware of just how hard it is to make it anywhere from here? How stuck we are?"

Her mother opened her mouth, but he cut over her. "And she is both. Accepting and graceful. I'm not sure I can say the same for a mother speaking this way to her only daughter, though."

"And who are you?"

"No one important to you, I'm sure."

Maya reached for his hand as though it were an anchor. "He's my home," she said. "You're right, it isn't this place. It isn't even the people inside, although some of them are my friends and they all deserve more respect from you than you've offered them. It's him."

247

"Him." Her mother sneered. "What, this is the best you could do, after all the work I put into you? Some common criminal bartender in the Ring? Oh, don't look at me like that. This whole area reeks of perversion. They're all the same out here, beggars or crooks, thinking they're above the law. Everyone knows it."

"And we're so much better, are we? Sitting in our lofty towers, pretending to fix the world's problems, pretending we're not standing on other people's shoulders? Picking people up, for what? Telling the truth?"

"The world's always been like that, Maya. Since the dawn of time, some of us have been stronger than others."

"Well, it shouldn't be."

"Just like your father. Just like him."

"Thanks," Maya said, "I'll take that as a compliment. I might never have known him, but it's good to know at least one of my parents might have been proud of me."

"Proud. Proud? Is that what you wanted? Someone to tell you well done and good job, you're so pretty and talented and special? It was my job to protect you, and I did. I'm still doing it right now. Do you have any idea how much blood, sweat and tears I've poured into raising you? How lonely and thankless it was? What else I could have done with my time? What else I could have been?"

Juan's thumb was a soft metronome over the back of her hand. Maya drew a deep breath and let the pace of it fill her.

"I'm sorry you suffered," she said. "But that was never my fault." She squared her shoulders. "I'm staying here. Where I'm wanted. Where I'm loved. And if they come and get me, then at least I'll know that I had that. I don't know what it was you thought you felt for me, but I don't think"—she swallowed heavily—"I'm not sure it was ever that."

Or maybe it had been, and somewhere along the way it had got lost. It had twisted. Maybe she'd never know. Her mother's face certainly didn't reveal it: frozen, contorted into an unreadable grimace. Maybe she didn't know, either.

"You'll change your mind," she said, after a long moment's silence. "Twenty-four hours, Maya. That's it, it's all that I can give you. Don't throw it all away for this... this shithole."

And she turned on her heel and strode off into the dusk, her bodyguards following like faceless ghosts.

Maya watched her go. Something was pressing down on her, something enormous, something she couldn't grasp. Some heavy blanket, some maelstrom of emotion. "Oh God," she said. She rubbed her palms across her face. "What are we going to do, Juan? This is all my fault. I should never have—"

"Shush," he said. "Maya."

"But Stuart. He—"

"I know."

"—but he's—"

"I know." He didn't blink. "He knew the risks."

"That doesn't make it any better!"

"No," he agreed, pulling her into his arms. "I know. It's not your fault."

It was, though. It was. She let them come, the tears, the wild, bitter injustice of it all. And in all fairness, Juan didn't ask her not to cry, didn't ask her to push anything aside. He held her through it all until the worst of it subsided.

He kissed her eyelids when she finally withdrew. Then her lips.

"What am I going to do?" she asked.

"We," he said. "Isn't it obvious? We have to leave."

"Yes, but… where? How? You said it yourself. Everyone is stuck out here."

Juan released his hold on her, turning towards the pub. "I'll contact Don. I'll find a way, don't worry. He owes me. So many times over."

She bit her lip.

"Trust me," he said. "You do, don't you?"

"Of course I do," she said, some tightness in her shoulders loosening a touch. "You know I do."

"Then all you have to worry about right now is staying quiet, all right? We can't drag Rina into this. Not before we even know."

Yes, that made sense. Maya nodded. "Of course."

He held her hand and squeezed it tightly one last time. "We'll find a way through this, I promise. Together. I'm with you. Don't you forget it."

"Ok," she said, and then, "I love you, too."

They were doused in looks the moment they stepped back inside the pub, the wash of curiosity from all sides not held at bay by Juan's refusal to meet anybody's eyes as he headed straight for the stairs. Well, maybe a little. At least nobody asked outright.

Nobody but Rina.

"Who was that?" she whispered as Maya slipped behind the bar. "What on earth was all that about?"

Maya shook her head. "No one. That was no one."

And although Rina's lips pinched tight, she said nothing further.

"And?" Maya asked in low tones when Juan returned from the office.

"He wasn't there. I've left a message."

"What if he doesn't get it? You know… in time?"

"He will. And either way, I've packed some bags already. We'll head out at first light. No use going at night without extra resources." He cast a glance at Rina who was fast approaching the bar. "Let's not discuss this any further in the open."

Maya hated waiting. She always had.

CHAPTER
TWENTY-THREE

There'd still been no word by the time they locked up. Maya threw some additional bits inside the duffel bags which sat within arm's reach of the bedroom door and gathered some loaves of bread and water canteens.

Juan was adamant they try to grab some sleep, although how he expected her to rest was anybody's guess. In the end, she gave in, anyway. He usually slept naked, but tonight neither of them undressed. She lay inside his arms until, by some miracle, a drowsiness found her.

She jerked awake with the dark pressing down on her. Juan's arms wound around her, too tense for him to be asleep. Had there been a noise?

A heavy knock thundered through the door.

"Stay," Juan said and slipped out of bed, grabbing the gun from beneath the mattress with one hand.

The door swung open. "Easy now," said Don, raising his hands in the air. "Is that any way to greet an old friend?"

Juan lowered the weapon. "If they let themselves into my bedroom at night, yes."

"Even if summoned?" Don smiled. "Wise. You called?"

Juan was already halfway across the room. "Not here," he said, and then they were both striding from the room.

There was no way Maya was going to stay put. No way. She waited until the door swung shut behind them, then she threw off the sheet and took a deep breath. Or maybe she should. She didn't want to make things worse. Then again, how much worse could they get?

He clearly wanted her to leave him to it. But she couldn't. This was just as much her business. More so, even. Still, she hesitated in the hallway. Until this point, she'd never crossed the implicit line into their conversations. This was a step into the dark. Unfamiliar territory. Something was tilting, shifting, changing.

God, who was she kidding? It had all changed already, hadn't it?

The wooden floor pressed cool against the soles of her feet. Their voices travelled, animated Spanish seeping through the door. Were they fighting? The hinges creaked when she pushed the door open, but they paid her no mind, their words picking up speed, their tongues rolling Rs into anger, their volume rising. Maya watched them spar for a moment, cutting across one another in rapid succession. She tried to catch the odd word, but all she could catch was the tension: the sharp gestures Don used to emphasise a point, the corded muscles of Juan's back shifting as he put his hands on his hips. Juan shook his head, the same melody of sound repeating for the second time in a row, but more strident, now. Demanding.

Don's gaze caught on Maya. He narrowed his eyes. Sneered. Turned back to Juan, dripping his next words into the space between them, too low to even guess at.

Juan punched him.

For a long moment, Don cradled his face, frozen in time. Then he laughed. "Siempre las mujeres." He spat out some blood, looking Maya straight in the eye. "Always the women."

Juan's eyes flicked to her for an instant. "Don't you dare mistake my position here," he said, his hands still curled into tight fists. His muscles trembled.

"Trust me, I'm not." Don continued to stare at Maya. "Congratulations, my girl. You just earned yourself a new life. That was what you came here for originally, wasn't it?"

"Juan?" Maya's voice sounded thready to her own ears.

Don rubbed his jaw. "You've won," he said, slipping his hand in his pocket and dangling a key in front of Juan. Juan plucked it from his fingers. "I suppose it was good while it lasted. Although it's a shame we should part on such terms, after all these years." Don tilted his head. Extended his hand. "¿No?"

She could see Juan's jaw working, the clench and release of his teeth. A long moment stretched, growing thin, thin, thinner. Then it snapped and Juan grabbed Don's hand, their palms locking in a grip which was too firm to be a handshake, too tight to be a sign of affection. Somehow, it still looked like one.

Don clapped him on the shoulder, a sudden, warm smile transforming his face, and then he was walking out of the room, Juan's eyes trailing him every step of the way.

"Juan?" Maya repeated once his footsteps had echoed away into nothingness. "Could you please tell me what's happening? Did he say yes? To what? We've got a way out of here?"

"Yes," he said, grabbing a bag from the shelf and unlocking the cupboard next to the table. Inside it, the safe slumbered. Juan opened it and began piling stacks of banknotes into the bag. "The keys are for the car. It's usually kept on standby."

That made sense. The bag was filling fast. Maya had never seen this much money in her life. "And the money?"

"Dropping some. Taking the rest."

She frowned. "He's just… giving it to you?"

His smile was tight. It didn't reach his eyes. "I negotiated it."

"By punching him?"

He laughed. "No. That was post settlement."

"You blackmailed him. With everything you know about him."

"Yes. I did." He held her gaze. "After all, if the Enforcers picked us up, what would I have to lose? Much better for him if they never get the chance to question me."

A shiver crept its way up her spine. "The rest of the money. He wants rid of it so nobody can find anything. When they come for me tomorrow."

"Correct."

"What is he going to do?"

"Probably play dumb. Easier that way to lie low if he convinces them that he's the victim, you know. Robbed by one of his most trusted confidantes. I took it all and then took off with you. It's probably your fault, in the end. You turned my head with all those revolutionary ideas of yours."

"Well. That's not entirely untrue," she said. "What about everyone else? Rina? Leroy? All the rest?"

Nobody would come after Beth. Surely not. Nobody could ever come after Beth.

"I don't know." He sighed. "I can only hope that it's in his best interests to protect them in some way because any extra investigation will shine the spotlight on him, too. And he's pretty extraordinary at protecting his best interests. Maya, we can't fix this one."

She bit her lip. "It's all my fault, though. None of them ever agreed to take this risk."

"We live with risk here every day. You think Rina didn't know the luxuries she got when working here came at a price? She isn't stupid. You think Leroy hasn't ever guessed at why I'm so good at pulling strings when it's important? All of this could just as easily have fallen apart because of me." He slung the bag over his shoulder. "We need to go. Don's arranging for passage out of the country as we speak."

He was right. She knew he was. She needed to leave this one behind. If not Stuart. That guilt was not so readily set aside.

"All right," she said and headed for their room.

This time, Juan drove the car all the way to the front entrance of the *Hope and Anchor*, where Maya waited with their packed bags. He'd separated the money into three separate piles and dashed off before she had a chance to question it. It took no time to pile all their valuables inside the backseats, within easy reach.

Maya looked out at the dark facade of the pub once she had settled in her seat, its lettering barely visible beneath the overcast sky. Its wooden edges seemed to blend into the dark, as if it might sink straight into the black night and vanish completely, swallowed by its own gravity. A pang shot through her chest, strangely bittersweet.

"Is it weird that I want to say goodbye to a building?" she asked.

"Yes," Juan said. "But that's always been part of your charm." He pushed the ignition. "Let's try and say goodbye to someone who'll answer back, instead?"

"You think that's safe?"

"I think it's necessary."

He made the drop first, a silent handover at some dilapidated building no more than five minutes away, then rerouted back to Rina's house. It took a while for someone to respond to their knocks, not nearly as long for Rina's father-in-law to get her to come to the door. Her hair was a tousled mess around her face as she pulled her bathrobe more tightly around herself.

"Well, I guess I wasn't sleeping anyway," she said. "For fuck's sake, will you finally tell me what is going on?" She motioned. "Come in first, maybe."

"We're not staying." Juan threw a look over his shoulder as they slipped into the corridor. "And we can't leave the car for long."

"Car," Rina said.

"We're here to say goodbye," Maya said.

"Car," Rina repeated. "Goodbye. This is getting better by the minute."

"It's a long story," said Juan. "The short version is, we're both leaving for good."

Rina's eyes flicked to Maya. "Who was that, this evening? It wasn't no one."

Maya pressed her lips together. "No."

"Who then?"

"I... I'm not sure how much I should tell you."

"Nothing," Juan said, at the same time that Rina said, "All of it."

Rina glared at him. "This"—she pointed a finger at him—"not at all helpful."

"Oh, I'm being extremely helpful, thank you very much," Juan shot back.

"No, you're being an arsehole," Rina said. "Do you have any idea how worried I've been since you both started slinking around like the world was ending this evening? I don't do bloody worried, you know that. And now you want to say goodbyes without a single word of explanation?"

"It's safer that way," Maya said.

Rina sighed. "I'd give my left leg, you know, if that wasn't your mother, this evening."

Maya bit her lip. Looked at Juan, then back at Rina. "Yes."

"Which means you aren't from the Counties. You're from inside. I mean, I've suspected that much for a while."

"You've kept that quiet," Maya said.

Rina shrugged. "It wasn't any of my business, was it? It was clear you wanted to keep some things to yourself. I mean, having said that, I can see what you were running from. God, if I ever speak that way to Sol, I hope someone slaps me silly." She shook her head. "Is it because of her? That you're leaving? She's trying to bring you back somehow?"

"It's irrelevant if it's to do with her mother," Juan said. "It really isn't safe for you to know more. The important bit is that I need to ask you to do something for me."

Rina leant heavily against the wall. "Oh, really?" she said. "Go on, then."

"Tomorrow, pretend that we were never here. None of this happened. Head to work. Be suitably surprised when nobody opens. Do whatever it is you'd do if you'd never seen us. There might be Enforcers there already, or maybe they'll show up later. But they will show. They might ask questions. You know nothing."

"Ok," Rina said. "Shouldn't be too hard seeing how I'm actually clueless." But she didn't sound as flippant as her words, a frown creasing her forehead.

Juan sighed. "To be honest, I'm not sure if we're doing you a favour by being here at all, but I couldn't just leave you without this, either." He dropped a small duffel bag on the floor before her. "They might well shut the pub down. I don't know. I don't know what Don is likely to do, either. I do know you're the best person to do something sensible with this. So let's hope nobody saw us tonight."

Rina dropped to her knees and zipped open the bag. "Jesus fucking Christ, Juan."

"It's not as much as it could be. I'm sorry it's not more."

"You're—fuck off, are you for real?" She turned some notes over in her hand, then stuffed them back in the bag. "You know what, this shit is getting so weird I'm not even going to ask."

"Finally," he said. "I don't care what you do with it, but please make sure it goes somewhere safe that isn't here, and quickly. In case they decide to search any of your houses. Unless you think it's safer not to take it at all. Your choice." He crossed his arms. "I assume making a run for it isn't really on the cards for you."

"Where to?" Rina asked. "It's fine, I'm keeping it. I'll find a way." She rose. "So you're both off. For good."

"I'm sorry," Maya said. Her eyes were stinging. "This is all my fault."

"Oh, don't be silly." Rina pulled her into a tight hug. "You're not responsible for your mum tracking you down."

Maya shook her head. "You don't know the half of it."

"No," Rina said. "But knowing you, whatever it was, you must have had good reason. I mean, you never even took a fifteen-minute power nap in the broom closet when you were extra tired, leaving this one to fight for himself. And trust me, I did that so many times."

"I'll pretend I didn't hear that," said Juan.

"Fire me," Rina said. She squeezed Maya tightly. "And you're definitely not responsible for the magic bags of money suddenly making an appearance."

"No," Juan agreed. "That one's all on me."

"So tempted to ask all the questions right now. All of them."

"Best not."

"I know. Being sensible."

Maya took a deep breath and clung to Rina. "I'll miss you," she whispered. It was sinking in, now she was standing here in a dimly lit hallway, holding on for the last time. Her eyes burned with sudden wetness. Would Rina be ok? And Solace? "I can't believe this is goodbye."

Rina gave her a last squeeze, then let go and stepped away. When her lips curved, her eyes crinkled: a thousand fine lines which Maya hadn't noticed before at a distance. Or maybe she'd never paid enough attention. "'Goodbyes are only for those who love with their eyes. Because for those who love with heart and soul, there is no such thing as separation.'"

Maya smiled. She brushed the tears away with the back of her hand. "That's beautiful."

"Isn't it? Very old. I'm glad I got to have you in my life for a while. I'll miss you, too."

"Thank you. You've been such a good friend to me. I— The best."

"Don't make my head explode." Rina looked at Juan. "And you."

"Yes?" Juan crossed his arms.

"Oh, no, you don't. You fuck off forever in some ridiculous cloud of mystery, I get a hug at least."

"I've never heard you swear this much," he said with a raised eyebrow. But the corner of his mouth quirked, and he folded Rina into an embrace, anyway.

"That's because you never took up my offer to come round for Christmas, either." Rina's words were muffled by the wool of his coat. "You know, when I was still trying. God knows what it is with me inviting people who fail to show."

"I know," Juan said. "It wasn't quite the right time or place. I always appreciated it, though."

"Idiot." They broke away from each other. "You take care of her, all right? Better yet, you two take care of each other. And whatever it is you're doing when you get all"—her hands mimicked a seesaw—"just cut it out. Trust each other. That's your one job."

Juan clasped her forearms. "We need to go. Thank you for everything. Please stay safe."

"Yeah," Rina said. "You, too."

"And say goodbye to Solace for me," said Maya.

"I will," Rina said. "She'll miss you, too."

Were her eyes wet, too, or was it a trick of the light? It was hard to make out in the cavern of the corridor. Juan slid past her and Maya followed, her fingers pressing against Rina's in passing. Then they were heading down the front garden path and Maya watched Rina over her shoulder: the shape of her dissolving, bit by bit, blending into the dark.

CHAPTER
TWENTY-FOUR

The car was darker, still. Maya buried herself in her seat. Houses flew by, soon giving way to wide stretches of trees as they hit the ring road, the first outcroppings of countryside meeting them along its sides. Juan turned on the car's lights, their sheen reflecting off the rain-doused asphalt. Here and there foliage spilled out onto the street, the remnants of a fallen tree turned bird-haven blocking part of the path. Hopefully, they could find their way through the concrete maze ahead of them without any true obstacles.

"Does it feel surreal to you?" Maya asked, after a long silence.

"To leave?"

She nodded.

"Yes. And no." The shape of him blurred in the low light, but his eyes were still bright. "In a way, I don't think I ever arrived. So there's not much to leave."

"But you seemed so tied into it. Rooted in the pub. Connected to them all."

"I suppose I did. Maybe I could have been."

"You won't miss them at all? Leroy? Beth?"

He hesitated for a moment. "Maybe I tell myself they are where they're meant to be. As am I."

"Leroy told me once that he thought of you as his best friend, you know."

"Did he, now."

Maya hummed an affirmative. She watched the world flow by for a few moments.

"Why did you punch him?"

"Leroy?"

"Don't be an arse. You know who."

His hands tightened on the steering wheel. "He called you a whore."

"That's funny."

Juan's eyes flicked across to her. "Excuse me?"

Maya shrugged. "That's what you called me, the day we met. I mean, not directly, but you implied that you thought I might be. So it's funny, in a way. Kind of… circular."

"I didn't mean it like that," he protested. "And I didn't know you then."

"I know."

"I don't always choose the right words. And sometimes I jump to the wrong conclusions."

"I know," Maya said. "Me, too. I wasn't trying to make a point." She paused. "He played on it as well, even then. Like he was trying to start me off on the wrong foot with you, or something. He had absolutely no reason to at that point."

Juan drew a deep breath. "Other than to play, that is. I shouldn't have shaken his hand."

"He meant a lot to you." Condensation crept up the windows, obscuring her view. Maya wiped a streak of it away with her palm.

"Whatever he did, he helped you once. They stay with you like that. People."

"The best and the worst of them."

The glass was cool against Maya's fingers. Solid. "Or maybe they're just people. Not good or bad at all. Maybe what stays is only the best and the worst of what they do." She rested her head against the windowpane. "I wish I could've hugged my mother goodbye. That's equally absurd, isn't it? With everything she's done. I should just hate her. Instead, I wish I could have really said goodbye. You know, not how we did. Without all this."

"I know," said Juan. "She'll always be your mother, in the end." Then, after a long pause, "Maybe for the best of her, you didn't need to. Maybe you've already told each other what you needed to. Without the hugs, without the words."

"Like Rina's quote."

"Yes." He veered out of the way of a giant pothole, elegantly circumscribing its arc. "Like that."

Then, after a long moment, he added, "Maybe she left it. The best of her. Within you. In who you are."

And, oddly, that was quite a comforting thought. True or not… She wanted to believe it.

"I wish I could have said goodbye to Stuart, too," she said, swallowing against the lump which suddenly blocked her throat.

"I know," he said, and she knew that was the truth, at least. "I know."

The night stretched on. They crossed the Thames, its thick, roiling waters a chasm beneath them. How long until this bridge would crumble to dust, too? When had they stopped building them to last?

Maya closed her eyes. The faint hum of the car enveloped her, warm air draping over her skin like a blanket. It had been warm in the train carriage, too, when she had fled from the Zone, pressed between boxes of cables. But her heart had been pounding, even the faintest gust of air setting her to tremble at the idea that someone might detect her. Now her breaths flowed even and slow. The slivers of night air which seeped through the cracks in the car drove a different kind of goosebumps over her body, Juan's presence tangible at her side. She could relax now. Let herself sink into heaviness. Just breathe…

She must have drifted off. When she next opened her eyes, they were no longer on a wide stretch of road, winding their way through dense woodlands instead.

"Did you sleep well?" Juan asked.

She rolled her shoulders. Unlocked the stiff joints in her fingers. "Was I asleep?"

"Looked like it." He caught a yawn with the back of his hand. "I admit, I'm a bit jealous."

"I'd drive if I could, you know."

"I know. Better not try to learn now. Not sure we've got the time."

"No," Maya said. They passed into a clearing where an ancient stone castle sank into its moat beside the road. Behind it, the sky was bleeding into the first hues of dawn, deep purples and pinks. "Nor to stop for the scenery."

Juan glanced outside. "Shame, right? There goes my chance to take you to beautiful places."

"Hopefully there'll be others." She craned her neck to catch a glimpse of the vista before the trees swallowed it again. "Where are we?"

"High Weald."

"I don't know why I asked. I was always rubbish at geography. Didn't seem to matter much if you're not going anywhere, anyway."

He laughed. "Down South."

"Where are we going?"

"To the coast. To the continent, by boat. I've got the name of a contact. Then, I don't know."

"An adventure." Maya sank deeper into her seat.

"Are you scared?"

"Not really. Not as long as I'm with you."

"Still questionable, in my opinion."

She nudged his thigh. "Well, nobody's asking you."

"Also, it's wise to be scared sometimes."

"Says Mr-I-hang-out-with-criminal-masterminds."

His lip quirked. "I never claimed to be wise myself. Only perceptive."

"See? And that's why nobody's asking you."

"Doesn't mean I can't spot wisdom. That's part of the perceptiveness."

"Well, I'm glad we cleared that distinction up." She brushed her hand along his thigh, resting it against the corded muscle for a moment. "Aren't your legs tired?"

"A bit. But it's better if we drive through."

"Do you think they'll follow us?"

"Stop worrying, Maya. They don't know we're gone yet."

"Maybe."

"Most likely. Your mother did say twenty-four hours. And you left your phone behind."

True. She'd stowed it in a drawer somewhere. Too much of a risk. Too much temptation. "I thought it was wise to be scared sometimes. Which would make worrying appropriate."

"See? If I was wise, I'd never be offering you all these own goals."

"Or maybe you're just trying to entertain me."

"Maybe."

Her fingers massaged little circles into his thigh. He reached across her arm to change the setting on the heating, the muscles in his forearm rippling with the motion. Outside, the blanket of darkness was beginning to lift, inch by inch.

"Maybe I am scared," she said. "But I'm at peace with the fear when you're here. If that makes any sense."

He swallowed, eyes fixed on the road. "It does."

"And then it becomes an adventure. Everything ahead. All we can discover." She sighed. "I just hope it won't go this wrong again."

His hand dropped down to cover her own. It was heavy. Warm.

"Maybe we'll find some castles that are still standing," Maya said. "Somewhere beyond the sea."

"I hear they're very draughty, you know."

"Spoilsport. We'll just have to go further south."

"Do they have castles there?" he asked.

"They must do," she said. "Some kind of stone building. I like the idea."

"Of stone buildings?"

"Of going south. Someplace sunny. Someplace bright."

"Let's do that, then. Maybe we'll even make it to Spain. At least I can communicate there." He wrinkled his nose. "Or we might get stuck in France."

"We'll manage." She hooked her thumb over his little finger. "But first, a boat. How far are we from the shore?"

"Not long to go now."

It wasn't. Soon the trees ran sparser, the woods opening out into marshland. Overgrown hedges embraced the curves of the road, wild and verdant, and then the hedges vanished as well and they were drifting alongside a solar farm. As far as the eye could see, obsidian panels stood sentry in the gloom, unmoving plinths raising their hungry mouths to the sky, ready to suck down the first rays of sunshine which dared to creep past the horizon.

Maya watched them slide by in silence. It wasn't even worth trying to count them.

Eventually, though, they drifted out of sight. They drove on until the road disappeared, until the grass thinned and turned to sand. Rows of sturdy bushes flanked the border where land merged into tall dunes. Juan brought the car to a stop, and as soon as Maya opened the door she could smell it, could taste it: the salt-soaked breeze like a crystal caress on her tongue.

She straightened and stretched, listening to the faint roar of the waves in the distance while Juan unpacked their bags.

"We should be able to cut through there." He pointed, handing her one of the duffels.

"And the car?"

He shrugged. "Not our problem anymore."

Maya slung the bag over her shoulder and walked ahead, cutting through the low passage between two dunes. A clump of thin reeds blocked her way, and she scrambled over them. Then the path ascended and transformed to soft sands, her boots sinking into its liquid grains. She fought her way up and past the peak, gravity easing her descent as the roar crescendoed in her ears, growing louder.

Before her, the beach spread white and wide, endless open swathes of stone cut apart by time. Maya stopped and stared, drinking in the salty air, her eyes drawn to the flat line of the horizon.

The sheen of the waves glistened. In the distance, the red-golden sun kissed the water as it rose from its depths. Juan stepped out on the sand beside her, awash within its glow.

"Look," Maya said, taking him by the hand. "It's the sea."

THE END

ODE TO REVIEWS

It is the barest truth:
As independent authors
Are all alone
I am in need of your support.

So if you liked this tale, then please:
Leave me a line or two,
Sprinkle some stars upon my dream
With a review or rating

So hungry Gods of rainforests may be placated.

And know, each word was crafted
With love
Within the deepest part of me.
(No, not *that* one. Honestly!)

I thank thee, kindly.

WANT MORE?

Then grab your free prequel short-story, *A different kind of sweetness*! Head to: https://bit.ly/32khihU or my website below. Exclusively available for subscribers to my newsletter only. You'll be the first to hear of any new releases, freebies and updates.

I promise I won't spam you. Or rhyme again. Not unless you ask me to.

Follow me on social media:
Instagram: @ambernightauthor
Facebook: @AmberNightAuthor
My website: ambernightwrites.wixsite.com/ambernight

COMING SOON

Compromised. A saucy Victorian tale featuring corsets, societal values, and men on horses. (Sorry, just the one. But some cliffs, too.)

GRATITUDE JAR

All credit for the poem which Rina quotes goes to Rumi who was an infinitely better poet than myself, not to mention a much wiser human being. You should absolutely check him out if you don't know him yet.

Gratitude goes to:

My daughter, for helping me grow every day.

My husband, for always making time, for supporting me on my journey, and for looking within.
#yourromanceneedslessromancewife

Kim, who kept reminding me that I could do this, when it was merely a glint within my eye.

The amazing alpha/beta squad for a true 360 view which made this a much more rounded novel: Maria, Gabi, Kim, Sarah McKenna, Amara Rae, Gina Griffin, K Archer.

Anyone else who has been a part of this process. Special shout-out to my Street and ARC teams, the Ricers, and the wider #indieauthor and #bookstagram community.

ABOUT THE AUTHOR

AMBER NIGHT

Amber has been owned by words for as long as she can remember. As a child, they drove her to the depths of the basement to bury herself in books. Now, they drive her to tell tales of diverse love, to dream of a day when the invisible boundaries which separate us need not exist at all.

A poet by heart, Amber explores the depths of what it means to be human. She looks beneath the surface differences which divide us to find the common ground which unites us in our struggles to be seen. She's also partial to a hefty dose of sensuality and steam.

And, of course, to tackling that timeless question: what does it really mean, to love and to be loved?

She hopes you like her rough drafts of an answer. Oh, and the hot men.

TRIGGER
WARNINGS

Please skip this page if you don't want to be spoiled!

I'll preface this by saying that, wherever I touch on darker themes within my writing, I aim to do so with subtlety. I often approach them from an implicit rather than explicit angle. None of these themes are present within the main relationship/between the main characters.

That said, we're all on different journeys, and if anyone prefers the certainty of knowing themes to spoiling themselves, then please read on below to find trigger warnings.

This novel alludes non-graphically to themes which might prove triggering to some people. None of these are present in the main relationship/between main characters. Themes include: past emotional abuse, past domestic violence (non-graphic), death of a loved one, brief physical assault.

Printed in Great Britain
by Amazon